# EZEKIEL'S WAR

T.W. MANES

# EZEKIEL'S WAR

## TATE PUBLISHING
AND ENTERPRISES, LLC

Published by Tate Publishing & Enterprises, LLC
127 E. Trade Center Terrace | Mustang, Oklahoma 73064 USA
1.888.361.9473 | www.tatepublishing.com

Tate Publishing is committed to excellence in the publishing industry. The company reflects the philosophy established by the founders, based on Psalm 68:11,
*"The Lord gave the word and great was the company of those who published it."*

Book design copyright © 2012 by Tate Publishing, LLC. All rights reserved.
*Cover design by Blake Brasor*
*Interior design by April Marciszewski*

Published in the United States of America

ISBN: 978-1-61346-815-9
1. Religion / Christian Theology / Eschatology
2. Fiction / War & Military
12.03.27

irst of all, I would like to dedicate this book to my parents. To my dad, who passed down his God-given ability to write and tell stories. Thanks for the genes, Dad. To my mom, who passed on her unrequited love for God and His Word to me. Thanks to both of you for showing me, through your examples, what being a Christian really is.

To my wonderful, ever-believing, ever-enduring, and patient wife. I'll never forget the day you "prophesied" that one day, we would live by me writing books and you painting pictures. You are truly more wonderful than words can ever say, and a fantastic artist.

Last, but certainly not least, thanks to my kids. I am truly blessed to have the most wonderful children and grandchildren in all the world. I am so proud of all of you.

I love all of you so much!

DEDICATION

ACKNOWLEDGMENTS

First of all, I would like to thank Trinity Tate of Tate Publishing for seeing "something" in my very rough first attempt at writing a commercial book and for picking it out of all of the other submissions to be published. From there, my sincere heartfelt thanks go out to all of the rest of the wonderful people at Tate Publishing. Without a doubt, you have had your work cut out for you in turning Ezekiel's War from a dark piece of hard carbon into a sparkling stone. It is the result of all of the tremendous hard work of all you at Tate Publishing who deserve the credit for what follows!

I know if I begin to list names, I will invariable leave someone out, but please don't take it as a slight in any way. It is just that I'm going off my faulty memory. But again, beginning with Trinity Tate, Dr. Richard Tate, Judy Abell, Rachael Sweeden, Kelsey Marcussen, Janey Hays, Lauren Downen, Kalyn McAlister, and especially, my long suffering and ever patient editor, Jessica Browning! If I have left anyone out, please forgive me. But *thank you* all so much!

# CHAPTER 1

It was 10:00 p.m. on Friday night. Lieutenant Colonel Ezekiel Cohen was frustrated; was upset; and, more than anything else, was almost bored to death. It had been three weeks since his last full day off. Now that he had finally gotten one, a huge storm had forced him to stay inside all day long. On top of that, he had been given two full days off together for the first time since he couldn't even remember. But now he heard that this storm was supposed to get worse before it got better. Everything he had been putting off so he could take care of it on his next day off was again going to be put off until another time.

*I'd rather have been on duty today than stuck inside here all day, doing nothing but house work,* he thought. At least then I might have had a chance of seeing Esther. In his boredom, he walked over to the large window in the front room of his apartment and peered through it. *Man, it's dark out there,* he thought.

No streetlights were shining, no cars were passing by; there was no artificial light at all to give any kind of illumination to the dark night. It was a really dark night, the kind of darkness that wraps its black tentacles around you in a tight, sightless cocoon; the kind that feels like it's going to smother you; the kind that makes it hard to breathe when you're in it; the kind of darkness that you wouldn't even know if someone was standing within two feet of you.

An involuntary shudder rippled up and down his back like the waves of the ocean. He knew he suffered somewhat from claustrophobia. But if anyone ever found out about it, he would be grounded, taken off flight status. It was his little secret he would carry to his grave.

As he continued looking through the window, he thought *This storm is miserable! Man, I feel sorry for our defense forces on the borders of Gaza and Lebanon. They're probably having fits with Hamas and Hezbollah right now. This weather tonight is perfect cover for those demonic terrorists to cause all kinds of havoc and bloodshed. Thank God Esther is stationed at our base instead on one of those outposts.*

On a normal night, there would be millions of stars shining brightly in the smooth, black velvet sky above the tiny country of Israel. There would be hundreds, thousands, even millions of them. There would be enough to equal the number of Abraham's descendants, just like God had promised him. But tonight, all of the flickering little diamonds God had placed in the sky and had told Abraham to count so he would know how many descendants he would have were completely hidden behind heavy, thick, ground-hugging storm clouds.

*I should be up there mingling with the stars, chasing them across the sky in my Raptor, playing tag with those fiery sparkling stones that are hanging in the beauty of God's bonnet. But because of this storm, I'm stuck here all by myself and bored to death.*

The storm had begun forming yesterday afternoon, way out in the middle of the Mediterranean Sea. It began moving inland late last night. By the morning, the sky was completely covered in thick, black clouds. The sun never broke through at all. The only difference between midnight and daylight was a small brightening in the sky. But every light in the country that works with light sensors to tell when the sun comes up were all still on.

*That is except here, where all of the streetlights are out,* he added.

The streetlights were all out for some reason, but his power was still on.

Ezekiel turned and slowly walked back over to his favorite chair, his very comfortable recliner, and sat down in it, pulling the footrest up as he did. The TV was already on, his only source of company. He glanced at it to see if there was any more news about the storm. The very pretty weather reporter had just come on the screen and was getting ready to give the forecast.

With her long, brunette hair and pretty, dark brown eyes, she reminded him somewhat of the love of his life, Lieutenant Esther Asher.

*The love of my life,* he thought and laughed at the same time. *I haven't even had a date with her. In fact, every time I ask her out, she turns me down. She won't even give me the time of day. But I can't help it, she is still the love of my life—and one day, who knows?*

His thoughts trailed off as the reporter began to speak.

"This is the largest storm to come ashore in a long time. In fact, this could possibly be the so-called storm of the century. If this storm were in another part of the world, it would be comparable to a hurricane or a typhoon. Winds are expected to gust in excess of two-hundred kilometers an hour with sustained winds of over one hundred and twenty-five kilometers an hour. This is a major and potentially very dangerous storm, viewers. Please be aware of this. Visibility will be down to zero in many places. In fact, we have already received several reports that all of the streetlights are out in different parts of our city.

"I hate to be the bearer of bad news but, if you're in any of those areas, I would very highly suggest that you not leave your homes or places of business unless it is an emergency. As all of you know, the terrorist clans of Hamas and Hezbollah love this kind of darkness so they can hide their evil deeds inside of it.

"At this time, to our west, the storm extends from way out past the island of Crete in the Mediterranean Sea. But to our east, it is covering all of us here in Israel along with all of Lebanon, Syria, and Jordan. It also extends north all of the way up to the Euphrates River in Turkey and all of the way south, where it is covering most of the countries of North Africa that border the Mediterranean. It also has entered into Saudi Arabia and will soon enter into Iraq and then Iran.

"According to the latest analysis and computer projections, the storm is expected to get a lot worse as it continues its eastward movement. Reports have been coming in to us that vast portions of Saudi Arabia, Iraq, and Iran are presently in the midst of *haboobs*, which, as you might know, are huge dust storms that can extend in width up to and even exceeding one hundred kilometers and as high as a kilometer and a half or, in rare cases, even more than that. These *haboobs* are blinding, choking masses of almost solid dirt. In the areas where these dust storms are taking place, there is zero visibility. It is total and complete blackout conditions."

Ezekiel glanced up from the TV. *There goes any chance at all to get the things done I needed to. Man! It could be another month before I get another day off!*

In the background, the TV continued to drone on. He was barely listening. But she suddenly said something about the wind, the sand storms, and the enormous amounts of static electricity from intense lightning strikes that were causing complete havoc with the early warning radars and sensors throughout the entire Middle East that caught his ear.

He sat up straight. *If the military radars and sensors for the Arab and Islamic countries that surround us here in Israel are down and not working, we will probably go on full alert. The Arabs always get very nervous when something happens that they can't keep an eye or an ear on us,* he thought.

He listened intently as the reporter continued speaking. "Viewers, the latest very disturbing item to happen in conjunction with this storm is that the sun has begun erupting with huge, vast solar flares. Some of these solar flares are so monstrous that they are extending out from the surface of the sun to almost the orbit of Mercury!

"People, I must tell you that when the sun erupts like this, it blasts enormous amounts of solar radiation into space, and that radiation only takes approximately eight minutes to reach us here on the earth! Just eight minutes! We must thank Yahweh that He put a protecting atmosphere around the earth plus a magnetic field that gives protection to us from this enormous radiation. Otherwise, we would all die very shortly after being blasted by it! But do not fear. As I said, we are mostly protected.

"But the things that are receiving full blasts of damaging radiation are the satellites in space. They are very vulnerable to these massive doses of radiation. They are shielded, of course, but with the size of some of these flares, the shields are probably not enough to fully protect them. Already, we have heard that communications and data transmissions all over the world have been severely disrupted, and some have stopped working completely. But again, thank Yahweh that none of our satellites seem to be harmed and that we are not having any of those problems here in Israel."

Ezekiel began thinking, *With none of the radars or sensors working in the Arab and Islamic countries surrounding us, none of them can see or hear us. This would be a perfect time for us to launch a strike and destroy the nuclear facilities in Iran.*

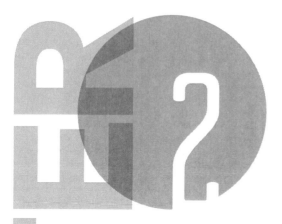

# CHAPTER 2

Ezekiel Cohen was a lieutenant colonel in the Israeli Air Force. The Israeli Air Force was the third largest in the world only behind the United States and Russia. That's why Ezekiel was very proud to be rated as his air force's best pilot. This earned him the position as squadron commander of the top-secret Master's Commission, 19th Aerial Fighter and Bomber Wing. This squadron was staffed with the rest of Israel's top pilots, their best of the best of their top guns. This gave them the privilege to fly the most advanced airplanes in Israel's entire fleet, which also gave them full access to the most advanced weapons systems in the Israeli inventory.

After spending all day cooped up, he wanted action! He needed action! But his thoughts, as they always do, quickly turned from action to Esther, the beautiful young lieutenant who often stood guard duty at the gate he drove through going onto his base. Without a doubt, he was in love with her, but she would not accept any proposal he extended.

*But I didn't get to be Israel's top pilot by giving up or being shy and timid. So...* His telephone rang. He quickly reached for it. "Hello. This is Ezekiel."

"Lieutenant Colonel, this is Cheryl Austin, General Green's secretary. I'm sorry to do this on your day off and this late at night, but General Green wants you back at the base thirty minutes ago."

"Yes, ma'am. Any idea what it's about?"

"No. He just said it was very urgent."

"Tell him I'm on my way."

"I will. I also have to call in your entire squadron. I don't know why, but I think something big is about to happen."

Five minutes later, he had climbed back into his flight suit and had hurried down to his ten-year-old Range Rover that was still in very good shape. Because of the massive storm, traffic was almost nonexistent. That allowed him to get onto the expressway quickly.

He got past the outskirts of town without any delays, going as fast as was safely possible to get to Sharon Air Force Base, where he and his unit were stationed. But now that he was off the expressway and on an old, rarely used road that would take him a back way, a shortcut, onto the base, he had to slow way down. His vehicle was wrapped in almost solid black clouds.

He glanced up through the top of the windshield. *Nothing but thick, black clouds!* He thought. Another involuntary shiver swept over him. An eerie feeling of being suffocated in a tight, black, choking cocoon suddenly began wrapping around him.

He shook his head to try to get his mind off it and forced himself to begin thinking about what the urgent call had been for. He again thought that tonight would be the perfect time to hit Iran and take out her nuclear facilities. He would find out for sure if that was it after he got to his base and met with General Green, but if he was allowed to put his two shekels in, he was going to say that they needed to do it. General Green would only need to make one phone call to the premier of Israel to get approval, and then being that General Green was also the top military officer in all of Israel, he could give the order to go.

Sharon AFB was located a stone's throw south of the Valley of Megiddo in northern Israel, not too far from Israel's border with Syria. It was supposed to be a secret base. It was never mentioned in any news release, and neither was it shown on any maps. In fact, most of the entire base was built underground with just a few nondescript buildings sitting on the surface that housed the sleeping quarters for the personnel who worked there. In addition to the few buildings were two parallel runways extending for three and a half kilometers straight out of the side of a solid granite mountain. The runways were paved with sand-colored asphalt in an attempt to blend in with the natural sand-colored earth surrounding them.

His thoughts again turned to what the reporter had said about the damage to the communication and data satellites circling the earth. She had said you couldn't even use a debit or credit card in most instances. She said that normal buying and selling had come to a complete stop in many places around the globe unless people were using paper money. But many merchants were beginning to refuse even this kind of buying and selling due to the fear of robbery and theft. She had said that people were resorting to the old-fashioned way of doing things by bartering.

But the last thing Ezekiel remembered the reporter saying was the ominous warning, "People of Israel, with this huge storm blasting through the Middle East, doing who knows what kind of damage, the sun going crazy and erupting like it's going to blow up, and the moon in the southern hemisphere entering into an eclipse that has made it appear to be the color of red blood, well…it almost seems like the entire world has suddenly passed into some kind of a crazy time warp or like some supernatural forces are gearing up for a huge climax between good and evil that will completely change the world as we know it. I mean, it is almost like the prophecies written in the books of Joel and Ezekiel are about to come true!"

Another involuntary shudder suddenly ran up and down his spine. *Yeah,* he thought, *between what Mother Nature is bringing on the world right now and what we might do later on tonight, by tomorrow morning, this old world is probably going to be completely different! It could even be the end of civilization as it's been known!*

He was gripping the steering wheel in a two-handed white-knuckle squeeze thinking about what the consequences would be if they were to launch a strike against Iran. His blood suddenly turned ice cold and huge goose bumps began splaying all over his body. At the same time, a burning, adrenaline-filled fever of excitement began sweeping over him. Sordid, drastic images of the almost unimaginable fiery hell he and his fellow warriors would unleash on Iran was sweeping through him … and it was almost scaring the literal hell out of him.

Ezekiel wasn't really scared. Not much of anything really scared him. He was very secure in his manhood! That's another reason he was Israel's top fighter pilot. But, he was very apprehensive about the amount of destruction him and his squadron were going to unleash on Iran.

Just yesterday, he and his pilots had been talking about this scenario. Ezekiel had said, "It's soon going to come down to it. The time we all knew would eventually happen is finally going to come."

"It has to come to it." Isaiah Goldstein, had replied, "There's no other way. None! Iran has left us no other choice. Listen. They made their bed when they began assembling a nuclear bomb. Now they have to sleep in it. But let me say this. It's going to be permanent sleep for them."

Isaiah's wingman, Billy Bartwaith, had replied, "No. It's not permanent sleep. Forever tormented in the fiery hot flames of *hell* is more like it. And if anyone deserves it, it's that madman leader of their country. He's the one who set their country on their own irreversible path to destruction. Listen, guys. Do any of you know what his name means in Arabic? No? Well, I'll tell you. His name, Malaku I-mawti means he is the *Islamic angel of death!* I looked it up in the Quran."

As Billy had said that, a shudder went through all of them. They all were thinking that if anyone deserved a name like that, it was definitely the insane leader of Iran who was bound and determined to set the entire Middle East on fire with the eternal flames of hell.

Ezekiel had replied, "When we do launch against them, we're going to bring something that will be burning hotter than any nuclear bomb they're building. I don't care what his name is! He's still an insane madman as far as I'm concerned. Guys, do you remember that American western movie, *Tombstone*, where Wyatt Earp yelled, 'You tell 'em I'm coming. And you tell 'em I'm bringing hell with me'? Well, that's exactly what we're going to do! We're gonna bring all of the fire, and we're gonna bring every bit of the evil, and we're gonna rain it down so hard on Iran that they will never rise from the ashes again. Iran will disappear just like Sodom and Gomorrah did. They'll become just like the jackal-infested destroyed city of Babylon. That insane leader of Iran made claims that they were going to wipe us off the face of the map; well, his very own words are going to do exactly that, but it won't be us who disappears. It's going to be Iran who disappears."

Just then, he began passing through several layers of thick, hail-embedded eerie-looking clouds. Through his rain streaked windshield and from the glow of his headlights it almost looked like green-tinged transparent ghosts suddenly were jumping up in front of him. He thought, *Yeah. There's going to be a lot of new ghosts and evil spirits floating around the earth later on tonight when we get done with you. And there's gonna be a lot of screaming and yelling as you descend into that hot, dark, bottomless abyss God made for Satan and his demons.*

*You fools think you're going to go to a place called paradise when you die. Well, I hope you like a burning lake of fire as your paradise, because that's exactly where you're going. And I guarantee, that you will not have twenty-one virgins, or whatever it is, waiting for you there. But you will probably have twenty-one different demons waiting to welcome you to the satanic abode.*

As he continued driving, jumbled, almost irrational thoughts continued to zip through his brain.

*Is this the beginning of the end of the world? No. The beginning of the end began a long time ago when that angel of death in Iran came into office. The beginning of the end began when he stood up and declared to the world that they were going to wipe Israel off the face of the world map. That was the beginning of the end right there.*

But what we are going to do in the next few hours could very well be the end of the end! It could very possibly be the hammering of the final nail into the crumbling coffin of human civilization as we have known it ...

As his thoughts rambled on, he came to a small dirt road angling off to his right from the highway. There had been no signs posted along the paved road to tell him where to turn. There was nothing to indicate that a dirt road even existed there except a large sign sticking up out of the ground about fifty meters down the path saying, "Warning. No Trespassing. Keep Out." Then, underneath that, in smaller letters, read, "This is an Israeli military area. Deadly force will be used to keep all unauthorized persons from entering."

From the turnoff, it took him almost a full half hour to travel the ten kilometers or so of the winding dirt trail from the old paved road down to the base. But as he finally got to the last half of a kilometer before arriving at the back guard gate, the road suddenly smoothed out to a flat, graded, maintained path. The military kept that section smooth and oiled to cut down on the dust.

At the end of the smooth section was a guard shack. Sticking out from the side of the shack was a heavy, reinforced steel crossbar capable of stopping a deuce-and-a-half truck traveling forty kilometers an hour. Two heavily armed military police personnel always manned the guard shack. As Ezekiel approached it, his heart skipped a beat. Tonight, both of the guards happened to be two of Ezekiel's favorites. One was a young man around twenty-five years old with ruddy cheeks and bright red hair. He was a staff sergeant. The other was Esther, a beautiful young lady in her late twenties. She was the girl Ezekiel was totally in love with. She held his heart in the palm of her hand in a vicelike grip that could never be broken.

As Ezekiel rolled his window down, he called out, "Hi, King David."

He called the young guard this even though he knew that was not his real name. The guard's last name was King, according to his nametag, but his first name was not David. Ezekiel didn't know his first name. But he had long ago told the young soldier that he was going to call him King David because he resembled the description of the real King David in the Bible, with ruddy cheeks and red hair. He had a feeling "King" David liked the nickname.

"How are you on this beautiful, rainy night?"

"Fine, sir," he replied as he was quickly glancing through Ezekiel's Rover to make sure he was by himself. "What brings you out on a night like this, sir?"

"Orders. You know how that goes."

He was trying his best to not betray the urgency he was feeling inside. He was also trying to not let them think that anything out of the normal was happening. He oftentimes got called in to the base at odd hours.

"They called and said for me to get here as quickly as possible. I hurried as fast as I could. Man, what a mess with this weather, huh? Now, though, I'll probably have to sit outside their offices and wait for several hours to find out what it's all about. You know, the old military way of doing things, hurry up and wait," he said with a grin.

Just then, Esther walked up next to his open window.

*She is beautiful, a living angel,* he thought.

She had been walking around his car, looking it over to make sure nothing was out of the ordinary.

"Oh. Hi, Esther," he called out.

The beautiful young lady consumed almost all of his thoughts. She was basically the first thing he thought about every morning when he woke up and the last thing he thought about before falling asleep at night.

From the beautiful covering of her hair to the way it framed her perfect face; from the dark brown glow of her eyes to the little, upturned nose; and from the high cheekbones to the soft circle of her mouth, he was totally infatuated with her. She was so beautiful that she didn't even need to wear makeup to be that way. She did, though, wear just a touch of blue eyeliner and a very light pink gloss on her lips.

"Hi, Lieutenant Colonel," Esther replied in a soft, semi-detached voice.

Esther consistently turned him down every time he asked her out, but he had to keep asking—his manly self-worth demanded that he did so. He cleared his throat and forged ahead. "Esther, after duty tonight, will you meet me at Benji Bahama's Place for a very late dinner—or an early breakfast, depending on what time it is?"

She stared at him for a moment without blinking. *This man is never going to give up*, she thought. Her eyes burned into his face.

Ezekiel thought she was glaring at him with anger. But what she was trying to do was see deep inside of the bothersome man who wanted companionship with her. He wanted to date her, and she was not sure she had any emotions left to give after her former fiancé was killed a few years back during a Hamas attack.

Her uncle, though, who just happened to be General Green, the commanding officer of the base and the highest-ranking officer in the entire Israeli military, had vouched for Ezekiel. General Green knew that she was still heartbroken over the loss of her fiancé, but he also knew that she had to move on if she was ever going to have any happiness in her life. And General Green knew Ezekiel. He knew that Ezekiel was a man of honor. He knew that Ezekiel was a very brave man, a strong man, a man who would sweep her off her feet and bring great happiness into her life if she would only allow him to. General Green had urged Esther to give him a chance and go out with him the next time he asked her.

She also knew that even though she had done everything in her power to resist the feelings, she too had long felt a huge attraction to him. Every time he drove through the gate, her heart would begin fluttering. But she was so afraid to allow her heart to love again after she had been hurt so badly before.

As she looked deeply into his eyes, her look softened. She felt a huge twinge of undeniable attraction inside as her heart began fluttering at breakneck speed. She had to finally admit it to herself that she had been very much attracted to him ever since she had met him almost a year before, the first time he had driven his old Range Rover through the gate.

She slowly moved her eyes up to meet his. His eyes were a soft, clear, deep blue color, and they were staring at her in earnest antici-pation. But it wasn't the color that softened her. It was the look of trust in them. It was the look of honor and respect in them. It was a look that she knew she would be able to trust the man whom she knew by his reputation and his accomplishments as a man of deep convictions who would right any wrong and demand justice for all.

And for the first time since Randy, her fiancé, had died, she felt huge sparks of human emotion return to her.

"Yes, Lieutenant Colonel," she replied. "I will meet you at Benji Bahama's Place for dinner. What time do you think it will be?"

Her answer took him completely by surprise. He almost didn't know what to say. He began to stutter and stammer like a little middle school student suddenly coming face to face with the prettiest girl in the entire school.

Finally, he blurted out, "Can I call you when I get off duty later on? I don't know exactly what it is that I have been called in for or for how long I will be required, so I am not sure when I will get off work. But I really would like for us to get together and have some of Benji Bahama's extraordinary prime rib. That is, if you like prime rib." He laughed nervously. "If you don't, you can order whatever you want."

She gave a soft, shy reply. "I like prime rib. That will be nice." She wrote her phone number on a piece of paper and gave it to him. "I'll be waiting to hear from you. Don't stand me up," she called out in a much more musical, laughing tone as she hurriedly turned and made her way over to the crossbar to lift it up so he could pass through.

As he drove under the barrier, she couldn't help herself and a huge, friendly smile crossed her lips. She glanced through his car window and saw that his entire face was one huge grin too. Her blood pressure suddenly shot up through the roof, and her face turned a bright red. She quickly turned away, hoping he couldn't see it.

But he did see the smile on her face as he drove through. A warm feeling swept all of the way through him that made his head get light. *Oh man. The most beautiful girl in all of Israel—no, in all of the world—has just agreed to have dinner with me!* As he drove on, he continued looking in his rearview mirror until he could no longer see her.

But just as soon as she passed out of his sight, the reality of what he had probably come there to do came roaring back to him with a screaming vengeance.

Just my luck. The girl of my dreams, my fantasies, my life has finally agreed to go out with me, and this might be the last mission I will ever go on.

# CHAPTER 3

He drove down the road next to one of the runways and disappeared into the side of the mountain. Inside this huge manmade cavern was the main area of the base. Even the bunkers where they kept all of the planes were located inside of the mountain, away from spying eyes looking down on them from high in the heavens.

He quickly made his way over to the building that housed General Green's office. Normally, it would have been locked up tight for the night and the weekend, but tonight, even the receptionist was at her desk.

He parked the Range Rover in front of the low, one-story, rectangular building next to several other vehicles. As he was getting out of his vehicle he looked over at them and was surprised to see that most were civilian vehicles. *What else is going on?* he wondered. Usually, if the military needed civilian approval for something, a phone call would suffice. But now, there were at least six civilian vehicles parked in front of the building. *They must be some high-ranking authorized civilians to be allowed on the base*, he thought.

He slammed his door shut behind him, and hurried inside the office.

Cheryl, the general's receptionist, looked up as he walked in. "Hello, Lieutenant Colonel Cohen. They said for you to go straight on in to General Green's conference room. They are expecting you."

Ezekiel paused for a moment, "Cheryl, who are *they*? There are a bunch of civilian cars parked outside."

"I was told to not say anything. You need to go on inside and you'll find out."

"Okay. But if I come back out here with my bloody head lying on a platter, just remember this: I'm gonna haunt you for the rest of your life." He laughed and winked at her.

She laughed and turned her face away so he couldn't see how red it had just become.

She knew that every female on the entire base was in love with the dashing figure of Lt. Col. Ezekiel Cohen. But even though he flirted around with most of them, he never tried to ask any of them out.

*Other than Lieutenant Esther Asher,* she said to herself, *and she won't even give him the time of day. Oh, what I'd give to be in her shoes. I would certainly give him the time of day if he would just ask me out. But for some reason, he's totally in love with a girl who doesn't even know he exists.*

He turned and walked over to the set of two very highly polished red oak doors in the middle of the far wall. Behind the doors was the general's conference room. He stopped in front of them and gave a quick, two-knuckle knock.

"Come," he heard as the word blasted through the solid wood doors in the general's distinctive deep baritone voice.

Ezekiel had seen very brave men cower and melt under the sound of that voice. He thought, *If there's a God, that must be what He sounds like.*

Without hesitating, he turned the knob, pulled the door open, and took a step inside. But after taking only a step or two, he stopped. He was stunned, to see who was sitting around the large rectangular table.

General Green, of course, was present. But the general wasn't sitting at the head of the table like he normally does. He was sitting one seat to the right. He was, though, facing the door that Ezekiel had just walked through.

Even though he had never met the man, Ezekiel instantly recognized the man sitting in the head chair. It was Prime Minister Emanuel Ben Joseph. Along with him sitting around the table were several of the high-ranking members of his cabinet, including the Israeli Defense Minister, Moshe Hezekiah. In fact, he had never met any of these men, but he recognized most of them from seeing them on TV.

Ezekiel was a big believer and supporter of these men and this particular government. *That's where all of the civilian cars came from,* he thought.

General Green stood up. At the same time, Ezekiel quickly regained his composure and came to attention.

"At ease, Lieutenant Colonel. Please come in and join us," General Green boomed.

General Green pointed toward an empty chair next to him. Lt. Col. Cohen began walking over to it. But before he got to it General Green said, "Lieutenant Colonel Cohen, before you sit down, let me thank you for coming so quickly. And please let me introduce you to Prime Minister Ben Joseph and the rest of the gentlemen here."

As soon as those pleasantries were completed and Ezekiel had taken his seat, General Green immediately got down to business. "Lieutenant Colonel Cohen, I'm sure you probably have a good idea why we called you here tonight. Let me assure you that it is not just to have you meet our prime minister and these other fine gentlemen, although I am sure that you will cherish this opportunity for the rest of your life."

He paused as this feeble attempt on his part to ease the tension in the room failed miserably. Prime Minister Ben Joseph seemed to be in a bad mood. He had just nodded his head at the lieutenant colonel when he had been introduced. He had not smiled, nor had he shaken Ezekiel's hand. Right now, a stony, hard look was plastered on his face and his jaw set like flint.

General Green continued. "You were called here tonight because you are a man with extraordinary talents and abilities. You have the ability to fly aircraft, unlike any of your peers. And you also have the ability to command and lead others like very few people have. For some reason, people gravitate to you, and they will follow you to the very steps of hell if need be.

"Lieutenant Colonel Cohen, I am going to be very blunt with you. Right now, as we speak, the very continuing existence of our country is at stake. You, Lieutenant Colonel, have the ability and leadership to make sure that Israel continues to live and prosper in this world long after this, this darkest night in our entire existence up 'til now, has passed.

"You know that ever since Malaku I-mawti came into power, he has made inflammatory statements such as they are going to wipe Israel off the face of the world map. In his murderous zeal, he has threatened our lives and our very existence as a nation. While at the same time, he has thumbed his nose at the rest of the world and laughed in their faces. And the castrated, impotent, do-nothing, cowardly appeasement leaders of the world have done nothing but make hollow threats toward him. They stood idly by while Iran was allowed to go ahead and develop nuclear weapons ... and as of this time, Lieutenant Colonel, I must inform you that we have unimpeachable evidence that this madman has now in his possession at least three of those weapons. But it is very possible they have more, maybe many more.

"I'm also sure that you already know the Russians have been sleeping in the same bed with the Iranians throughout this entire process. After building the atomic reactors for them, they also helped them enrich their fuel to turn it into weapons-grade material, even though both countries stringently deny it. But as you well know, both countries are very determined liars."

He paused for a brief second and looked at the men before continuing. "Gentlemen, it is a very, very real possibility that after we attack Iran, we will shortly thereafter be attacked by the Russians. The reason for this is because we are completely on our own without any help from any other country in the entire world. But let me state this as clearly as I can, other than the fact that we too are a formidable and powerful nation, I truly believe we have the great God of Israel on our side who will go before us and fight for us. He is Yahweh, El Shaddai, Elohim, *the great I Am.*

"But, gentlemen, what is discouraging is that we should have been able to trust that the United States would step up and help us stop this *angel of death*, but the United States has turned her back on us too. We have certain treaties with the United States that require them to protect us, or at least give us the means to protect ourselves. But this new president seems to want to appease the Muslims at any and all costs. Plus, he is more concerned about what the world thinks of him than what the treaties we have between our two countries actually say. So it basically makes these treaties meaningless."

He briefly stopped again as he gathered his thoughts together. He didn't want to go too far and step over the invisible line of proper diplomacy and enter into the political arena where these other men dwelt on a daily basis. He didn't want to say something he shouldn't say or didn't think he had the authority to say in front of these men. Finally, he continued.

"I guess we can't blame the American president completely, what with the economic problems the entire world has been going through lately. I'm sure his attention and focus has been diverted toward finding a solution for that."

Prime Minister Ben Joseph let a huge snort blast out of his nostrils. No way was he going to give this wannabe world dictator president any slack or make excuses for him. Not after the way he had been treated by him.

He jumped to his feet and immediately took control of the floor. As he did the soft, comfortable calf leather chair he had been sitting on went flying backward and crashed hard against the far wall, landing upside down. He raised himself up to his full height of six feet two inches tall and stuck his chest out in a proud display of courage and strength.

Prime Minister Emanuel Ben Joseph had still not gotten over the snub by the president of the United States when, after a meeting between the two leaders in Washington, DC, the president had made the prime minister exit the White House through a door in the back that is used specifically by servants and delivery men. The prime minister had to walk past several outside garbage cans to get to his chauffeured car. The prime minister had felt like the president was sending him a direct message that he considers the prime minister and Israel to be nothing more than his servants. After what was discussed in the meeting between the president and him and the slight that followed was when the prime minister knew that the president of the United States was a full-fledged Muslim lover who hated Jews, just like most all Muslims. In fact, the prime minister wondered if the president was really a full-fledged Muslim hiding behind lies and deceits of being a Christian.

After the prime minister arrived back home in Israel, it took several days of intense negotiation by his most trusted advisers to keep the prime minister from sending his Mossad Intelligence Agency's top trained killers to go after the Muslim-appeasing fool, as he had called him. But diplomacy and common sense had eventually won out as it did again.

Inside of the conference room tonight. He hesitated just long enough to gather his emotions back under control before allowing himself to speak. Even though everyone in the room was well aware of the intense anger running rampant throughout him, the prime minister was ever the gentleman and cordial politician. But they all knew too that he was also a very tough former military hero whom they all respected very highly for his bravery and tenacity. They all knew that he was a living man of true steel, not like some comic book superhero.

He took a deep breath, cleared his throat and began. "Gentlemen, let me tell you this. With this president the United States now has, there's only one thing I am sure of: the fool's entire focus is finding some way to get re-elected when his present term expires. In his selfish, conceited, and narcissistic mind, he assumes it will be so much easier for him to reach his ultimate goal of becoming ruler of the entire world one day if he remains president of the United States.

"As you all are aware of, I'm sure, his ruling party was astoundingly defeated in the last elections that were held during the middle of his first term. Now all of his concerns and worries are on that instead of worrying about the survival of a tiny country in the Middle East that he loathes. In fact, I am sure he believes that if we were to suddenly disappear off the map like Iran wants us to do, that would be just one less problem he would have to spend five minutes worrying about."

Prime Minister Ben Joseph stopped to take another deep breath. As his huge barrel chest expanded to an even larger size, he moved his gaze slowly around the room, stopping for a brief instant on each man's face before moving on to the next one in line. No one questioned the man's great love for his country. No one doubted his leadership either. Nor did they question his determination that Israel will continue to exist, even if every man, woman, girl, and boy above the age of sixteen in the country has to lay their lives down for that to continue to happen. They knew without a doubt that Emmanuel Ben Joseph would be at the front of the line, ready and willing to lay his own life down first to keep his precious country free. They all had heard him say, "Never again! Never again will Israel be dispersed or defeated! All of Israel will fight to the last breath of the last person before ever surrendering again."

As his gaze finally reached Ezekiel, his voice suddenly rose several octaves. "But Lieutenant Colonel Cohen, we are not going to go away, nor are we going to allow ourselves to be destroyed either. Are we? So, we have come to the conclusion that we must act alone. We must demonstrate the awesome power we have in our own possession to these rogue nations. If we do not do this, these satanically inspired corrupted nations will all bind themselves together and come against us and try again to destroy us.

"You and the rest of your brave pilots were asked to come here tonight to carry out a daring—" He again paused, unsure just how to proceed. He knew exactly what the consequences could be and very possibly were.

Finally, he said, "Lieutenant Colonel, I'm going to be very blunt here. Your mission tonight might even be described as possibly suicidal. But it is to defend Israel from total destruction. Listen, my good man. We have been advised by our intelligence agents, who have been embedded in place for many years inside Iran and in whom we have absolute, one hundred percent confidence, that Iran has in her possession three nuclear bombs. We do not know how many kilotons these bombs possess, but we know this much: if they launch them against us, no matter what amount of destructive power they possess, Israel might very possibly cease to exist as a nation."

As those words were coming out of his mouth, his eyes were glaring into Ezekiel's eyes with a look that was hotter and more intense than an arc welder torch. After a moment, he continued, "But now for the most disturbing news of all. Our intelligence has also learned that Iran is preparing to launch these bombs against us shortly after the sun comes up tomorrow morning. They will be launched atop a new rocket they have recently developed in conjunction with North Korea, and they have great confidence in this missile. But tomorrow is Saturday, our Sabbath, and much of our nation will be congregated at synagogue.

"Your mission tonight, Lieutenant Colonel Cohen, is to make sure they will not be able to launch those weapons of mass destruction against us. We must totally destroy the weapons plus their means to launch those weapons. Now, you already know this, Lieutenant Colonel, but other than my defense minister, Moshe Hezekiah, this is something my other cabinet members are finding out for the first time tonight."

He turned to face his cabinet members. "Gentlemen, there is one thing that we will be eternally grateful for that the United States did for us. You see, before one of their former presidents left office, he made arrangements for us to receive ten of their most advanced F-22 Raptor stealth aircraft. Plus, he made arrangements for us to buy two B-2 stealth bombers. These aircraft have been conscripted into the Lieutenant Colonel's squadron. The Lieutenant Colonel and his brave pilots have been training on these new aircraft for the last several months.

"The United States' former president believed that the newly elected 'messiah of the world,' as he called him, who would soon take over his office would never stand up to Iran, its murderous leaders, or any other Muslim nation for that matter. He also believed, because of the new president's Muslim beliefs and background, that this new president would never agree to give us the weapons that we need to protect ourselves with. So, he made arrangements through what they call their Black Ops department—which is off the budget books, out of public record, and without their congress's knowledge—for us to receive these advanced fighter and bomber aircraft. We received these aircraft and all the weapons of mass destruction common to these aircraft that we need to destroy all of the nuclear facilities inside of Iran, plus their means to launch those weapons against us.

"Now the time has come to put you, Lieutenant Colonel Cohen, and your squadron into operational mode. Your ten fighter aircraft and the two B-2s are right now being equipped with these special weapons you will need to complete your task. In just a short period of time, you will use these weapons on various targets inside of Iran. And if all goes as planned, the stealth qualities of these F-22 Raptors and the B-2s will allow each of the aircraft to fly undetected all of the way across Iranian airspace and then fly home unscathed. Do you have any questions, Lieutenant Colonel?"

"Yes, sir. Just one. Where do we get enough fuel to fly this distance?"

"Good question. Allow me to say that, uh … certain very delicate discussions have taken place between …" The prime minister took a minute to clear his throat and then said, "Well, let me just say that some very high-ranking individuals, one of them an American general, are willing to put their entire careers, and possibly even their lives, on the line to provide a secure secret runway inside of Iraq, along with plenty enough fuel for your planes going to and returning from Iran. Is that good enough for you?"

"Yes, sir. I'm sure we'll be briefed as to where this secret runway is located."

"You will. So, if there are no other questions, Lieutenant Colonel Cohen, our hearts and our prayers go with you and your brave pilots. May the Elohim of Israel, the almighty El Shaddai, the Yahweh who led Israel out of Egypt, and the great *I Am*, go with you and protect and keep you. And may He also keep our entire nation protected under the shadow of His mighty wings as we continue to dwell in the shelter of the Most High. Shalom."

orty-five minutes later, Lt. Col. Cohen was strapped into his F-22 Raptor aircraft, the most advanced stealth fighter and bomber airplane in the world, and began taxiing toward the end of the runway. Each of the aircraft had been assigned different targets in different parts of the country. The plan was for each aircraft to take off in an order and time sequence that would have them all dropping their bombs at approximately the same time, no matter where in Iran the targets were located. Some of the planes had farther to fly than the other ones, so their take-off times were adjusted accordingly. This meant that each plane, other than the two B-2s that would have two F-22s escorting them, would be flying on its own all of the way to its assigned targets.

Ezekiel eased the throttles forward a notch so he could pick up more speed as he rolled down the taxiway. He quickly reached the end and made a U-turn back onto the actual runway and expertly lined the plane up on the white center line running the length of the runway. He reached out with his right hand and jammed the throttles all the way forward until they hit the stops to give full military power to the powerful twin engines. The afterburners kicked in, and like a rocket, he went shooting out of the mountain and down the runway.

As the plane quickly accelerated, it was just a few short seconds until he reached the speed needed for takeoff, and he gently pulled back on the stick. The nose instantly rose up off the ground, followed by the rest of the plane a second later as it left the restraints of the earth and became the magnificent mechanical flying bird it had been created to be. As soon as Ezekiel felt the wheels leave the runway, he quickly hit the switch, bringing the wheels up into their tucked and locked position.

As they locked in place, he pulled back on the throttles to slow his ascent and then pointed his plane to do a low-level fly-over of the guard station where King David and Esther were. As he approached it, he glanced out of the cockpit. He could see their faces as they were looking up at him. They had been watching for his plane to take off. Both Esther and King David smiled and waved up at him. In return, he gave the universal symbol of acknowledgment by an airplane pilot by waving his wings from side to side.

Ezekiel was not a religious man, nor was he a praying man. God just had never been a part of his life. He had gone through Bar Mitzvah, and he had chanted the sayings he had been required to do, but God or religion was something that he never paid any attention to.

Tonight, though, he suddenly felt differently. After both the Prime Minister and General Green invoked the names of God, he felt the need to try to communicate with this God they both knew and respected so much. *El Shaddai,* he prayed, *you are the almighty God of Israel and we are your chosen people. I humbly ask for you to keep your protecting hand on all of my men and myself tonight as we undertake this dangerous mission. I also ask you to allow us all to return safely back from this mission, unharmed and undamaged in any way whatsoever. I ask for you to personally go before us, be our guide, and take us to our targets. I ask for you to go before us and prepare our way so that it will be successful. And I ask for you to personally fight for us like you always did for the patriarchs of old. And finally, I ask you to please keep Esther safe too. Please keep her wrapped up in the palm of your hands, as I ask for you to do for all of Israel. And especially, I thank you for having her say yes for our dinner date.*

As long as he could, he kept his gaze on her while a huge smile wrapped itself across his face. He leaned over against the cockpit canopy and blew her a silent kiss. "You don't know this, little sweet one, but I have been in love with you ever since the first time my lonely eyes had the inexpressible pleasure of focusing on you," he whispered. "You have held my heart so captive that my eyes have not been able to even look upon another woman. *I love you.*"

At the same time, unknown to him, she was uttering her own prayer. Both she and Sergeant King knew something big was going on tonight. The prime minister and his cabinet had arrived first at the base, followed by Ezekiel and his squadron not long afterward. Then, within an hour's time, Ezekiel and all of his men had taken off into the air in a staggered manner. Because of this, they knew something huge was happening or was soon going to.

She prayed, *Oh mighty Yahweh, God and keeper of Israel and Father to your Son, Jesus Christ, please keep Lieutenant Colonel Cohen safe under the protection of your wings like a mother hen keeps her chicks safe as he goes forth tonight on this mission. And please keep all of your people in this country—yes, this country that you created by your own awesome power—safe and free from all harm. And if it be in your perfect will, please allow Lieutenant Colonel Cohen and myself to find peace and happiness in each other's company. I thank you that you have allowed me to once again feel the sweet presence of unrestrained love in my heart for this wonderful man you have allowed to come into my life.*

Even though Ezekiel didn't want to leave her beautiful presence behind, he knew he had to. He had a mission that all of Israel was depending on him to successfully complete. He and all of his squadron knew that if they failed, by that time the next night, Israel would no longer exist. Malaku I-mawti would succeed in wiping Israel off the map. He pointed the nose of his plane upward and increased the throttles forward enough to bring him up to an altitude of thirty-nine thousand feet. This put him above the huge storm that had continued blowing in.

Neither Ezekiel nor any of the military leaders in Israel knew at that time that every radar in every country anywhere within a thousand miles of Israel was malfunctioning. They had no way of knowing this. Everything was functioning perfectly normal inside of the entire borders of Israel, except for some streetlights that were out. They had no idea that El Shaddai, the Almighty, had already gone ahead of them and was preparing their way.

Ezekiel turned his plane to head east, but once he reached his cruising speed, he moved his plane back down directly inside of the storm clouds and flipped the switch for the automatic pilot to take over. At that point, he also began flying without any lights, radar, or transponder.

His eyes wandered up through the top of the canopy. Again, an eerie feeling swept over him like he was trapped inside of a smothering cocoon. This is also how his plane would have appeared on radar if it had been noticeable. It would have appeared as a little caterpillar wrapped up inside a huge cocoon. But his plane wasn't on anyone's radar. After shutting off his transponder, even the Israeli radars couldn't see him anymore. As far as the world was now concerned, he didn't exist. Neither did any of the other planes in his squadron. None of them existed any longer and wouldn't until after they had all dropped their bombs on the unsuspecting targets below them and then returned home.

As far as Israel knew, no one else in the entire world—except for a very few, very tight-lipped people in the United States—knew that Israel was in possession of ten F-22 Raptors and two B-2 bombers. They were hoping and praying it would remain that way, even after using them for the first time tonight in war.

Of course, they all knew that even if their planes did all return safely and undetected, Israel would still be the first to be blamed for these attacks and condemned by the entire world. It would not matter to any other country that Israel had just rid the world of the weapons of mass destruction that a tyrant and terrorist had accumulated and planned on using. They would still be condemned and vilified by everyone else. Thus was the hatred of the world toward Jews.

To get his mind off the claustrophobic enclosed feelings, he turned his attention back to his instruments to make sure he was still on target. He was. The computer in his airplane had been programmed to fly by a very highly sophisticated, secure GPS satellite guidance system that would take his plane, without any help or direction from him, to the targets he was to destroy. This would not have been possible if God had not gone before them and prepared the way by keeping their own satellites in space protected from the huge solar flares that were creating havoc throughout the rest of the world, and allow them to continue working unabated. At the precise time, it would alert him to drop his weapons where they would then be guided down to their actual target by the same sophisticated GPS guidance system to within six inches of dead center of where they had been aimed. After all targets had been destroyed, he would take over the flying duties and head his plane to meet up with the rest of his squadron.

Even though his plane was very capable of much more, he would be flying at a speed just under the speed of sound. They certainly did not want any sonic booms to give away their presence or their positions. Also, the plane had very sensitive sensors on it that would automatically readjust its altitude to remain as much as possible inside of the dark layer of clouds. Even though the plane was basically invisible to radar, they didn't want anyone to look up in the sky and spot a fast-moving, unidentified flying object. So if the weather cooperated and the sky remained covered in clouds, he should be able to successfully complete his assigned mission and eventually get back to his home base so he could call Esther.

He leaned his head back and got as comfortable as he could for the long flight still ahead of him, making sure to keep his gaze inside of the plane. As he did, he let his mind wander back to Esther and the date she had promised him.

*Will the date ever happen?* he wondered, *or will Iran retaliate?*

If they did, he, along with his squadron, would certainly have to quickly rearm their planes and rush back in an attempt to repel them.

He thought, *How in the world have things gotten this bad so quickly?*

In just the last few months, everything had degenerated to the point that twelve of the best airplanes and pilots in the world were on their way at that very moment to drop the fires of hell onto another sovereign country.

How many people are going to die tonight? What if some of the ones who die are Russian scientists and technicians? If that happens, will Russia send their troops to retaliate against us?

All twelve planes were in the air and on their way to Iran. They had taken off with as much fuel as possible, so they'd had to use almost every foot of the runway to get up in the air. They still had to meet up with a flying tanker plane to top off, but they wanted the time spent in that position to be as minimal as possible. They knew that during the time they were hooked up, they would be reflecting radar back to anyone who was looking. And all of the pilots assumed that there would be hundreds of pairs of eyes from a bunch of Arab countries looking for anything suspicious coming from the Jews. None of them were aware at that time that it was impossible to see any of them due to the unusual weather phenomena taking place on the earth and the monstrous solar flares on the surface of the sun, which had caused all of their enemy's radars and systems to be inoperable.

After the planes took off, General Green, Prime Minister Emanuel Ben Joseph, and the other cabinet ministers made their way to an underground command bunker built inside of the solid granite mountain, where they would stay until the mission was over, and even longer if Iran retaliated. The bunker measured one hundred feet wide by three hundred feet long. It was a large place consisting of thirty thousand square feet of the latest, most sophisticated electronics and surveillance equipment found anywhere in the world. It rivaled anything that the United States and Russia had. It was also equipped with sleeping quarters; a complete kitchen; and enough food, water, and purified air to last a year. It was a complete underground little city.

In the middle section of the bunker was a large observation room that measured a tad over ten thousand square feet. Along one wall were several large, flat-screen monitors. Ten of them, at that moment, were showing what the pilots inside of ten aircraft on their way to Iran were seeing. Basically, all they were seeing at that time were dark black clouds rushing rapidly past the canopies. But later on, when they reached their targets, they would be able to follow the path of the smart bombs all of the way down to their targets. Even if the planes remained inside of the cloud cover, they would still be able to see if the bombs found their correct targets by infrared technology and by the tiny cameras mounted on the tips of the bombs themselves. They would also hopefully be able to see with the high definition cameras mounted on the planes of the amount of damage the bombs caused after they hit. These cameras had the ability to *see* through clouds or most other obstructions.

This observation room was where the attack and any follow-up war action would be monitored and directed from. It was also where the government of Israel would be conducted during this time, if necessary. Prime Minister Emanuel Ben Joseph would assume ultimate responsibility for everything that happened, good or bad, from then on out.

General Green and his command staff and Prime Minister Ben Joseph and his cabinet gathered around a large, rectangular conference table. They sat down on comfortable padded armchairs. They knew it was going to be a long night. From that area, they could see all of the large monitors and also listen to reports as they came in.

The pilots were on very strict orders to maintain radio silence. But Israel still had several intelligence operators in place in Iran to send encrypted coded messages back to them where they would be received and decoded inside of the bunker.

Prime Minister Emanuel Ben Joseph was sitting with both elbows on the table, holding his head in both of his hands. His eyes had a far off look in them. He wasn't thinking about the operation taking place. He was thinking about what the entire world was going to be saying the next day after the news was broadcast about what they had done.

*Will they all condemn us?* he wondered. *It seems like everyone in the world already hates us now. What will it be like after this? What will the United States say and do? The United States is basically the only friend we have, even if they no longer show it with their new power-hungry elected leaders they now have. If they turn against us, our existence is basically doomed no matter what we accomplish tonight. That is, unless God shows favor on us.*

Colonel Jeremiah, General Green's chief of staff, walked into the room holding a large stack of papers in his hands. He nodded at General Green. General Green acknowledged him back with a nod, then leaned over and said, "Prime Minister, sir, Colonel Jeremiah is here with the projections of our analysts, if you care to hear them."

Prime Minister Ben Joseph jerked like he had been shot. Then as his thoughts returned back to the room and where he was, he said, "Yes. Please fill me in on what our analysts believe is going to happen."

"Colonel Jeremiah, please proceed," General Green said.

"Yes, sir," he began. "General Green, Prime Minister Ben Joseph, and all of the rest of our distinguished guests, first of all, let me say thank you for being here tonight. Now, as I begin, let me emphasize that the projections I am about to give to you are from the brightest and most brilliant minds in all of Israel. They have actually spent the last several months, and in some cases even years, preparing these for us. Because of this, we believe them to be very accurate.

"Let's start with the mission taking place right now. We believe there is a ninety-nine percent favorable probability that we will attain complete surprise in this operation tonight. Most of that is due to these wonderful planes the United States sold to us. But another is that we have just learned that right now, throughout the entire Middle East, all other countries have lost complete radar and imaging capabilities. This is due to the monstrous storm blowing in off the Mediterranean and also because of the very unusual solar activity taking place on the sun. This solar activity is causing havoc throughout the entire world."

He stopped for a moment and glanced up from his notes to look around the room. General Green was looking back at him with an attentive look on his face, along with several of the prime minister's cabinet members. But the prime minister was still holding his head up with his right hand and had a faraway look in his eyes. It appeared almost like he hadn't heard a word that had been said.

Colonel Jeremiah glanced away from the prime minister and allowed his gaze to go to the monitors on the wall to see if anything was happening there. But there was still nothing but gray-black clouds rushing by. He turned back to his notes.

"Gentlemen, we here in Israel are not experiencing anything out of the ordinary. We have complete communications and radar and imaging capabilities. Therefore, we believe we will be able to accomplish our mission tonight without what we had originally projected. We had originally projected that we would lose two of our aircraft and pilots.

"We also believe there is a ninety percent favorable probability that we will succeed in destroying all of Iran's nuclear weapons since we are aware of their so-called secret locations. Likewise, we believe there is a ninety percent favorable probability that we will destroy at least seventy-five percent of Iran's capability of launching any nuclear weapons of any sort back against us.

"That leaves a twenty-five percent chance that they will be able to get at least one of their missiles launched back against us before we have the opportunity to destroy it. If that scenario happens, we have projected that anywhere from a hundred thousand to two hundred and fifty thousand of our people will either die or be severely injured. We also project that the damage to our economy will run upward of twenty billion *shkalim,* or almost ten percent of our gross domestic product."

"My God," Eleizer Oranson, the Israeli finance minister blurted out with disbelief. "Ten percent of our entire gross? That will devastate our economy!"

Mr. Oranson was a dapper little man. He stood five feet four inches tall in his elevated shoes, the shoes he tried to keep covered by allowing his pants to drape over them enough to drag on the floor. But other than that, he was always immaculately dressed in the finest suits, shirts, and ties that Seville Row in London could custom tailor for him. If he hadn't been so good with finances, he would have been gone from the prime minister's cabinet a long time ago. All he ever thought about was money and how to produce more of it. His outburst had shown his callousness by being directed at the monetary loss with not one word spoken of the tremendous loss of lives and injuries projected to happen.

Colonel Jeremiah was momentarily taken aback by Mr. Oranson's outburst and his brusque, callous manner. But after quickly regaining his composure, he jumped back in, directing his remarks toward the finance minister.

"Mr. Oranson, sir, we know we can absorb the monetary loss without too much difficulty. But the number of our people we will lose will be the most damaging of all. No matter how many or even how few lives we lose, a nuclear bomb explosion will have a devastating effect on the morale within our country. Our people are very tired of this constant battle, of staying alert at all times with the fear of a terrorist attack taking place at any time. But our people are and have always been very resourceful people. They will, after the initial shock wears off, come back strong with full support for us and our military.

"If the enemy is not able to or chooses not, at this time, to retaliate against us, we believe we will have ninety-eight percent support for our actions inside of our country. But at the same time, unfortunately, we believe that we will only have a small number of countries throughout the world that will support us in our actions. But in reality, gentlemen, there might not be any.

"Unfortunately, this includes the United States. With the president they have now, we are certain that he will immediately go before the cameras and condemn us, in no uncertain terms, for our defensive actions. And this is even though a lot of the intelligence we have received concerning Iran's preparations to launch these nuclear weapons against us has come from the United States itself.

"We are certain that even though this is so, their president will still go on camera and condemn us. But, gentlemen, we also believe there is at least a fifty-fifty chance that if Iran does retaliate against us with nuclear weapons, the military leaders within the United States might pull together and institute a coup to replace this president. Without a doubt, this is our extreme desire.

"So, Prime Minister Ben Joseph, sir, this kind of leaves us in a quandary. If we dare to hope for Unites States support, that means we probably have to absorb a nuclear attack against us. But without their support and their unlimited help, there is no way we can face down the entire world, because that is exactly what we will be doing come tomorrow morning."

Prime Minister Ben Joseph finally lifted his head and nodded toward Col. Jeremiah and then, slowly and very tiredly, rose to his feet. His shoulders were no longer straight and unbending. They were slumped forward as if he was carrying an enormous weight, which was exactly what he was doing. His head was bent down. He was not making eye contact with any other person. Finally, he slowly turned and moved around his chair until his back was facing the rest of them. After that, he slowly put both of his hands behind his back and grasped them together. He then stood there, rocking back and forth on the heels of his feet, in deep thought.

Finally, after a couple of very long minutes, he turned back to face the men, all who had been sitting there, watching him and not saying a word.

"Let me ask you a question, Colonel Jeremiah. Are you saying that the best scenario for us would be if Iran were to launch a nuclear missile back against us?"

"Uh … yes, sir. I guess that is what I am saying … unfortunately."

"Well then let me ask another question. General Green, have any contingencies been built into this operation that will allow us to be attacked with a nuclear missile?"

"Yes, sir, it has. But as of right now, our twelve airplanes are on their way that will, if they are successful, destroy all of Iran's nuclear weapons and their ability to launch any missiles back at us.

"We can, though, with your approval, send a coded message to Lieutenant Colonel Cohen's plane that will reprogram it to allow Iran to retain at least one bomb and the ability to launch that bomb back at us. You see, sir, Iran already has one missile loaded with a nuclear weapon sitting on the launch pad ready to be fired. If we reprogram Lieutenant Colonel Cohen's plane to not bomb that site, then Iran will probably launch that missile against us as soon as they realize they have been attacked. That launch site is Lieutenant Colonel Cohen's first target."

"I see. Tell me this, General. How much time do I have to give you the … the … yes or no … to destroy or not destroy this launch site?"

"Approximately one hour, sir," General Green replied after glancing at his watch and doing some quick calculations.

"One more question. I guess this is directed at you, Colonel Jeremiah. How sure are you that a coup will take place in the United States?"

"Our analysts believe there is a fifty-fifty chance a coup will happen. But if you are you asking me what I personally believe, sir, I believe the odds are much greater than fifty-fifty. I believe with a seventy-five percent favorable probability that a military takeover will occur in the United States if we are attacked by a nuclear weapon.

"You see, most of the top military leaders in the States are just sick about the direction their country has taken since this new president has come into office. A large percentage of them think this new president—along with his so-called czars—are going to declare a state of emergency and assume full and complete power for themselves, just like Hitler and his band of Nazi thugs did back in the nineteen thirties. If that were to happen, with a one hundred percent favorable response, it would be assured that a military coup would take place within hours. But I personally believe that for the time being, these two groups are in a sort of standoff, not unlike the Cold War between the United States and Russia when they operated under the assumption of mutual destruction if one were to have made an attack against the other."

"All right. I understand," Prime Minster Ben Joseph replied with resignation in his voice. "So then, if you gentlemen will excuse me, I am going to go find an area where I can have some privacy so I can have a little talk with God. I must say, it is not easy to give an order that will allow upward of a quarter of a million of your own people to die. General, could you show me where such an area might exist?"

"Of course, sir. Please use my quarters inside of this bunker. I guarantee that you will not be disturbed. Also, there is a copy of the Holy Scriptures on the night stand if you so desire to consult them."

With that, Prime Minister Emanuel Ben Joseph, with the slumped shoulders of a ninety-five-year-old man, shuffled his way out of the bunker and into the general's quarters.

CHAPTER 6

zekiel glanced down at his watch. In another four minutes and thirty-two seconds, he would be coming up on his first target. His bomb should release at that time.

Ezekiel knew that this first location was the most important target of all of the ones that had been assigned. Ezekiel was willing to allow the onboard computer to do the work, but he was still manually making sure all of the coordinates were correct to assure a dead-on hit. One bomb, one destroyed nuclear missile; that was the plan.

With approximately thirty seconds to go, he felt something had gone wrong. His bomb release mechanism should have already been activating the bomb doors but he hadn't heard anything that would have signaled that.

Something was wrong.

*This isn't right*, he thought. *Should I manually override this?*

He didn't know what to do. He had not received any notification that this target was being bypassed.

Another thirty seconds quickly ticked off the clock, and his plane made a slight adjustment in its trajectory to go on to the next target. He knew this was according to the program already in the computer. He also knew that he had about another six to seven minutes before his next target would come up.

*But why hasn't the bomb released?* he wondered. *Is something wrong with the mechanism? Or maybe the computer is messed up. Should I break radio silence and notify the command bunker? That missile is sure to be launched as soon as the missile battery receives word their country is under attack. And if that were to happen… Oh God. Please don't let it be targeted at the Sharon Air Base. Please… but please don't let it hit my country anywhere and explode.*

He couldn't bear the thought that maybe Esther could possibly be targeted by that missile. After her finally agreeing to go out with him he couldn't even allow a thought to run through his mind that something might happen to her. He knew if that missile were targeted at Sharon Air Base, every living thing within twenty-five miles of it would all be dead, including Esther.

*Should I turn around, go back, and manually fly my targets? Should I personally take out that missile? Is there a flaw in my program?* "God, please tell me what to do," he screamed.

In the bunker, Prime Minister Ben Joseph finally returned with only about five minutes left before the time ran out to reprogram Ezekiel's plane. Even though the signals would be traveling at the speed of light, there would still be a few seconds of delay due to having to travel twenty-two thousand miles up into space to reach their geostationary satellite and then to return back to Lt. Col. Cohen's plane. So it was imperative if he was going to make a change in plans that he give the order now. And all of this depended on if the solar flares shooting off the sun had not damaged or destroyed their satellite.

As Prime Minister Ben Joseph shuffled into the room, his face was drawn and gray. He looked like he had an Egyptian death mask covering his face. It was totally devoid of any emotion whatsoever. He was a man who had become a stone-faced statue moving slowly into the room.

He stopped as he finally managed to reach the back of his chair.

He slowly reached out and grabbed the back of it. His body was trembling like a man with advanced Parkinson's disease, so badly that he needed to hold onto the back of the chair to steady himself. Before saying anything, he slowly glanced around the room at each of the men sitting around the table. Then, in a voice almost devoid of sound, he mouthed the words, "General Green, please send the order to change the target away from the missile."

General Green nodded his head in the direction of Col. Jeremiah.

"Consider it done." Col. Jeremiah replied over his shoulder as he was hurrying to complete the task.

At the same time, Prime Minister Ben Joseph let go of the back of the chair and collapsed down to the floor onto his knees. His legs could no longer support the enormous burden on his soul. He suddenly fell forward onto his hands and began sucking in huge gasps of air like he was going to be sick. Then, he let all of it explode out of his mouth in a bellowing howl of tormented anguish that reached down to the very bottom of his being. "Oh God. What have I done?" he screamed. He balled his hands into a pair of fists and began pounding the floor as hard as he could. "I've just given the order to kill a quarter million of my own people. I am no better than Hitler. I too am a mass murderer of Jews. I too have just sent multitudes of innocents to their graves unaware."

As those anguished words painfully tumbled from his mouth, he fell face forward to the floor. He was a mass of human sobbing, a man with so much sorrow no other man could ease or comfort. No one moved to try to comfort or console him. They all knew that it was impossible to do such a thing.

General Green thought, *How do you tell someone who had just given an order like he had just done, "It's going to be all right"? It's absolutely not possible.*

The prime minister suddenly began making a noise like he was gagging or choking. General Green quickly knelt down beside him. But the prime minister wasn't choking. What he was doing was repeating over and over again a statement made two thousand years ago by Caiaphas, the Jewish High Priest at the time of Jesus: "It is better for one to die than for all to die."

Most of the men in the room, other than General Green, were not religious Jews. Even so, through their study of Jewish history, they all knew certain stories and tales about Jesus, the ancient Jew who had claimed to be the Jewish Messiah but had been crucified on a cross by the Roman authorities over two thousand years ago.

Most of them were aware of the story that on the same night Jesus had been arrested by the Jewish religious authorities and had been forced to stand before the Sanhedrin Council, the judges had consulted amongst themselves and had finally declared, because of the Roman occupation and their sure and swift brand of justice, that it is better for one to die than for all to die. That was the exact feeling they all felt that night. It is better that a few die in Israel than for all of Israel to die.

General Green knew this was a plan concocted by humans. It was a plan to allow a few—possibly two hundred fifty thousand people—to die in their own country in the hope that another country would come to their rescue. General Green could not say so, but he was thinking that if only the prime minister would have put his faith and trust in God and His ability to deliver them, these unbearable feelings of despair would have never come upon him.

As the prime minister lay there in a pitiful heap, he continued crying out to God to please be merciful and to forgive him. He also begged God that the innocents would not hold him accountable and that their blood would not be held against him. He begged God to make the casualties as small as possible. He begged God to allow him to die.

As soon as the prime minister had given him the order, Col. Jeremiah sent the order to change the program in Ezekiel's plane to not drop any bombs on his first target. He knew they were cutting it very close. The prime minister had not given him much time to reprogram the plane. He hadn't yet had time to notify Lt. Col. Cohen of the change. He also knew Lt. Col. Cohen had the ability to override the computer and drop his bomb on the missile anyway. General Green knew this too. The two men looked at each other. Neither knew what was or what possibly had already happened.

zekiel was confused. All of his training, all of his military-instilled discipline, everything he was about as
a man told him that a malfunction
had happened in his computer. If
so, he knew he had to take manual control of the plane and return to destroy
the missile. He also knew that if he didn't
do that very thing, it was a very real possibility that his home base, Sharon Air
Force Base, would be targeted, and if
that happened the love of his life would
surely die. He also knew that it was a possibility that Tel Aviv might be the target
instead. If that was it, then it was almost
assured that his parents, his two sisters,
and his younger brother would all die.

He sat there for only an instant
longer, but that instant seemed to last
an eternity. Every pore in his body was
sweating profusely! His stomach was
doing flip-flops, filled with the nauseating bile of his last meal. He could, he
knew, send a coded computerized message back to command headquarters to
get their take on what to do. But by the

time his message was sent and the time it would take to get a return message, he would be too far away from the target to go back. His fuel situation would not allow him to go back. He needed to make a decision. He needed to make it *now*.

He made up his mind. He was going back. His reached out with his right hand to flip the manual override switch to retake control of his plane and weapons systems. But as soon as his forefinger barely touched the switch, he heard a beep in his helmet alerting him to an incoming computerized message.

He quickly jerked his hand back. Then as the sudden release of the almost crippling tension began flowing out of his body, he suddenly felt like he was going to pass out. It was like the raging surge of a million gallons of water pouring out of a broken dam.

Finally, the message began to scroll across his monitor: "Attention. Code Green. Do not. Repeat, do not, return to missile and destroy. Allow computer to guide plane to completion of mission. Repeat, Code Green."

Code Green was the password assuring that it was coming from command headquarters. Part of him was relieved that he hadn't had to make the decision. But the other part was in total turmoil about whether everyone he loved were all going to perish.

As he read the words another sudden burst of fear and anguish surged through his body. He knew he was still within the bubble of time where, if he were to choose, he could still flip the manual switch and go back. If he were to do that, more than likely, both Esther and his family's lives would be saved. But he had been ordered to continue on with the plan as programmed from that point on. He had never, throughout his entire thirteen-year air force career, ever broken a direct order or refused to carry one out. But lives that meant more to him than his own were at stake.

"What do I do?" he screamed.

He leaned his head back against the headrest of his flight seat. It had originally been custom molded to fit his body perfectly, but it was anything but comfortable at that moment. It felt more like he was sitting on a pile of six-inch-long metal spikes being driven deep into his entire body, like he was being crucified all over. He slowly closed his eyes for just a second. If he was going to go back, he only had about ten more seconds to flip the switch and make the turn. After that, it would be too late.

"Oh, God. What do I do? What do I do?" he prayed.

As his words were barely fading into silence, it seemed like he heard a small, quiet voice speak to him. But it wasn't a voice that he audibly heard speaking into his ear. It was just a voice speaking to him somewhere inside of his being, centered right around his heart.

"Ezekiel, continue on as ordered. You asked me earlier to take care of Esther. I will do as you asked. I will also protect your family because of your concern. Continue on, and I will keep all of my people safe under the shadow of my wings."

A surge of relief suddenly flooded through him as all of the tension and indecisiveness emptied out. One replaced the other. A huge smile wrapped itself across his face. He knew everything was going to be all right. He couldn't explain it. But he just knew inside of him what was going to happen. He also knew that the voice he had heard had come from God. And in all of his life, that had been the first and only time he had ever heard the voice of El Shaddai, Almighty God, speaking to him. *But,* he suddenly thought, *God doesn't have the voice of General Green. He has a very small, quiet voice instead of a deep, booming baritone like I always thought He would have.*

eneral Green suddenly stood up. His eyes were fixed on the flat-screen monitors lined up on the wall in front of him. "Look. They're all dropping their ordnance right now." He glanced down at his watch. Then, he looked back up and continued. "They're all dropping their ordnance at the *exact* time we had scheduled. This is fantastic, gentlemen. We have never had an operation take place that began at the exact *second* we had scheduled for it to begin. And for all twelve of them to do so at the exact same time is almost unbelievable. It's just uncanny. In fact, I will proclaim that it is *supernatural*."

He stood there immobile with a smile in the beginning stages of wrapping itself across his face.

At the same time, Colonel Jeremiah suddenly jumped up out of his chair, sending it flying backward against the wall with it landing upside down, just like the prime minister had done earlier.

He just couldn't help himself. He cried out, "Great God of Israel, we *thank you* and give praise to you."

At that same time, Prime Minister Ben Joseph lifted his head up from the floor. His face was a total mess. His eyes were bright red, swollen, almost to the point of being closed from the constant flow of tears he had been shedding. He was sucking in huge gasps of air. His chest was heaving up and down. But as he tried to focus on the screens, he too had a sudden surge of relief beginning to flow through him while some of the tension and emotions began flowing out.

In Iran, at that exact same time, things were going absolutely crazy. Malaku I-mawti was the craziest of all of them. He was screaming at his defense minister who was standing in front of his desk, trembling so bad he was about to urinate in his pants.

"What do you mean *you have no idea what is happening* or *who* is doing this to us? You know it can only be two countries. It is either the United States or Israel … or maybe both combined. But surely we have whoever this is on radar, don't we?"

"No, sir," Arash Shakiba, the defense minister replied. "We do not have anything on radar at this time. Nothing at all. As far as we know, this attack might have come from outer space. Sir, all we know for a fact is that all over Iran at this exact time, in a very coordinated effort, explosions are taking place that are destroying our entire nuclear weapons program, including the nuclear bombs, plus our ability to deliver those bombs via missiles.

"Everything has been destroyed … except … we have just received a report that says one of our missile silos has been spared. And if that is the case, we believe it is the one silo that already has a nuclear bomb attached to the missile and the missile is already fueled and ready to be launched. The problem with this is *why*." the defense minister continued. "Why would this one site be spared when all of the others have been destroyed?"

"I don't care *why* this site has been spared!" Malaku I-mawti screamed. "If that is the case, I order you to arm that bomb as quickly as possible and then set the target to destroy Tel Aviv. And do it *now*."

"But, sir, we have no confirmed reports that Israel is behind this attack. If we launch an attack against her and she is innocent, then the rest of the world will condemn us to death by restrictive sanctions."

"I don't care. It does not matter. We were going to attack her tomorrow anyway. Well, we have just moved up the date and time. Do what I ordered you to do. And do it *now*."

Malaku I-mawti slammed his fists down so hard onto the top of his desk that it shattered several pieces of little glass figurines he had sitting on it. They broke into a million different pieces. He had never in his life felt such fury, nor such extreme hatred. He continued screaming! "With every cell, molecule, and atom in my body I absolutely hate the blood-sucking, money-grubbing Jews of the world. I want to kill every one of them no matter where they live or what gutter they hide in."

At this moment, he actually even hated his hero, Adolph Hitler, for not finishing the job of exterminating every Jew in the world. Hitler had made a huge dent in the Jewish population of the world at that time, but he had failed to finish the job. Because of that, Malaku I-mawti truly believed, *Hitler's mantle has fallen on me. It's now my job, given by Allah himself—all praise be to him—to complete the job Hitler had begun.*

His hatred for the Jews had no rhyme or rational reason for it. It was just an extreme hatred that he had grown up with in his family. His father had hated the Jews and passed that down to his son. Possibly, it went all of the way back to when Abraham sent Hagar into the desert to die with Ishmael instead of splitting his inheritance with them.

But, it didn't matter anymore. Nothing mattered except for his complete desire to totally exterminate all of the Jews inside of Israel. And if he destroyed the entire country at the same time, well so be it.

He wanted so much to totally destroy the entire country of Israel and leave it nothing but a barren, radioactive wasteland for the rest of eternity. That attack was going to happen tomorrow on their so-called Sabbath. And he knew that if he could accomplish that goal, his place in paradise would be assured.

But as that thought flowed through his mind, another suddenly entered in; one that had filled him for his entire life with terrifying fear; one that he had tried his entire life to suppress, so far with success. But he began wondering if the twenty-one virgins he would receive as his reward in paradise would be of the male variety—but more than just male, the very young male variety—since those were the only kind he ever fantasized about or was attracted to. He suddenly licked his lips as that thought came to him. Ten to eleven years old were the perfect age for him, and this is who he fantasized about constantly. But it suddenly appeared that his plans, his goals, his dreams, his fantasies had all been shattered. It was a total nightmare. It was worse than any dream he had ever had before in his life.

Arash Shakiba, the defense minister of Iran, after speaking with Malaku I-mawti hurried back to his office and immediately picked up a satellite phone to call General Rostami, the commanding officer of the missile battery that had been miraculously untouched—*All praise be to Allah*, he thought to himself—by whoever was bombing them.

As soon as General Rostami picked up, Minister Shakiba cut right to the chase without any pleasantries. "General Rostami, I am calling you upon orders from our great leader, President Malaku I-mawti has given the order for you to arm the weapon and to set the target for Jerusalem as quickly as you can.

"I am sure you have been monitoring the reports coming in from all over our country that we have been under attack, but we do not know by whom at this time or even how they are accomplishing this. But whoever it is and by whatever means they are doing so, all of our nuclear facilities and weapons have now been destroyed. All but yours. The fate of the Iranian people rests on your shoulders, General. By *inshallah*—if god wills—it shall be done. *Allahu Akbar*."

"Yes, Defense Minister Shakiba, god is great. *Allahu Akbar*. And we have heard the reports. Because of these, we have already taken the initiative to arm the weapon. We had just been waiting for a target to be given to us. Within five minutes, sir, we will have the target set for Jerusalem; and as you say, *inshallah*, by god's will and with Muhammad's blessing—may peace be upon him—it shall be done. Jerusalem will soon become a smoking heap of radioactive refuse within the next thirty minutes. *Allahu Akbar*," General Rostami yelled as he hit the stop button on the satellite phone.

After that, he quickly called the commanding officer who had been standing by at the missile silo for the target to be given to him. But General Rostami, in his hurry to give the coordinates for Jerusalem, made a small mistake and accidentally wrote one number of the coordinates down wrong. He didn't realize his mistake and quickly repeated these coordinates to the commanding officer, who immediately transferred the coordinates into the computer controlling the missile. Within five minutes, with a flame stretching behind it for over thirty feet, the missile blasted off the launch pad.

But unknown to anyone at that time, that one small numerical mistake General Rostami had made would be enough to spare all of Jerusalem. Jerusalem had been a mistake in the first place. President Malaku l-mawti had ordered Tel Aviv to be destroyed. That is where the government of Israel was located. Defense Minister Shakiba had given it wrong to General Rostami. General Rostami had given a wrong coordinate to the missile crew. Ten minutes later, there was much wailing and gnashing of teeth in the camps of the Palestinians inside of the Gaza Strip, along with the deaths of hundreds of thousands and the wounding and burning of hundreds of thousands more as the fires of *hell* were suddenly unleashed upon them.

# CHAPTER 10

All forms of military discipline had temporarily ceased inside the underground command bunker at Sharon Air Force Base. Everyone was yelling, clapping, and slapping everyone else on their backs. Even General Green was being congratulated and slapped on the back by much younger and lower-ranked officers. He, though, was doing the same thing.

Prime Minister Ben Joseph was absolutely ecstatic. His emotions had completely run the gamut from such agony he never knew could possibly exist to the joyous and ecstatic atmosphere taking place in the room. His right hand was plastered over his heart. It was beating a million miles a minute. Even though he was totally ecstatic, he was experiencing a small amount of pain in his chest along with a small portion running up and down his left arm.

He thought, *I'm getting way too old for this. A much younger man is needed to make these kinds of decisions.* But with a huge smile on his face, he thought, *I'll keep doing this job as long as God gives me the strength to do it.*

With that, he raised his voice and called everyone to order. As soon as he had their attention, he said, "Men, we have won a great battle tonight."

As these words were barely out of his mouth, he was again interrupted by yelling and clapping.

But the prime minister raised his hand again. "As I was saying, or at least trying to say, we have won a great battle here tonight. But it was not by our own doing. No. We won this battle only because *El Shaddai*, Almighty God, went to battle before us and prepared our way. And since He was already on the scene, I guess He just couldn't help Himself and He decided to go ahead and fight our battles for us.

"Yes, we have twelve very brave pilots who had the courage to fly straight into the mouth of the lion's den. But it was by the grace and mercy of Yahweh, who again shut the mouths of the lions just like He had done for the patriarch, Daniel, many years ago inside of that same godless country that allowed all of our brave young heroes to return back here tonight, safely and completely unscathed. Gentlemen, we must all take a moment out of our celebrations and give Yahweh our complete thanks and appreciation."

All quickly either bowed their heads where they stood or fell down to their knees with their faces bowed to the floor and began to give praise and thanks to the God of Israel, the great *I Am.*

Later on, the pictures began to flow across the screens of the utter devastation and carnage that had taken place in the Gaza Strip. Along with these pictures that were being provided by both, ONE, One World News Network, along with Al-Jazeera, the Arabic news provider, came the screams and denunciations of the "terrorist" Jewish state throughout the entire world. Even though there was plenty of proof that Israel was not behind the nuclear attack and had absolutely nothing to do with it, everyone was still condemning her. Not one country was willing to stand in the gap with the tiny country that occupies a small strip of land at the very center of the world.

That especially included the United States. And since Israel itself had not been hit by a nuclear-tipped missile, no military coup took place. But as had been predicted previously, Hussein Anwar, the president of the United States, immediately took to the airwaves.

"My fellow Americans, I'm sure most of you have heard by now that the anti-peace, pro-war fanatical faction in Israel that makes up the majority of their people launched a totally unprovoked and surprise attack against Iran last night. This criminal act has all but devastated Iran's military, along with killing multitudes of innocent civilians. But thanks to Allah, Iran was able to launch one missile back toward Israel in defense of her borders. Unfortunately, that missile went off course and landed in the Gaza Strip. That has created massive numbers of deaths and injuries of other poor, innocent Muslim people.

"I want you to know, my fellow Americans, that Israel's actions are criminal beyond human terms! I declare that Prime Minister Ben Joseph and the rest of her leaders should all be brought before the world court for trial and then condemned to a public execution. But until then, I declare that all aid to Israel is completely discontinued until further notice, *which might very well be permanent,*" he declared.

Even though this had been expected, the news was still devastating to the leaders of Israel. That had been the sole reason for sparing the nuclear-tipped missile from destruction in the first place.

But after watching the new enemy of the Jewish state make this announcement, Prime Minister Ben Joseph declared, "Men, do not lose hope and do not forget that we have our God going before us and fighting for us. You saw the actual hand of God fighting on our side tonight. And just like the Holy Scriptures say, 'If God be for you, who can be against you?' So, my friends and colleagues, we do not need the United States, nor anyone else for that matter, to come to our aid and help us. Our God desires to have the glory. This is His opportunity for Him to achieve it."

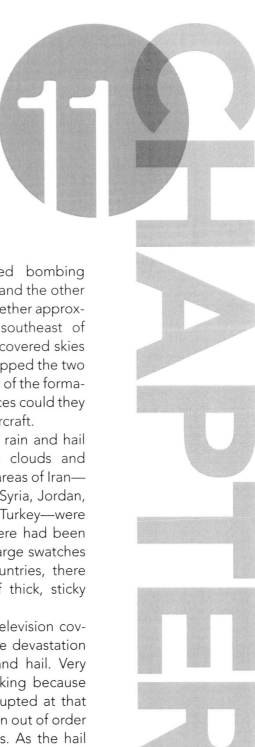

After they completed bombing their targets Ezekiel and the other pilots formed up together approximately fifty miles southeast of Tehran in the cloud-covered skies over Iran. They quickly wrapped the two B-2 bombers in the middle of the formation. Under no circumstances could they afford to lose these two aircraft.

A furious downpour of rain and hail was blasting out of the clouds and drenching the earth. Vast areas of Iran—and, for that matter, Iraq, Syria, Jordan, Saudi Arabia, and even Turkey—were being flooded. Where there had been huge *haboobs* covering large swatches of the earth in these countries, there now were huge areas of thick, sticky mud covering the land.

No one had radio or television coverage to warn them of the devastation accompanying the rain and hail. Very few electronics were working because electrical service was disrupted at that time. Power grids had been out of order for over twenty-four hours. As the hail swept down out of the sky, many of the chunks of ice were so large that entire houses and buildings were being destroyed just like they had been hit by artillery shells. The gusting, swirling winds had, in many areas, formed into very damaging tornadoes that were destroying everything in their paths.

By the time the storm finally passed, Iran would have suffered over twenty billion dollars in damage and over forty thousand lives lost. That was in addition to the damage and deaths the Israelis had rained down on them.

But it was not just Iran that suffered this damage. It was every country throughout the entire Middle East, North Africa all along the Mediterranean coast, and even up into Turkey and the former Russian satellite of Georgia. Hundreds of thousands of people would have died in the tumult before it finally blew over. Plus, billions and billions of dollars in damage will have been done.

Without a doubt, this would end up being the most expensive storm to ever be recorded in the history of mankind, both in dollars and in deaths.

All countries in that entire area suffered catastrophic damage and casualties; that is, all countries but one tiny country that sits in the very center of all of this turmoil: Israel. Not a single death or a single shekel in damage took place in the country God created for His own chosen people.

As Ezekiel and his men formed up over Iran, no one reported any contact with the enemy or even any problems of any kind whatsoever. They reported that all targets had been successfully destroyed and put out of commission for the foreseeable future. All of these were huge miracles, they knew. Everyone knew that some kind of a supernatural force was fighting alongside them. Too many things had happened to just be coincidences.

All twelve pilots made it back home to Sharon AFB safe and sound. Being the squadron commander, Ezekiel was the last to land. After he did so, he hurriedly shut the engines down, climbed out of his plane, and quickly called Esther.

"Hello," she said.

"Esther? This is Ezekiel Cohen. I'm so glad you answered. I need to speak with you for a brief moment. In a second, I have to run in to General Green's office, but I wanted to call you first."

"Oh. Hi, Lieutenant Colonel Cohen. How was your flight?"

As she heard the sound of his voice come through her phone, her heart began beating a million times a minute and an enormous weight of relief quickly fell off her.

"It's Ezekiel, Esther. *Ezekiel.* Call me Ezekiel. Anyway, I don't know if you've heard what has taken place tonight."

"Yes, I heard. You and your squadron bombed Iran. Actually, I haven't really heard that, but it's something Travis and I were discussing and believe is what happened."

"Travis? Who's Travis?"

"Travis King, the other guard at the gate, dummy. You call him King David, but his real name is Travis King."

"Oh. *King* David. Now I know who you mean. I never knew his first name. Anyway, yes, you're right. We did bomb Iran tonight. We took out all of their nuclear bombs and their missile batteries. Now they no longer have any nuclear weapons to threaten us with."

"That's wonderful, Lieutenant Colo—uh … Ezekiel. But you're wrong about one thing. Apparently, they were able to get one nuclear missile launched before you destroyed them all. You see, we heard on a radio that Iran had launched a nuclear missile toward us. Oh, I tell you, Travis and I were so scared. We believed that Sharon AFB would be the target. But we heard a little later on that the Gaza Strip had been hit instead. Lieutenant Col—uh … Ezekiel, why would they shoot that missile at Gaza?"

"I don't know, Esther. I hadn't heard about what you have just told me." A loud gasp of surprise escaped through his lips. Hearing about the missile striking Gaza shook him all the way down to his core. *How many people died or were injured?* he wondered. Then he said, "Esther, maybe you should come along with me to give the general a briefing. It seems that you know more things than I do. Anyway, I don't know why they shot a nuclear-tipped missile into the Gaza Strip. Uh … do you know how many casualties there are?"

"No, not yet, but we all know that with the extreme overcrowding over there, the number has to be in the hundreds of thousands, doesn't it?" Esther asked.

"Yeah … I guess. Say, I do have to run. The general is going to have me shot if I don't. But before I go, I gotta tell you that more than likely, I am going to be restricted to the base for a while. If Iran retaliates against us, I will need to jump back in my plane and fly back to attack the enemy forces."

"I know, and I understand. Everyone on the base is being restricted until further notice. That includes me too. But, Ezekiel, I just now got off duty. So if you would like, I could still meet you at the base officers' club later on after you meet with General Green. The food might not be up to Bahama's, but that's okay, isn't it?"

"Of course. Oh, I'm so glad you're still on the base. I mean …"

"I know what you mean. Don't worry about it. I think I want to see you as much as you want to see me. I don't know, Ezekiel. I just have an awful feeling that something very, very bad is about to happen soon. And … I guess I … just want someone … to share that with. I don't want to be by myself if something bad does happen. Besides, I guess I could do a whole lot worse than you," she said, laughing.

"Wow. I guess I don't really know what to say after that. I mean, of course I want to be with you too. But by what you said, am I like … I don't know … am I, like, playing second fiddle here?"

"No, of course not. I didn't mean it like that. In fact, I haven't even been on a date for over two years. Ever since … uh … I don't really want to get into that."

"No, Esther. I understand. I really do. Why don't you go on and head over to the officers' club and I'll meet you there just as soon as I can."

He hung up the phone and then just stood there. Over and over and over again, all he could think of was, *Wow. Wow. She talked like she has wanted to be with me for a long time now, but why didn't she ever show it? I mean, all of those times I invited her to go out, and nothing. I mean, she barely even gave me the time of day. But now, I mean, wow.*

He was five minutes late for the debriefing with General Green. The rest of his men were already there. As he finally burst through the door, General Green slowly turned his head and looked at him.

"Well, Lieutenant Colonel Cohen, thank you for blessing us with your presence. May I ask as to the reason why you're late?"

"Uh, sir … uh … it's … kind of a long story, sir."

"Aw, get over it, Lieutenant Colonel Ezekiel," Captain Tommy Barnes yelled. "Uh … General, may I answer for Lieutenant Colonel Cohen?"

"Proceed."

"Uh, well, you see, General, it's kind of like this. You see, uh … Lieutenant Colonel Cohen is in love, sir. Yes. That's what it is. He's in love."

"I see," General Green replied as he turned his face and attention directly onto Ezekiel. "Lieutenant Colonel, is this correct? Have you suddenly been struck with the need to nest, son? I mean, have you been struck with Cupid's arrow?"

"Uh … yes, uh … maybe … no. Uh … I mean …"

"Oh, good God in heaven. Lieutenant Colonel Cohen is in love. Well, son, congratulations. I'm happy for you. But we have a lot of unfinished business to take care of here. So, if you think you're ready to contribute to this meeting, we'll go on from here."

"Yes, of course, General. Ready and raring, so to speak."

"Yes. Well … ready and raring, are you? Good. Good."

Before Ezekiel and his men had taken off for their bombing runs into Iran, Ezekiel couldn't help it and blurted out to all of his men that Esther had finally agreed to go out with him. He had said, "After almost a year of asking her out, she finally decided I was worth it and has agreed to go out with me. I tell you, guys, I'm already in love with her, and I haven't even been out with her yet!"

All of his men had slapped him on the back and congratulated him, along with a lot of yelling and teasing. This was always the way they kept loose before any mission.

After the debriefing, General Green asked if there were any questions. Ezekiel raised his hand.

"I have just one, sir."

"Go ahead."

"Yes, sir. Well, It has come to my knowledge, that a … a …"

"Go ahead, son. For God's sake, what's on your mind?"

"Well, sir, is it true that Iran was able to launch a nuclear missile back at us?"

"Yes. That is true. They did return one missile at us."

"Well, sir, If I may, was it the missile my plane was ordered to not hit?"

"Again, son, that's correct. But what difference does it make?"

"Well, sir, it's just that … well … that you just do know how close I came to overriding the computer and destroying that missile. Could you tell me, sir, why my plane was ordered not to hit that site? I mean, even though it didn't hit us and instead hit Gaza, it still could have hit us. I was directly over the target. I was there. I could have easily taken it out. Why wasn't I allowed to do that?"

General Green's eyes burned into Ezekiel until Ezekiel could no longer hold his gaze and glanced away. "Lieutenant Colonel Cohen, you and all of your men in this room right now are all national heroes. You have all completed a most dangerous mission, and you have all returned safely from that mission by what I truly believe was divine intervention. Therefore, likewise, while you and your men were flying inside of enemy territory, all of us inside of the command bunker were deep in prayer, asking El Shaddai for divine guidance in what to do. And all of us believed we received His guidance. Therefore, that is your answer. It might not be the one you wanted, but it's the only one you're going to get."

"But, sir—"

General Green held up his hand, immediately stifling any and all comment. "That's all for right now, men. But you are all requested to remain on this base and available for immediate recall for any mission that might come up. I do not know how long you will be restricted here. But I suggest that you all get some sleep."

Ten minutes later, Ezekiel was sitting in a corner booth inside of the officers' club. Next to him was the girl of his dreams. She was no longer wearing her helmet and had allowed her thick auburn hair to flow down across her shoulders and down to the middle of her back. It perfectly accentuated her beautiful features. Ezekiel looked at her and knew that no other woman in the entire world was as beautiful and gorgeous as the living angel that was sitting next to him.

He leaned in close to Esther to speak quietly into her ear. He was close enough to smell her perfume. As the sweet aroma of lilacs and roses, with just a touch of vanilla, wafted up into his nostrils, his heart quit beating for a full moment and it took all of his extreme, disciplined military willpower to stop himself from asking her to marry him right then and there. But somewhere in the back of his mind, his head was telling him not to do that just yet. It was the first time she had even agreed to see him. He couldn't very well ask her to marry him within the first five minutes of sitting down next to her.

Can I?

But something was also sending a warning to his mind that had put an extreme urgency into everything happening around them.

Esther was feeling the same urgency. She had always felt like she had some kind of a sixth sense or a well-attuned female intuition. This sixth sense was telling her to let her reservations go and allow this very brave man into her life and her heart forever.

But instead of saying anything romantic, Ezekiel asked, "Esther, how detailed was the report you heard about the Gaza nuclear missile strike? Did it say anything about which direction the radioactive fallout was heading or anything like that?"

She turned her head to look at him. For the first time, she noticed how blue his brightly shining eyes were. It took her breath away for just a second. But she quickly regained her composure and said, "No. Nothing that I can remember. I too wondered about the fallout. But I haven't heard anything."

Listen. I don't know what your level of security is. I would think being in the guard detachment it must be relatively high, but I am going to tell you something that you need to keep to yourself only. Do not—I repeat, do not tell anyone else. Okay?"

She nodded her head.

"The missile that landed on Gaza was one of my targets earlier tonight. It was supposed to be my very first target. I was actually over the target, and my computer was programmed to drop the bomb that would have destroyed it. But nothing happened. I had no idea why. I could have overridden the computer and manually dropped the bomb anyway. In fact, I was reaching my hand out to flip the switch to do just that when I suddenly received a coded message saying to not do that and to allow the computer to fly the rest of the mission as already programmed."

She looked at him, stunned. "You mean … you're telling me … I mean, what you just said is that our own government made a decision to allow that missile to be fired at us?"

He nodded his head. "Yes. That's exactly what I'm telling you. It must have been authorized at the highest level to allow that nuclear missile to be fired into our country."

"But how … why … I mean, did they know it would land on Gaza and not on us?"

"I don't believe they did. I mean … well … this is why I don't want you to say anything. It just doesn't make any sense, does it? Why would our own leaders purposely allow a nuclear missile to be shot at us, knowing that it could very possibly kill hundreds of thousands of our own people? Esther, as I sat there in that plane, with my finger reaching for the switch to manually override it, my first thought was about you."

She quickly looked up and stared into his eyes.

A little embarrassed smile crawled slowly across his face as he quickly continued, "Yes, you were my first thought and my first worry. I mean, this was the first time you had ever given me the time of day, and I just couldn't let something happen to you before I had a chance to show you how wonderful a person I really am."

He laughed. She did too.

"My next thought was about Tel Aviv. My family lives there. My dad, mom, two older sisters, and a younger brother all live there. I didn't know what to do, but I was going to override the program and destroy the missile if I hadn't received the message when I did. But I still can't figure out why they did what they did. Tel Aviv could be a smoking pile of nuclear waste right now, and so could Sharon Air Force Base. I couldn't bear it if that were to have happened. But I just don't understand."

"Neither do I, Ezekiel. Neither do I. But I'm so glad that nothing happened to Tel Aviv either. My mother lives there in a convalescent home. She is almost the only family I have left, although she doesn't know I even exist anymore. She was severely injured in the head by a piece of shrapnel in a terrorist bus bombing attack four years ago in Bethlehem. My father and brother were killed in the same bombing. They were all there for the Christmas service at the Church of the Nativity.

"You see, Ezekiel… and I hope this doesn't make a difference with us, but my family is Christian. We are Messianic Jews. So, I don't know what all of this was about tonight, but I fully believe that Jesus has everything under control. You know, Ezekiel, there are so many prophecies in the Bible that have to do with what is happening right now. In fact, if you believe the prophecies, the next step in what is going to happen will be that Russia will move in force against us to try to destroy us. But God will intervene and send Gog, who, in the Bible, is mentioned as the king of the north, to almost total defeat. Ezekiel, this can be found in the book of Ezekiel in the Bible in chapters thirty-eight and thirty-nine. I have spent several years in small Bible study groups, studying about these end-time prophecies."

"Esther, I'm sorry about your family. I'm so sorry. But… do you really believe that Bible stuff?"

"Yes, I really do. You see, Ezekiel, I know inside of me that Jesus really lives. Yes, he did die on a cross over two thousand years ago, but I truly believe that He then rose from that grave, that He ascended into heaven and that He now lives in my heart too."

"Well, Esther, I believe you. I have never made any decision one way or the other about God. My family has never been religious. So I accept your beliefs and respect them. Maybe you can help me to find what apparently you have."

She looked at him for a long time to make sure he was serious about it. She was very attracted to Ezekiel, but she could not give her heart to someone who didn't share her beliefs. That was why she was so devastated when her previous fiancé, Randy, had been killed. They had not only shared their love for each other, but they had also shared the love of Christ too.

As she was looking into Ezekiel's face, she was surprised that all of a sudden, he brought Randy up. It was like he had been reading her thoughts.

"Esther, I truly hope that I am not opening up old wounds, but I know about your fiancé, Randy. I didn't know him personally, but I knew about him and about his very deep love of God. That had to help cement your love for each other since you feel the same way about God as he must have. I truly would like to find the same thing that both of you had."

"Ezekiel, do you know how he died?"

He shook his head no. "All I know is that he was killed in a Hamas attack."

"Ezekiel, he died a hero! But the thing is he didn't have to die at all. He died to protect his platoon when he threw himself on top of a grenade. He died so his men wouldn't have to."

"I am so sorry, Esther. I really am. That does really take a hero for someone to do something like that. I knew that he held the highest honor our country has to give, but I never knew what it was for. To tell you the truth, I don't know if I would have it in me to sacrifice myself for others … uh … that is, other than you.

"Yes, Esther, I know this is the first time we have ever even been out, but since I met you eleven months and seven days ago, I have so much wanted to hold you in my arms and try my best to comfort you, to tell you that I am not Randy, but if you would just let me in, I could take so much of the pain away and maybe … and maybe bring some happiness back into your life."

She looked at him for what seemed like several minutes. A little tear swelled up in her left eye and then slowly rolled down her face. "Ezekiel, yes, I was in love with Randy. He was the one and only man I have ever loved … up 'til now anyway. But … Jesus has helped me to get through the pain I have felt for so long. At first and for a long time afterward, I actually hated Randy. I knew that he gave his life as a sacrifice for his men.

"And my dad did too. My dad gave his life trying to protect my brother, my mom, and the rest of the people on the bus. My dad actually saw the suicide bomber reaching for the detonating cord before he pulled it. My dad jumped the man and tried to tear the cord out of his hand, but to no avail. But the time he was fighting with the bomber was enough to allow all but seven people to get off the bus. Unfortunately, my brother would not leave my dad's side. My mom was completely shielded by my dad's body, except for a small portion of her head where she got hit.

"But you see, Ezekiel, both Randy and my dad gave their lives as sacrifices so that others could live. And that is exactly what Jesus did too. Jesus gave His life so we—everyone in the entire world if they so desire—can have eternal life with Him. Jesus is the one who has taken all of my hatred and most of my pain away. I can breathe again. In fact, I can now live again and…love again."

Ezekiel was staring into her eyes, her face, her heart. In that very moment, he felt something deeper, more special, more…wonderful than anything else he had ever felt in his entire life! *This beautiful, gorgeous woman is going to become my wife somehow, some way, if only she will have me,* he thought.

Just then his beeper went off, interrupting everything. It was alerting him to return immediately back to the command bunker. "Esther, I have to hurry back over to General Green's office. Something has come up."

Just then, she quickly reached over and grabbed him by his arm. "Ezekiel, please be careful. I…don't want anything to happen to you like…well, you know. I don't think I could live if I had to go through all of it again."

He gently laid his hand on top of hers. At the same time, he leaned in against her and gave her a very gentle brush of his lips against her forehead. "Don't worry. I am not the sacrificing kind. I am not a hero. I like living, my love."

As he was standing up, she quickly stood up next to him. She reached her arms out and put them around his neck as she leaned gently in against him, tilting her face up to put her lips against his, kissing him deeply and passionately.

*Oh, man. This is it. I am never leaving her side for the rest of my life. General Green can get another flyboy to take my place.*

But he knew he couldn't do that. His country depended on him. So did Esther. But from that moment on, he was going to do any and everything in his power, or even beyond his power, to protect her and to keep her safe, along with his country.

She took her arms from around his neck and leaned back and said, "I'll be waiting when you return, my love. Come back to me, okay?"

"I will. Oh, I will. I give you my word on it."

Five minutes later, he was standing inside the command bunker next to General Green and watching little, red LEDs begin to light up everywhere all over the map of the world. The map was like a hologram. It showed all of the countries of the world and their alert status. Green meant the country was in a neutral status. Orange meant the country's military forces had increased their alert status above neutral. Red meant the country had come to full alert. Red was now the predominate color almost everywhere. Very few remained orange, and none were green.

Israel's attack against Iran and Iran's launch of a nuclear missile back toward Israel—even if it hit Gaza instead—had triggered a full worldwide military alert. Every Arab nation surrounding Israel was on full military standby, for whatever that was worth. Due to the effects of the huge storm destroying their countries as it slowly made its way eastward, they were but remnants of what they normally were.

Even so, every radical Muslim throughout these countries was screaming for an immediate *jihad*. Every moderate Muslim was demanding immediate retaliation against Israel. Every other Muslim was following along like little lapdogs with an intense desire to see the day every Jew was dead.

Across the entire world, Jewish embassies, Jewish synagogues, Jewish businesses, in fact, Jews everywhere were coming under attack. Some were being firebombed with Molotov cocktails. Others were being fired upon by gun-wielding radicals. Some were just being swarmed by vast human waves of people who were driven like they had some kind of supernatural mind-control mechanism inside of them.

What was happening across the world was a repeat of *Kristallnacht*—night of the broken glass—that the Nazis had perpetrated against the Jews at the beginning of World War II, only this was on a worldwide basis this time. The *entire* world had turned against the Jews. Within the next full day, twenty-four hours, over a million Jews worldwide would be killed, injured, homeless, or have their businesses destroyed.

As Ezekiel stood next to General Green, watching the entire world turn into a satanically inspired evil never before seen in history, both men shook their heads in disbelief.

"Never in my wildest imagination did I expect something like this to happen," General Green said, basically to himself but loud enough for Ezekiel to hear.

General Green turned to look at Ezekiel. "You don't understand why we did what we did when we allowed that nuclear missile to be launched against us, do you, Lieutenant Colonel?"

Ezekiel looked hard into the general's eyes. "No, sir, I don't. It has made me wonder though."

"It was something that, at the time, we all felt needed to be done. It is that simple. We were willing that some die to make sure that the rest of the nation survived."

"You mean you were willing to sacrifice some people so that more would be able to live?"

"Yes. Exactly."

"I've been hearing a lot about sacrificing tonight," Ezekiel said. But then he asked, "Why? What could have made all of you willing to sacrifice Tel Aviv? You could not have possibly known that the missile would hit Gaza instead of Tel Aviv."

"No, we didn't know that. In fact, we fully expected the missile to hit somewhere inside of Israel. It was a total surprise to us that it hit Gaza instead of us."

"But why, sir? Why?"

"You see, we all fully expected for a good portion of the world to turn against us, especially the Arab and Muslim countries and possibly even Russia. Therefore, we felt we needed the one country that always, up to now anyways, has been our friend and protector: the United States. We had a lot of intelligence coming to us that if Iran succeeded in launching a nuclear missile against us, a military coup was very likely to take place within the United States that would replace this... this socialistic, appeasement-pleasing president they have now. And if that had taken place, we felt very confident that they would then continue their friendship with us and honor the treaties between our two countries. But that didn't happen, did it? Anyway, Lieutenant Colonel, that is the reason we made the decision to allow that missile to be launched against us."

General Green looked wearily down toward the ground. His emotions had run the full gamut tonight too, from the mission these brave pilots had flown to being part of a decision to allow a nuclear missile to be launched against his own country, thereby possibly killing hundreds of thousands of innocent civilians, to the ecstatic release of extreme joy after hearing that the nuclear missile had landed in the Gaza Strip instead of in the actual country of Israel, to now seeing that it was going to be Israel and only Israel against the entire world.

Just then, his assistant, Colonel Jeremiah, walked up to him. He had a phone in his hand. "It's for you, General. Prime Minister Ben Joseph."

Prime Minister Ben Joseph and all of the rest of the civilian government members had left and returned back to Tel Aviv a couple of hours ago. The prime minister was now calling from his office.

"Hello. This is General Green."

"Yes. General, I am calling to get your input. I'm sure you're aware about what is happening in the world right now. In fact, I'm sure you're probably even more aware of it than we are. But be that as it may, I am calling to see if you have noticed what is right now taking place in Russia? It appears to us that Russia has gone on a full military alert across their entire country. And the word has just reached us a few minutes ago that they have expelled our entire embassy, staff and all, everyone. Russia has given just twenty-four hours for us to get all of our personnel and equipment out of their country. They are severing all contact with us. I have never seen such anger directed against us.

"And, General, we have also just received word that the president of the United States has summoned our ambassador to an immediate meeting at the White House that is to take place in another fifteen minutes. As you're aware, I'm sure, it is going on seven thirty in the evening in Washington, DC, right now.

"I personally spoke with our ambassador in the States just after he got off the phone with the president's appointment secretary demanding his presence. Our ambassador told me that the secretary was furious and said the president was also. So much, I guess, for there being a coup, huh? Anyway, your response, General?"

"Prime Minister, you know we were all aware of these possibilities beforehand. But we had no other choice, sir. Our country's survival required us to do what we did. Sir, if I may say so, I firmly believe that God fought on our side tonight. And I firmly believe that He will go before us and fight for us the rest of the way too, whatever that way is or wherever it leads."

"Yes, General, I agree with you. It seems like God is the only one who is on our side right now. *Shalom*, my friend," Prime Minister Ben Joseph said.

"*Shalom*, Prime Minister. But, sir, before you hang up, let me say that I feel it might be better if you were to return to this bunker until we can see what is going to take place."

"I appreciate your concern, General Green, but for now, I want the country to see me in person, not hiding safe and sound inside of a bunker."

The general handed the phone back to Colonel Jeremiah with a deep sense of admiration in his heart for such a brave man. Surely God had placed the man in this position for such a time as now.

He turned to face Ezekiel again. "I suppose you heard most of that conversation or were able to get the gist of it."

"Yes, General, I heard your response to the prime minister concerning your belief that God is fighting on our side. Let me ask you, General, if I may be so blunt, sir?"

"Go ahead, Lieutenant Colonel. Ask whatever you will."

"Well, sir, it's just that ... well ..."

"Go ahead, son. You're free to speak anything on your mind."

"Well, sir, I was just wondering, do you really believe that? Do you really believe God is fighting on our side?"

"Lieutenant Colonel, let me think about how best to answer your question. First of all, yes, I do believe He is on our side and will fight for us in the future, just like He's done in our past. You see, son, you're too young to remember the nineteen sixty-seven war with the Arabs. That war has often been labeled the Six-Day War because that is the amount of time that it lasted, just six days. In fact, you were not even born yet. But at that time, I was a young, eighteen-year-old army corporal assigned to a tank unit.

"At that time, we were totally outnumbered and completely surrounded by enemy Arab forces. On the surface, we had absolutely no chance, and the Arab armies were marching without hesitation on their way to capturing the entire city of Jerusalem. Nothing we could do could stop them. In fact, there was absolutely nothing in their way to keep them from accomplishing their target. But for some unknown reason, the Arab armies stopped and waited. Who knows for what? At the time this happened, some of them were actually within visual sight of Jerusalem. But for some reason, they all stopped their advance.

"That gave us time to regroup and launch a counterattack against them. Because of that we were able to totally route the combined armies and send them back to their own territories with their beaten and whipped tails tucked between their legs. So, Lieutenant Colonel, again, yes, I do believe that God will fight for us, just like He did then and just like He already has done for us tonight.

"God is the reason those armies stopped. In fact, some Arab soldiers interviewed afterward said that they saw huge masses of men, a much, much larger army than our entire forces combined, surrounding the entire city of Jerusalem. They said they knew they were well out-numbered, and many of them wondered where all of the fighters came from. They assumed we had hired mercenaries. But, Ezekiel, those fighters were part of the angelic host of angels that surrounds the throne of God in heaven. God sent them here to fight for us. He did it then. I promise you He will do it again now."

Ezekiel stood there, taking it all in. He was nodding his head as huge goose bumps were running rampant up and down his body. Of course he had heard about the glorious win for the Israelis and the total defeat of the combined Arab armies back in 1967. In fact, it was a subject that was very heavily taught in history classes in school. He had also heard that it was a great miracle from God that the Israelis had won that war. It was just that Ezekiel had never really even believed in God before.

He turned back to the map of the world. Every light on the entire map was red. Seeing those, he knew that it would take nothing less than another miracle from—well, at least, some kind of a God for Israel to continue to survive.

He could almost allow himself to believe that there might be a supernatural God who did certain favors for some people, but he was having a real hard time believing that this same, God had a son whom He allowed to come to earth as a human being instead of as a God and then allowed that same son to die a horrible death on a Roman cross. No matter how much he was in love with Esther, this was something that he had to take with a grain of salt and just allow Esther to have a few idiosyncrasies. But he also knew that he had heard not with his ears but a voice earlier that night that told him that Esther would be all right.

During the time he was standing there, thinking, General Green was speaking with Colonel Jeremiah. Eventually, he turned back to Ezekiel. "Lieutenant Colonel, I've just been given some information that means ... well, it means that Israel is going to need God to fight on our side more than He ever has before or ... or we are all doomed. We have just received word that Russia is coming to the aid of Iran. And as such, the two countries have vowed ultimate revenge against us. In fact, Russia has now gone on full alert status. She is recalling all of their troops who might have been on leave, plus they are calling up all of their reserve troops right now. In addition to this news, every, I repeat, *every* other Arab and Muslim nation in the world has now declared war, or *jihad*, against us.

"Again, though, Ezekiel, our sincere hope is that the United States will stand by our side with us against the world. If they do, I don't believe any other nation would be willing to go against our combined strengths. But at this moment, our ambassador in the United States is meeting with their president. We shall wait to hear what he has to say."

"General, would you mind if I run out and grab a quick bite to eat? I won't be gone long. And if you need me, I have my beeper and cell phone, and can be back here within five minutes."

General Green looked into the troubled nervous eyes of Ezekiel. Yes, they were troubled and nervous, but nowhere did he see any fear. But he also knew what the real reason was for Ezekiel's request.

"Yes, Lieutenant Colonel. You have my permission to go. And while you're … uh … eating, please give my regards to Lieutenant Asher too."

Ezekiel stood there staring at General Green with a blank look on his face. He didn't have any idea who the general was talking about. But then, slowly, it dawned on him. Just loud enough for the general to hear, "Esther," escaped out of his mouth. He had no idea the general even knew who he was interested in, much less that the general knew Esther personally.

General Green smiled and nodded his head, "Yes, Ezekiel, Lieutenant Esther Asher."

As soon as Ezekiel stepped off the elevator, he grabbed his cell phone and called Esther. She answered on the first ring, but he could tell she had been sleeping.

"Oh, Esther, I'm sorry to have woken you up."

"No, Ezekiel. No. It's okay. I didn't even realize I had dozed off. Where are you?"

"I just left the underground command bunker. General Green allowed me to have a brief break in order to grab a bite to eat. Would you feel up to meeting me again at the Officers' Club?"

"Sure. I'm on my way."

"Okay. I'll see you there. Oh, and by the way, General Green told me to give you his regards, Lieutenant Asher. Could I ask how General Green happens to know you so well?"

"Yes, of course. General Green is my uncle on my mom's side of the family. He is my mom's older brother. He has always taken a liking to me, but I sometimes feel that I haven't received the promotions I should have because he is afraid of being accused of nepotism. But, oh well. As the Muslims, say, *inshallah*—as God wills."

A few minutes later, they were both sitting in the same booth they had been in earlier. But this time, they were sitting scrunched up so tight against each other that you couldn't have squeezed a piece of paper between them.

Ezekiel turned to face her.. "You're just full of surprises, aren't you? Is there anyone else you either know or are related to that I might need to know about before I stumble over my tongue?" He laughed.

"No. I don't think there is anyone else I know or am related to. But I will tell you one thing though. The only reason I allowed myself to meet you earlier tonight is because my uncle told me that I should. He convinced me that you were a man very much worth taking a chance on and that I should give you that chance. He said you are a man of honor. He said you are a very brave man. And he said that if you were to break my heart, instead of flying secret airplanes from secret airfields, you would be cleaning latrines with toothbrushes as a private for the rest of your military career." As she said that, she leaned into him and began giggling. He sat there for a moment, shaking his head while, at the same time, marveling at how life works at times.

Ezekiel smiled. "I promise you, my little bewitching beauty, that I will never break your heart. Especially now that I know what my future holds if I do." He laughed before continuing. "Seriously though, I am, even if I do say so myself, a man of honor. I don't know what the future holds, but this I do know. I will never knowingly do anything to hurt you. But speaking of the future, have you heard any more news about what is happening in the world right now?"

"No. For some reason, our country has instituted a full news blackout. That even includes the Internet. It is impossible to even turn it on right now."

"Well, that is probably for the best. I mean, again, please keep what I am saying to yourself. I guess as General Green's niece, he would not mind me sharing this with you. I mean, he didn't tell me to not say anything. So, I assume he thought I would confide in you. Anyway, because of what we did earlier tonight, the entire world has turned against us. That probably even includes the United States. Our ambassador is in a meeting at this very moment with the president of the United States, but from all indications, they are going to condemn us too. That means they will not do anything to stand in the breech with us. So it really will be us against the world.

"Esther, we have our own nuclear weapons. We are not impotent. But we cannot stand up to the entire world. Before leaving the command bunker, General Green confided in me that Russia is mobilizing all of her troops. She is recalling everyone that is on leave and bringing up all of her reserve personnel, just like you said would happen. Without a doubt, we probably killed several Russians tonight in our raids. We had anticipated that would happen. You know that the Russians helped them build their nuclear plants and also to enrich their fuel. So, it's very conceivable that many Russians were still working in or around the places we targeted. But we did not really believe they would move against us. Then again, all of her moves right now might just be a stunt to try to scare and intimidate us. We'll have to wait and see. But we might need your God and your Jesus before this is over. That reminds me. Is your uncle, General Green, a believer in Jesus too?"

"Yes. He is a Messianic Jew like me. Why do you ask?"

"Well, he talked a lot to me tonight about God and how God has fought on the side of the Jews several times in our history."

"Yes. He is a firm believer. Ezekiel, he saw God fighting for us during the Six-Day War. I mean, he didn't actually *see* God, but he definitely saw the miracles God did."

"Then tell me this, Esther. Where was God when the Nazis were killing all of the Jews throughout Europe? Huh? Tell me that. Where was He, and why did He allow it to happen in the first place if He's so intent on fighting for us?"

"Ezekiel, I know where God was. He was in heaven, where He always is. But as to why He allowed such evilness to occur, I cannot tell you that, for I don't know the reason."

"Well, you know, Esther, I'm not condemning Him or anything like that. In fact, until I met you, I never even thought about God. He just hasn't ever played a part in my life before now, at least not that I'm aware of."

Esther didn't reply back right away. She was in deep thought. Suddenly, she looked up at him, "You know what, Ezekiel? Maybe I do have an answer for you. You mentioned earlier tonight that our own government actually allowed a nuclear missile to be fired at us. At the time they made that decision, they knew full well that it was probably going to kill and injure multitudes of our people, but they made the decision to allow that to happen anyway. Why, Ezekiel? Why did they make that decision?"

He started to say something, but she raised her hand to stop him.

"I'll tell you why that decision was made. It was made knowing that multitudes would be killed and injured, but it was also made in the hope and belief that the United States would launch a military coup against their own government and then would come to fight alongside us. Am I correct?"

"Yes. But how did you know about that? I know you haven't spoken with General Green tonight, so how did you know?"

"There have been rumors to that effect for a few weeks now. My uncle discussed it with me over dinner not too long ago."

"Okay, but what does that have to do with what I asked you about God?"

"Here's the tie-in, I believe. You see, yes, six million Jews died in the Holocaust, but because of that, millions more from throughout the world returned back to their Jewish roots and religion. It also is the reason why we Jews were finally able to re-establish our homeland here in Israel after being dispersed for over two thousand years.

"Ezekiel, there is a scripture in the Bible that says to the effect; 'What Satan meant for harm, God meant for good.' Our patriarch, Joseph, made that statement while he was curator over the entire land of Egypt after his brothers, the same ones who had sold him into slavery many years before, came before him and were reunited with him. So, I believe that sometimes God allows—He definitely does not send it—but He allows evil to take place so that He can then turn the evil around and defeat Satan by turning everything to good. In other words, our prime minister made a decision tonight knowing that extreme evil was probably going to happen against the Jewish people again. He made that decision to allow that evil to happen in the hope that good would come out of it by the United States coming to our aid.

"But first of all, Ezekiel, know this. God is fighting on our side in this war, and he did not allow that evil to come against us this time. He stood up and declared that He is going to go to war for us and fight for us. Don't you see, Ezekiel? God didn't allow that missile to strike us. He purposely turned it away from us. But if it would have hit us, it probably would have sent the United States into a coup so they could use their incredible military might to cause all nations to cower down before them and leave us alone. God didn't want that to happen. You know why? Because He wants to show the entire world that He is the savior of the Jews, not the United States, and especially not their evil president.

"Now, I don't know what that president is saying right now to our ambassador, but I bet it is not good news. I bet he is telling him he is going to stand by and allow whatever must be to take place. And as I already told you, the Holy Bible says that in the latter days, Russia, who I truly believe is the Gog mentioned in the book of Ezekiel in chapter thirty-eight in the Bible, will come against us with all of her might, just like a *storm cloud* covering the land. And Ezekiel, I truly believe with all of my heart and soul that we have just entered into those latter days."

Ezekiel just sat there, thinking. He was shaking his head from side to side, in awe of Esther's insight. But he didn't know what to think. He had never once in his entire life even picked up a Bible, much less opened one to read what it has to say. Finally, he turned to look at her.

"You know, Esther, you might be right. Someone has given you a lot of insight into things, especially tonight, when you have not had any news or contact with anyone else but me. But it still stuns me that a so-called good God would allow millions of people to die just to get people's attention turned back toward Him. I just don't know."

"I don't know either. But His word declares, 'God's ways are not our ways.' I don't completely understand it either. But just as our prime minister had to make a decision to allow multitudes to die, God had been forced to do the same thing. In other words, maybe it's as the old saying goes: 'the greater good far outweighs the greater evil.'"

"Yes. I see your point. I guess it makes sense. But if God is really going to go to war and fight for us, I hope He comes prepared for a real bloodbath because that is exactly what is probably going to happen."

Right at that moment his cell phone rang. It was General Green.

"Yes. Hello, General Green."

"Lieutenant Colonel Cohen, I called to see if you are taking good care of my niece."

"Uh … uh … yes, sir, I do believe that I am."

"Then I want you to take the hand of that extremely beautiful young lady and lead her back here to my bunker ASAP."

"Uh … yes, sir. Yes, sir. On my way, uh … on *our* way, sir."

He closed his phone and looked at Esther and said, "Your uncle just told me to take you by the hand and lead you back to his bunker."

A thousand sparkling diamonds suddenly exploded in her eyes and all across her face.

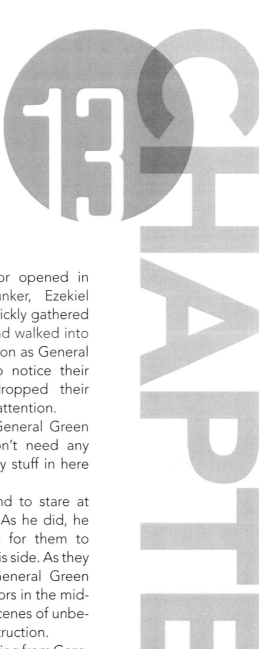

CHAPTER 13

As the elevator door opened in the command bunker, Ezekiel reached out and quickly gathered up Esther's hand and walked into the room. But as soon as General Green turned around to notice their presence, they both dropped their hands and came to rigid attention.

"At ease. At ease," General Green quickly replied. "We don't need any more of that strict military stuff in here for the rest of this night."

He turned back around to stare at the flat screen monitors. As he did, he motioned with his hand for them to come up next to him, by his side. As they stepped next to him, General Green pointed to the two monitors in the middle. They were showing scenes of unbelievable carnage and destruction.

"Those scenes are coming from Gaza. It's the carnage caused by the nuclear missile." He stopped for a minute, unable to go on as his voice suddenly choked up. His eyes misted over, and unashamedly, tears began running down his face.

*My Lord, please have mercy on those poor people,* he prayed. "Excuse me, Esther and Ezekiel. These people are our avowed enemies, and they hate us with their entire might, but they are still children of God. They have souls and bodies just like we do. They have just been deceived by the god of this world, the one who is responsible for the creation of such devastating weapons of such mass destruction. And this carnage, these deaths, these injuries… oh, again, I'm sorry for this display."

Tears flowed freely and abundantly down his face. They didn't originate in his eyes; they had worked their way up out of his heart, a heart that was breaking because thousands, maybe even hundreds of thousands of God's own original creation had just died and were already on their way sliding headlong and face first into the fiery-hot flames of hell unless they had made Jesus their Lord and Savior. General Green knew that Jesus had declared, "I am the way, the truth, and the life. No man comes to the Father but through me!"

Finally, a few moments later, he gathered his emotions back together and continued. "We have now gotten a very rough estimate of the number of dead and injured. Initial reports are saying that an estimated five hundred thousand people are probably already dead, with at least another five hundred thousand injured. Oh, my precious God. And those figures do not include the number that will eventually die from radiation poisoning."

He again briefly paused, "I have to say that the casualty rate is solely because of the huge compacted density in population inside Gaza. As you well know, those people have chosen to live on top of each other, almost like rats, even though they could have moved and lived elsewhere. Over many years, we have made many concessions that would have allowed the Palestinians to have their own state if they would only reject their terrorist ways and give full recognition to us to live and exist. But the terrorist leaders of Hamas, Hezbollah, and Al Fatah have purposely chosen to ignore our peace offerings and have continued their terrorist activities to try to drive us out of our land. Thus, their own demonic activities have brought this disaster on them. It did not come from us!"

Ezekiel took a moment to clear his throat, and then asked, "General Green, do we have any reports saying which direction the poisonous radiation cloud is moving?"

"Yes. This storm that has been coming in from the Mediterranean Sea has inexplicably changed directions and is now moving in a southwest direction. That means that the radioactive cloud is moving toward Egypt and possibly on toward Libya. But the forecasters are predicting that this is only a temporary change. They are saying that within twenty-four hours or so, the winds should reverse back toward the east again. If that happens, then the cloud should move into Saudi Arabia. And after that, who knows where it will go? But because of this southerly direction it's now moving, Israel should be spared from any of it.

"Ezekiel," General Green continued, "this is what I was talking with you about before. This is a sure sign that El Shaddai, the almighty great Yahweh, is fighting on our side. Yes, due to the hatred against us worldwide, many Jews have lost their lives and their businesses around the world this night, but there has not been any report of a single Jewish casualty happening tonight inside of Israel. Our troops along the Gaza border have all been able to don radiation warfare suits and seek shelter inside of our bunkers. Inside of those bunkers is enough food and water to last for the next two weeks. Plus, we have air scrubbers installed in all of them that will give the brave men and women fresh, pure air to breathe. Plus, due to the extreme intensity of this storm, every soldier was already down inside of those bunkers when the nuclear explosion took place. Yes, Ezekiel, God is on our side. If you don't believe me, just ask this very beautiful, young niece of mine that's standing next to you."

Ezekiel kept his gaze on the general's face, studying him for another minute before he turned to look at Esther. She had only what Ezekiel could describe as an angelic smile on her face.

"Yes, Ezekiel, God is on our side. You'll see. You'll see with your very own eyes before this mess is all over." she said.

In that moment, he wanted so much to believe like these two did. In fact, his entire being was aching in so much anguish that he was sure it was as powerful as childbirth would feel. If Esther had known about this, she would have told him he was in the throes of being born again.

But for his entire life up until now, he had never had a need for God. It wasn't so much that he didn't believe in God; it was more that he just didn't know for sure that God existed. *But if He does, I'll be very happy to accept His help in all matters,* he thought.

Just then, Colonel Jeremiah walked up to General Green. Colonial Jeremiah had been over in the far reaches of this big observation room. He had been standing next to a bank of twenty computers, each one with a military analyst of some sort working on it. He had been conversing with several of the analysts before one of them handed him a message for General Green.

"General Green, sir, we just received notice that Iran has launched several squadrons of fighters and bomber jets into the air. We believe they are heading toward us. We estimate there are over one hundred of these planes in the air as we speak. From what we have been able to determine so far, they're all in a single formation and on a bearing heading for Tel Aviv. But if they maintain their present course, they will pass directly over the top of us here at Sharon Air Force Base. Also, sir, I suspect they're carrying every type of bunker-busting bomb they have in their arsenal. Personally, I don't believe they have anything that can damage us down here in this bunker under the granite mountain, but if they reach Tel Aviv, it is no telling what kind of havoc and damage they can cause there."

General Green turned to look at Ezekiel. "Lieutenant Colonel Cohen, what kind of havoc do you think you and your band of merry men can bring against these planes?"

"Sir, first of all, they can't see us, so they can't shoot what they can't see. If we go up strictly as fighters, without bombs, we should be able to fly circles around them and create a total mess up there, sir."

"Then get your men and go, son. My prayers will be with you and your men. And if I turn my back for a minute, I won't mind if you were to give my niece here a quick peck on her cheek."

With that, he turned his back to them. Ezekiel quickly leaned over to do exactly what the general had suggested. But Esther reached out and grabbed both of his arms and lifted them over her head and placed them around her back. Then she stood up on her tiptoes to be able to place her lips fully against his. They remained in this position until the general finally cleared his throat in a loud, grunting manner.

"Yes, sir. Yes, sir. On my way, sir. On my way."

Ezekiel quickly turned and ran out of the room into the elevator. As soon as he stepped into it he reached over and picked up the secure telephone mounted on the wall. He quickly punched three numbers on the phone. Those numbers were a code that sent out an emergency message to the rest of his squadron to immediately report to the ready room.

By the time Ezekiel arrived, seven of his men were already there. The other two came bursting through the door less than ten seconds later. The B-2 pilots were exempt for this action. They were only taking the F-22s up as fighters to engage Iran's planes.

Ezekiel walked up in front of the men and grabbed their attention. "My brothers, Iran has launched a counterattack against us with her air force. It is estimated that she has over one hundred planes in the air right now, and it appears they're heading for Tel Aviv. But as you know, that heading will place them directly over the top of this base. General Green wants us to go up and cause a little havoc with these planes before he unleashes the rest of our fighters. I don't know about you men, but I'm really looking forward to this. I have been dying to see what our F-22s can do in a real dogfight. So, any questions? Anyone? Then let's go have some fun, men."

# CHAPTER 14

Their planes had already been refueled and rearmed. They had been sitting inside of their reinforced concrete bunkers just waiting to take back into the sky, where such magnificent mechanical flying birds belong. After they climbed in the cockpits and the canopies had been lowered, Ezekiel came over the radio and told his men that after they got into the air, they would receive their coordinates to where they would find the enemy planes. Shortly after that, in side-by-side formations, they turned down the runways, lit their afterburners, and blasted up into the clouds. Less than five minutes later, all ten planes were in the air and quickly assembled into formation.

In addition to being the most advanced stealth aircraft in the world, the planes also had the most advanced computers and avionics in the world. Their radars, lasers, and sensors were more advanced by decades over what Iran was flying against them with.

Plus, they also carried the most sophisticated weapons ever developed.

Ezekiel knew they were basically outnumbered by at least ten to one, but it didn't matter. The Iranians couldn't shoot what they couldn't see. In addition to being completely stealthy, they were also buried deep inside thick, smothering clouds.

He was completely relaxed, not afraid at all. He leaned his head back against the padded seatback and again glanced up through the canopy. But instead of seeing dark clouds, vivid visions of Esther were floating past his eyes. He laughed out loud. At the same time he accidentally placed his finger on the squadron call button that went out to the other nine planes, which was also heard inside of the command bunker, where Esther was standing next to General Green. He turned his face up toward the top of the canopy and sang out loud, "Yeah. I'm in love. I'm in love." But he quickly realized what he had done as soon as the yelps and catcalls began coming back at him through his radio.

As Ezekiel's very off-key rendition of a love song blasted out of the loud speakers situated all throughout the bunker, Esther instantly ducked her head and buried her face in her hands. It was a failed attempt to hide the hundred different shades of red she had just turned She was absolutely horrified and thought she was going to faint.

General Green noticed her embarrassment. He quickly reached out and put his arm around her waist, supporting her and keeping her from falling down. Then he said, "Well, hon, you will never need to fear him becoming a singing star and leaving you with a voice like that! But, my dear, how do you feel about him?"

"Oh, Uncle, I love him too. I really do. I just didn't know it until you talked me into seeing him. Now my heart is totally wrapped around his."

"I see. I do. And let me say this. I approve too."

While this was going on in the command bunker, Ezekiel and his men received their coordinates and made their plans. Half of the squadron would come in above the enemy planes and then drop down and fly directly toward them as soon as they made visual contact. The other half would come in below and loop around behind the advancing enemy planes. This means they had to fly either above or below the advancing swarm until they came into range of them. They chose to go down to the deck and fly treetop level. At that low height, and at the speed they were moving, even if they hadn't been stealth aircraft, the Iranian planes would not have been able to look down on them with their ancient radars and pull them out of the ground cover clutter they were lost in. But Ezekiel and his men had nothing to worry about anyway. None of the radars and sensors on Iran's planes were working at that time. They were flying above the storm on visual sight and talking on their radios to keep each other informed where they all were.

The five planes that were going to come in behind the enemy flew on that level until they were a good thirty miles past the Iranian planes. They then pointed their noses straight toward the heavens and quickly accelerated up into the thick clouds, where they all performed the Immelman Loop to perfection so they could come in behind and below the enemy planes. Ezekiel was part of this group. He came over the communication band and gave instructions for each plane to follow.

Each of their planes was carrying eight of the most advanced Israeli air-to-air missiles their scientists had invented. They had taken the best the Americans had developed and had then drastically improved on the design. No one else in the world knew about these new missiles or had anything comparable.

Each missile had the unique ability to lock on to a separate individual target. That meant with Ezekiel's squadron of ten planes, in theory, they had the ability to knock eighty Iranian planes out of the air.

Ezekiel came over the radio again. "Men, let's see if these Screaming Demons can do what the white coats in the labs say they can do, okay?"

Screaming Demons was the nickname given to the new missiles.

"On my mark, we shoot all eight. Then we cruise slowly behind until the carnage falls out of our way. After that, let's stagger behind while our other planes that are coming straight on mix it up with these guys. Okay? Whaddya say, men?"

Everyone replied, almost in unison, "We're with you, lover boy. Let's go for it."

A few seconds later, Ezekiel gave the order to fire. Less than a minute later, thirty-six Iranian planes suddenly realized a missile was on their tails. Four missiles failed to lock onto a target. The Iranian pilots had no idea where the missiles were coming from. They seemed to just come out of thin air. But before they had the ability to react, thirty-six enemy aircraft exploded and fell out of the sky. Two minutes after that, while they were still in complete shock and total disarray, the remaining planes were suddenly attacked by something the remaining Iranian pilots had never seen before. For many of them, it was the last thing they ever saw as they were cut to pieces by either cannon fire or missiles.

Not long after that, Ezekiel and the rest of his men ran out of ammunition. But they still decided to hang around to try to create even more havoc. They decided to fly through, around, over, and under the Iranian jets. They wanted to keep the enemy in confusion and disarray and stall for time until the Israeli reinforcements arrived on the scene.

Since the Iranians had no ability to see the F-22s on their radar, and since they were all flying in very heavy cloud cover in very high winds, within seconds, all of the Iranian planes were completely disoriented and out of any sort of formation. They began flying haphazardly in all directions to try to find some way to get away from these UFOs who were intent on killing them all.

Ezekiel, and his men, had their radios tuned to the Iranians' frequency. Most of them could understand a smattering of Arabic and Farsi But all of a sudden, they heard several of the Iranians screaming something about 'Foo Fighters' attacking them.

All fighter pilots were aware that during World War II, many pilots from every country involved in the war would sometimes see bright, unexplainable lights suddenly appear out their cockpits and windshields, and many pilots claimed they were attacked by these unexplained or unidentified flying objects. In fact, Ezekiel knew that one of the Apollo space craft on their way to the moon encountered some of these foo fighters in outer space. But Ezekiel and his men found it funny that the Iranians believed that they were being attacked by foo fighters.

When all was said and done, less than twenty Iranian planes out of the original one hundred and three were able to make it back to their home base in Iran. The others had either crashed into each other, hit the ground and exploded, or been knocked out of the air by the F-22s' unique weapons systems. Every one of Ezekiel's men, including him, became multiple aces in this battle.

All of this action took place in the skies above Iraq. For some unknown reason, the Iraqis had been able to partially monitor this battle. Their radar and other systems seemed to come on and work intermittently. But they had no idea why the Iranian planes suddenly began going crazy flying in all directions and angles, crashing into each other, or falling out of the sky. They never saw the F-22s and didn't realize the Israelis were involved in the massacre.

Because of this huge victory, Ezekiel came over the squadron frequency. "Men, you were wonderful back there! You did a fantastic job! Listen, I want all ten of us to do a low-level, high-speed, supersonic flyover of Sharon Air Force Base. What do you say?"

Not all thought this was a wonderful idea, but they figured Ezekiel was in good with the general, so they would be able to get away with it, even though it was completely against the rules. Ezekiel did not have, nor did he seek, permission to do the flyover. But he figured him and his band of flying merry men had earned a little spending capital with the general by having totally destroyed this attempt on the Iranians part to retaliate, and also by his love for the general's beautiful niece.

General Green had just poured himself a cup of freshly made steaming hot coffee. He picked it up with his right hand and was in the process of bringing it up to his mouth when all ten F-22s made their supersonic, earsplitting booming flyovers at the same time. Even though his bunker was over a hundred feet below the surface of the earth, and even though it was extremely hardened with reinforced concrete and steel, the entire base had very sensitive listening devices all around it, and the sonic bursts inside of the bunker were just as loud and jarring as they were on the surface. The loud, booming, earth-shaking noise make him jerk his hand straight up and dump the steaming coffee all over his starched and pressed dress blue military uniform.

If this had happened several years before, quite a few very explicit expletives would have instantly flown out of the general's mouth and exploded over the entire room in his deep, baritone voice. But now, he stood perfectly still like a statue, barely even breathing. His body was locked in this position, unable to move until the searing pain from the hot liquid had a chance to somewhat dissipate.

Finally, he slowly sucked in a deep calming breath. At the same time, a small smile slowly tilted the corners of his lips. He turned to Esther. She was standing forward on the front of her feet with her shoulders scrunched up almost into a rounded ball with her hands clenched tightly against her mouth. Her eyes were staring straight down at the floor, unable to look up at her uncle. She was terrified of what was coming next.

General Green turned all of the way until he was standing right in front of her. He then reached out with his left arm and gently put his hand under her chin. As he slowly applied a little pressure and lifted her head up so she had to look directly into his eyes, he whispered, "Boys will be boys, I guess."

CHAPTER 15

ollowing their exuberant display, Ezekiel and his men landed and parked their planes back inside of the underground caverns that served as their hangers. He ordered all of his men to come back to the command bunker with him. He did this for a couple of reasons. One, he didn't want to face the general alone after their little display. Two, he was extremely proud of his men and wanted the general to greet them as returning heroes, which they most certainly were.

The other nine pilots weren't sure this was a good idea, especially since this was Ezekiel's idea only and they hadn't been invited by anyone else. But Ezekiel convinced them that they would most certainly be welcomed. He was counting on their heroic deeds they had done earlier, and also that Esther could protect them from any wrath that might come from the general for his brashness.

As the elevator doors opened, General Green was just walking back into the room from changing his clothes.

His face was still red and splotchy where the hot liquid had splashed him. Ezekiel jauntily began to lead his men out of the elevator. But as soon as he saw the look on Esther's face, which was still a horrified mask of total shock and terror, he stopped and glanced around the room until his eyes finally landed on General Green. His first thought upon seeing the general was that he had never seen a face made out of such hard, solid stone on a living person before.

The general stood perfectly still, rigid, not even moving a muscle. His eyes were like two welding torches of flaming fire burning right through Ezekiel.

Ezekiel quickly looked from the general and quickly glanced back to Esther. She met his glance for only a second and then quickly looked away as she began shaking her head from side to side. He slowly looked back at the general. He hadn't moved either. He was still standing in the same place he had stopped after coming off the elevator. But then he suddenly decided that it might be better to come to military attention.

He quickly raised himself up to his full height and then yelled, "Attention."

His men, who also had already stopped in their tracks, quickly came to attention too. But they were all wondering just what their crazy flight leader had just gotten them into.

As Ezekiel stood there, he noticed that the general had, for some reason, changed his uniform from the one he had been wearing earlier. The general was dressed in camouflage fatigues, the kind you wear in combat. He wondered why.

General Green cleared his throat in a loud baritone grunt. It was the type of grunt or snort that could be heard in every nook and cranny of the huge underground building. If any poor soul had been trying to sleep at that time, well, it was too bad for him, as he certainly would have been awakened by now.

After General Green was assured he had gotten everyone's attention in the entire room, he let his dark, grayish-green eyes slowly roam over the ten men standing in front of him. By this time, all of them were just about to urinate in their pants. No one else in the room was even breathing, as all work had suddenly ceased. Everyone wanted to see what was going to happen next.

As his eyes slowly came back around and settled on Ezekiel, he stopped and stared at him for what seemed like an eternity. Finally, General Green could no longer help himself and allowed a small smile to creep across his face. He finally yelled, "At ease, men."

All ten pilots slowly sucked in a small breath, but none of them moved more than putting one arm behind their backs in the parade rest position.

General Green walked over to Ezekiel and stopped directly in front of him and said, "Son, I'm sure you will have no problem paying to have my dress uniform dry-cleaned, the one I had been wearing before you and your merry band of heroes decided to make me spill coffee all over it. That will not be a problem, will it, son?"

"F-for sure, sir. Absolutely, sir. Uh … I'm sorry, sir," he stuttered.

The general couldn't help himself any longer, and he reached out and wrapped Ezekiel up in a huge bear hug, pulling him in close to his chest. "Well done, my boy. Well done." All along, General Green had always felt that if he ever had a son, he would want him to be exactly like Ezekiel Cohen. He loved the brash boy. It was what made him who he was!

He patted Ezekiel on the back and then let go and hurried over to the rest of Ezekiel's men. He reached out and wrapped each one of them up in a big bear hug too. He also told each of them, "Well done. Well done." After that, he played the good host and showed all of the men around the bunker, explaining all of the intricacies and answering all questions.

In the meantime, Ezekiel broke away and hurried over to Esther.

She said under her breath, "You made him spill a whole cup of hot coffee all over himself. I thought he was going to kill you guys."

"He seems to have gotten over it. But where can we sneak off to? I'm dying to hold you in my arms and get a kiss from you."

She laughed. "Ezekiel, I don't know. I've never been in this bunker before. But I really would like one too."

General Green eventually made his way back around to them. He said, "I want all of you to go get some sleep. I said *sleep*. That's directed at you, Ezekiel and Esther. But that also goes for the rest of you. As you men just saw on the alert screens, Russia is in the process of pulling up her entire armed forces. It looks very much like she is going to use our raid against Iran as an excuse to come against us. When that happens, as it surely will, not only will Russia be coming against us, but you can be sure that all of the rest of the Arab countries will join with her and come too.

"Men, and Esther, the Bible says in the book of Ezekiel that the king of the north will come against us with so many troops it will be like a storm cloud covering the earth. It also says that at the same time, the king of the South will arise and come against us. That's Sudan, Libya, Egypt, and the rest of her allies along the north coast of Africa, including probably Somalia. But the Bible also says for us to not be afraid. That's because God says He will fight for us. In fact, it also says that only one sixth of the kingdom of the north will be left spared after he brings his troops against us.

"The Bible also says that in this time of the end before the King of kings and Lord of lords comes back again, that one third of the earth's inhabitants will be destroyed. My people, unfortunately, I truly believe that God's Word is speaking of this vast throng of forces that are mobilizing even now as I speak. You see, God's Word very plainly declares that there is only one way into the kingdom of God, and that is through the redeeming blood of His only Son, whom I believe with my entire being is Jesus, the Holy Christ, the Anointed One. A very large portion of the vast throng coming against us is Muslim. And Muslim people do not believe that Jesus is God's own Son. They believe in Jesus. But they believe that He was a good and important prophet, but not God's Son. So when Jesus himself declared, 'I am the Way, the Truth, and the Life. No man comes unto the Father but through me,' the Muslims believe He was just blowing hot air.

"Well, I truly believe that He will most definitely be blowing hot air very soon, enough to burn the billion or so Muslims in the world to a very burnt crisp in the eternal fires of hell, along with the kings of the north and south. Without a doubt, Satan is going to stir these people up, and they will all band together to come against us. You will see this with your own eyes. So I want all of you completely rested up and ready to go and fight alongside of God when these enemies come against us."

"Uh … sir, may I ask a question or make a statement?" Major Jonah Malachi asked.

"Sure, Major. Ask away or make your statement."

"Uh, sir … well … uh … I don't really know how to say this …"

"Say it. Anything. Anything at all, Major."

"Okay, well … uh … I'm not too sure I agree with what you just said, sir. No offense."

"No offense taken. Of course you don't agree with me. Not too many people here in Israel do at this time. But I want all of you to do something for me as we progress together down this rough and winding road that is ahead of us. I want all of you to keep your eyes wide open and your hearts willing to accept what your eyes see. That's all I ask. If you do that—in fact, if all of Israel will just do that—I promise every one of you, and Israel too, that all will see with their own eyes the glory; power; and, most of all, the love that God has for us, His people. If you will be willing to do that, you will see God's Son, Jesus, leading us to victory.

"One more thing. You will see this because we, little, tiny Israel, will be going up against the rest of the whole world all by ourselves. There will not be another country in the entire world that will come to our aid. You will see."

"Sir, what about the United States? Won't they come to help?"

"No. Absolutely not. Their president has his eye on becoming the dictator of the world after all of this mess is over. Do you think the world would want anything to do with him if he decided to give so-called help to us?"

General Green stood there, shaking his head from side to side. "No. I'm afraid it is just us and God against the world. So, keep that in mind as we win this war against the world. And we surely will. We surely will. Now, all of you go get some sleep so you'll be ready and raring when God calls you to His side to fight along with Him."

Esther stood there, listening admiringly as her uncle stated his beliefs without wavering. Warm, wet tears were rolling down her cheeks. In her heart, she was praying so hard that the message would get through to all of them, but especially to Ezekiel. She knew in her heart that the world as it had been known had suddenly entered into the final stages of its existence. The final nail in the crumbling coffin of civilization under the rule of Satan was being hammered even at this very moment.

She knew that basically, Satan only had another seven years of time left of being god of this world. Therefore, she knew that the next seven years would be unlike anything the world had ever known before up to this time. The next seven years would be the worst years ever to exist in the history of mankind. She remembered the statement that Jesus had declared, "If those times had not been shortened, no man would be left alive." Esther knew without the slightest doubt at all that Satan is going to do any and every thing he possibly can to totally and completely destroy this world and everyone in it to keep it out of the hands of Jesus, who is going to come back to rule the world as King of the world.

She knew that Jesus had come the first time a little over two thousand years ago to be the Son of Man instead of the conquering king like most Jews believe the Messiah is to be. The scriptures are confusing, but if you really read them and study them like it says to do in 2 Timothy 2:15, "Study to show thyself approved unto God, a workman that needs not to be ashamed, rightly dividing the word of truth," then God would show you the truth. That is why she believed with all of her heart that Jesus was the Messiah. But the first time He came, He was the mild, meek-mannered Son of Man who proclaimed, "Love your neighbour as yourself," and was willing to turn the other cheek. But this time, when He comes back again, He is coming in all of His glory as the Son of God to totally destroy all of the works of Satan and to claim this world as His own.

That was why she so much wanted Ezekiel to believe in God, and especially in Jesus. God had some way, somehow filled her heart to such an overflowing depth of love for that brash and brave young man that she could hardly stand it. After the next seven years were finally over, she knew they would then enter into a millennium reign with Jesus, the Christ, as He rules the earth during those years from a throne right in Israel, in Jerusalem.

And oh, what years they will be. Oh, God, I pray, please, please, please open Ezekiel's eyes and his heart. He just has to spend those years with me, God. But he won't be able to unless he accepts Jesus as your Son and accepts Him into his life as Lord over it. So please, my Father, deal with his heart. Deal with his thoughts. And please bring him to salvation in Jesus.

# CHAPTER 16

After they left the bunker, Ezekiel's men headed over to the officers' barracks to their rooms. Ezekiel put his arm around Esther's waist and walked her over to the women's officers' barracks. Just before they got there, he glanced down at his watch. It read 4:45 a.m. He was bone tired, both physically and mentally. He had been awake for over twenty-three hours straight. He had flown a bombing mission into Iran and had later gone back up to attack a squadron of more than a hundred enemy warplanes.

Exhaustion was not the right word for it. But he had the woman who held his heart captive and he was very reluctant to let her go. But she was every bit as exhausted as he was, maybe even more so. He had the ability to live on adrenaline during his times in the air. She had to sit, wait, and worry for him to return. All things considered, he preferred doing what he did instead of the waiting and worrying.

He leaned in and slowly placed his lips against hers. She reached up, put her arms around his neck, and pulled him tight against her. He took her breath away. She was doing the same to him.

"Oh, Esther, I love you. I love you."

"I love you too, my Ezekiel. You do not know this, but you have held my heart captive for almost a year too."

He leaned back and looked at her with amazement. "I have? But...but...but you never said anything. You never gave me any indication at all."

"I know. I'm so sorry. I really am. I was afraid. I was afraid with what you do, and...and of who you are that you would die and break my heart again. I was afraid I couldn't live with that. So, I just allowed my heart to love you and kept it to myself. Also, every woman on this base would give their right arm just to have a single date with you. I didn't have the emotional capacity to compete with that until now."

"Oh, Esther, there will never be anyone else but you. You're all I ever think about when I'm off duty. In fact, you're the last thing I think about before I go to sleep at night and the first thing I think about when I wake up in the morning." Suddenly, he got down on one knee and took her hand in his and stared into her face. "Esther, my forever love, will you marry me? I mean ... I mean, I don't want to be rude or anything or ... to push you into anything, but if General Green is correct about what he said, I want with all of my heart and soul to be married to you as we go through this journey. I want you by my side as well as in my heart."

"Yes. Oh, yes. I'll marry you. I love you so much, my brave hero."

She suddenly jumped up into his arms and began smothering his face with kisses. He was so surprised he lost his balance, and they both fell to the ground in a big heap, laughing like little kids.

Finally, Ezekiel said, "I sure hope the general doesn't suddenly walk by and see us like this."

Eventually, Esther made herself let go of Ezekiel and walked slowly and sadly into her barracks to try to get some sleep. But she knew that would be an almost impossible thing for her to do. Her heart had never felt like it did now. She thought she had experienced love before, but it was nothing like the love she was feeling for Ezekiel. Her heart was just about to explode with happiness.

Ezekiel somehow made his way over to the men's barracks, but he had no recollection how he had accomplished that. He was so drunk with love that his mind was working on instinct only and not rational thought.

When he got to his bed, he pulled his boots off and lay down on top of the covers still fully clothed. On his face was the biggest smile he had ever had. But suddenly, he remembered that he needed to find a way to buy Esther a ring … and to set a date … and to … to … well, there were just too many things to think about right now. He did remember that the only family Esther had was her mom and General Green. So, since her mom was incapacitated, he decided he would ask the general for Esther's hand. It would be the right and honorable thing to do, and the general would probably really appreciate that. He also remembered that he needed to call his parents and tell them the good news too.

He lay there with a million and one things floating through his mind. But the exhaustion of the long night swept over his body, and his eyes slowly closed. The next thing he knew, his secure beeper was going off. A groan slipped out of his throat as his eyes slowed popped open. With an extreme effort, he managed to sit up and look at the clock sitting on the end table next to his bed. He couldn't believe it; he had been asleep for exactly two hours and ten minutes.

*Oh well,* he thought. *That's why God made adrenaline.*

He quickly jumped out of bed and grabbed a clean shirt and threw it on and then hurriedly pulled his boots on. He ran out of his room without taking a shower, brushing his teeth, or changing his underwear. As the door slammed behind him, for some reason, he remembered how his mom had always told him as he was growing up to always make sure he was wearing clean underwear and had brushed his teeth: "Because, son, you just never know. You might be in some kind of an accident and would appreciate having clean teeth and clean underwear on."

*Well, Mom, I'm just not going to be able to have an accident today. I didn't have time to do those things. Oh, and by the way, Mom, I'm getting married to the most wonderful girl in the entire world very soon,* he thought. He was laughing as he approached the elevator that would take him to see Esther's uncle; his commander; and his soon-to-be uncle-in-law, if there was such a thing.

The elevator quickly reached the bottom floor to the command bunker. As the door opened, he walked out of it; but unbeknown to him, he had the biggest grin on his face a man could ever have.

General Green, who had only gotten about two hours of sleep himself, turned to look at him. "Well, aren't you the cat who has eaten the canary?"

"Excuse me, sir? Uh ... why do you ask that, sir?"

"Well, you just happen to have the biggest grin on your face that I have ever seen on a man. That's all, and that's why I ask."

"Oh. I didn't know I was grinning. But since you mentioned it, sir, I was wondering something. I was wondering if I could ask you something."

"Of course, son. I have always said all of my men can ask anything they want at any time. What can I do for you?"

"Well, sir, I was just wondering ... uh ... uh ..."

"*Ask,* son. I don't have all day here."

"Well, sir, I was wondering if I could have your niece, Esther's, hand in marriage? Uh ... sir?"

General Green stared at Ezekiel, unsmiling, unflinching, unblinking for what seemed like an eternity. At General Green's sudden stony reaction, Ezekiel thought he had just made the biggest mistake of his entire life. He stood there, immobile, paralyzed, just about emptying his bladder into his pants for the second time in less than twenty-four hours' time.

Finally, General Green spoke at the same time a huge grin began wrapping itself across his face too. "Have you, Ezekiel, asked Esther about this? Or do you just think your handsome looks, your suave personality, and your brave heroics will melt her heart and she will just fall into your arms?"

"Uh ... yes, General. I asked her last night after we left here. And, uh ... sir, she said yes."

"Well then, if that is the case, I'll have to have her go see a psychiatrist to make sure she hasn't totally lost her mind. No! I'm only joking! I'll be most happy to give you and her my blessing along with her hand in marriage. Have you set a date yet?"

"No, sir. I … uh … I'm not sure how to proceed with this."

"Well, son, I personally say the sooner the better, what with the way the world is shaping up. But as for right now, we have another little problem to take care of first. It's how best to prosecute a war that's about to suddenly engulf us all. While we were trying to get some sleep, Russia declared to the world that she was not going to stand idly by while the Jews kill and maim hundreds of her innocent citizens, supposedly like we had just done in Iran. They claim over three hundred of her 'innocent' citizens were killed in our raid.

"They announced to the world that they were going to, once and for all, take care of the Jewish problem that has plagued the world since Abraham begat Isaac and Isaac begat Jacob. Russia also declared that no country had better come to Israel's aid, or if some nation were foolish enough to try to do so, that nation had better be prepared to feel the wrath of her nuclear power too.

"As of this time, Russia is preparing to move on the ground with hundreds of thousands, if not millions, of troops heading our way. Some of them will be moving toward the Black Sea and will come down through Turkey to get to us. Of course, Turkey, being a Muslim country, has declared her own intentions to go along as an ally to help Russia in her quest to destroy us. It also appears that the rest of Russia's troops will be moving down through Afghanistan and then on into Iran. It's too bad, Ezekiel, that the United States has already pulled all of her troops out of Afghanistan. But even there, that would be wishful thinking on our part for the US to use them to help us.

"So, after Russia moves down into Iran through Afghanistan, they will probably take some time to reorganize their troops with Iran's. They will have to combine their forces with all of the different Muslim and Arab armies into one massive single army under their command.

"After they complete that task, they will then move into Iraq until they come to the Euphrates River on their way to us here in Israel. That area should slow their march down considerably due to the massive amount of flooding that has already taken place as the result of this enormous storm system that has dumped more than thirty inches of rain on portions of Iraq and Iran.

"We have been trying to decide if we should move against them before they get here and, if that were to be the case, should we hit them with our own nukes or stick to conventional weapons? Ezekiel, I trust your opinion in this matter. Since you are soon to be my nephew-in-law, please give me your opinion about what we are faced with."

Ezekiel stood there, stunned and shocked. What he had planned as a lifetime of being in love and living with Esther suddenly looked very much like they might only have a few days at most of life left in them or of life left in the whole country of Israel as it was looking.

"Uh ... sir, I have very little insight into this. As you're well aware, I'm not in the intelligence service. But, well ... you know, as you were saying last night about how God is going to fight for us ... well, I just think that maybe we ought to concentrate all of our efforts and energies into protecting our own country.

"You see, I just feel like if we attack these troops while they're on their way here, and especially if we drop nuclear weapons on those troops in whatever country they happen to be in at the time, well then, most definitely, the whole world will be against us because we will be seen as the aggressor again. But if we stay here, reinforce our borders as best as we can, we'll be seen as only trying to defend ourselves. That way, maybe, just maybe, some other countries will offer to help and step up.

"Plus, sir, if you are right about God fighting for us, well, it just seems to me that since He gave this country to us originally, He will be more than willing to keep it from falling into any other hands. Am I making myself clear, sir?"

General Green stood there, nodding his head up and down. He was even more pleased with Ezekiel now. He turned to the other men inside of the bunker. "Everyone, look at me and listen. I want all of you to know that this man right here is soon to be my new nephew."

Ezekiel couldn't have been prouder. But then another thought suddenly popped into his head. "General, sir ... well, I have another idea. I mean, I don't know how practical it may be, but—"

"Say it, son. Don't hesitate."

"Well, sir, you said that part of the Russian troops will be crossing the Euphrates River when they're moving through Iraq. Also, the others will be coming down through Turkey, where, again, they will have to cross the Euphrates. Well, consider this. Would it be possible for us to send in a small, covert team, unannounced and unseen, into Turkey that could possibly blow up a couple of the dams on the Euphrates River? I mean, if we could somehow time it to be right around the same time the Russians are getting ready to cross it, maybe there would be enough water to flood the land and drown many of them. At least it would certainly slow them down and cause a lot of confusion."

"Hmm. Maybe you have a point there," General Green replied.

"Sir, I'm sure you're aware of the fact that inside of the border of Turkey, there are six huge dams that have been built along the Euphrates. If we could take out the top two dams without anyone's knowledge that it was us doing it, well, maybe the rushing walls of water would be enough to take out the remaining dams downstream from those two all along its path. And if that were to occur, it would have to certainly play havoc with the Russians and whoever else is coming with them."

"Do you have any idea how much water is in storage behind those dams?" the general asked.

"Well, sir, the water that is held behind all those dams all along the Euphrates River from Turkey down through Iraq must be close to at least a quarter of what the Mediterranean Sea holds. I'm guessing about that, of course, but it has to be a tremendous amount of water, sir. And if all of that quarter of an ocean of water were to be suddenly let loose without any restraint, combined with all of the rain water from this huge storm; well, sir, in my way of thinking, I believe it could be enough to flood the entire land of Iraq, or at least a vast, vast portion of it.

"Also, General, here's one more thing. If the enemy troops do still make it to us here inside of Israel, they will have to come down through the mountain passes of Lebanon and Syria, plus the mountain passes inside of our own country. So, maybe it could also be possible for us to send some demolition specialists to preset explosive charges that would cause the mountain passes to collapse down on top of the advancing armies as they're traveling through them. If we could do that, they would be sitting ducks for us to destroy as they try to escape out of our ambush."

"Yes. I like it. I like it all," General Green replied. "I will see what we can do to accomplish those things. But there's one other aspect of this that we must consider and be aware of. Colonel Jeremiah, would you be so kind as to go into my room and get my Bible off my nightstand? I want to read something out of it for all of us to consider in addition to this. In the meantime, Ezekiel, you go get my niece and tell her I want to see her immediately. Ezekiel … tell her you asked me for her hand in marriage. But don't tell her what I said. I want to have a little fun with her first. She needs to laugh a little more."

Ezekiel hurried out of the command bunker and then hurried over to where Esther was still sleeping. When he got to her barracks, he walked quickly through the front door and entered into the foyer. He hesitated until he spotted the receptionist's desk and then quickly walked over to it. As he got to it, he smiled.

"Hi. Could I get you to do me a favor and call Lieutenant Esther Cohen? Please have her get up and get ready as soon as possible. Tell her General Green wants to see her as soon as possible. Also, please tell her that Ezekiel wants to see her as soon as possible too."

The receptionist knew who he was. As soon as he walked in the door, her heart began to flutter. But as soon as he asked for Esther Asher, she knew she had no chance to ever make him see her. She thought about ignoring his request and not calling Esther. But she quickly thought better of that.

If Esther's uncle wants to see her, I better do what he wants.

Ezekiel turned around and walked back outside to wait. A concrete bench was setting on a barren spot of earth beneath a big elm tree. He ambled over to it and sat down. He figured he had a few minutes to kill, so he thought he would call his parents and tell them about Esther while he was waiting.

His mom answered the phone on the third ring. "Hello."

"Mom, it's me, Ezekiel."

"Ezekiel. Oh, how good of you to call. Your dad and I were just talking about you. We were wondering if you had any idea at all about what is going on in the world right now?"

He had never discussed anything with his parents about what he did, or for that matter, with anyone else. Much of what he did was classified because of the F-22s they flew, and he couldn't talk about it. All his parents knew was that he just flew planes for the air force. They had no idea what kind of planes he flew.

"I know about some of it, Mom. I've been trying to follow as much as I can. But let's get off that for just a minute. I have some other news to tell you and dad, some good news."

"What is it, son? Oh, I hope it really is good news. Oh my. What a crazy old world we live in right now."

"Mom, yes, it definitely is good news. At least it's good news to me, and I hope it will be good news to you too."

"Well, tell us, son. Don't keep us waiting."

He rolled his eyes. *Mom, I love you, but sometimes...,* he thought to himself. "Mom, listen. How would you like to have a new daughter in you and dad's lives?"

"What, son? What are you saying? I'm not pregnant. In fact, I'm way too old to have any more children, so how can we have another daughter?"

"No, Mom. I guess I should have said how would you feel to have a daughter-*in-law*?"

"Oh... oh..." She turned around to face her husband. "Solly, get over here and get on the extension phone. It's Ezekiel... and... he has some wonderful news for us."

His dad lumbered up slowly out of his favorite recliner and moved unhurriedly into the kitchen to pick up an extension phone mounted on the wall next to the counter. "Ezekiel, What news? What are you telling your mother?"

"I just asked mom how she would feel if she had a new daughter-in-law very soon."

"No. I mean... I mean, I just never expected you to settle down so soon. You're only thirty-one years old.... But yes, we are very happy for you. When is the big day? And how long have you known this girl? I mean, we didn't even know you were dating anyone. Also, Ezekiel, she is Jewish, isn't she?"

"Dad, I've known Esther for almost a year now, and yes, she is Jewish. I asked her last night if she would marry me, and she said yes. As for how long we have been dating, well, that's kind of complicated…I mean, we really only started dating just yesterday, but we have both been in love with each other for almost a year now. We just never let the other one know about it before yesterday."

"Uh…Ezekiel, let me see if I got this right. Let's see. You asked this girl to marry you after you have been dating her for only one day? Is that correct?"

"Yes, Dad…I know, it's kind of weird. But, Dad, we really love each other. And, Dad, her uncle is General Green, the commanding general of the base I work at. Plus, he's the commanding officer over the entire Israeli military, and he has given his blessing on our union. General Green and his wife, plus Esther's mom, are basically the only family Esther has anymore. Her dad and brother were killed in a homicide bombing in Bethlehem a few years ago. Her mom was hit in the head with shrapnel from the same blast, which has left her incapacitated. Esther is like a daughter to General Green, so, Dad, Mom, you must be happy for us too, okay?"

There was nothing but silence on the line for a couple of minutes.

Finally, his mom asked, "Ezekiel, when is the happy day? And how soon can we meet this lucky woman?"

His dad popped in, "Ezekiel, you say she is the niece of the commanding officer over the entire military?"

"Yes, Dad."

"Well, son, you could have done worse, I'm sure. Maybe you can finally move up in the world from flying those transports that you do. Maybe you can get into a real plane or something and fight for our country like the other brave men do. So, anyway, tell us, when is the big day?"

"Yeah, Dad. Maybe knowing General Green will help me move up in the world, as you say. But as for everything else, well, it's all up in the air right now. You've seen the news, I'm sure, so we're kind of restricted to our base right now. But as soon as we know anything more, we'll let you know, okay? Just be happy for me, okay? You'll love Esther. I'm sure of that."

As soon as he finished saying that, Esther came bounding out of the front door of the barracks. Ezekiel saw her and hurriedly said his good-byes. He was so happy to get off the phone. He rolled his eyes straight up to God and wondered why he had even called. He loved his folks but sometimes they drove him nuts.

Esther came running toward him and jumped up into his arms as he was just standing back up to his feet. That time, he caught her in midair and their momentum made them begin spinning around in circles. Finally, he stopped and set her down before he fell down from being too dizzy.

"What does my uncle want to see me for?" she asked.

"Well, uh…I felt like I should…it's like this, you see. I spilled the beans to him. I asked your uncle for your hand in marriage. Now he thinks you're crazy and you need to go see a psychiatrist."

"No…He would never say that…would he?"

Her face was a mixture of horror. At the same time, her heart suddenly seized up and felt like it was going to explode. Her breath caught in her throat, making her feel like she was about to gag. She knew General Green was not only her uncle but he was her commanding officer too. He could, if he so willed, stop her from marrying Ezekiel and even stop her from seeing him.

It took everything he could do to keep a straight face. But he said, "You need to talk with him, convince him, see if you can make him see it our way. Okay?"

"Oh, yes. Yes, for sure. Oh, Ezekiel, I don't care what he says. I love you. And I'm going to marry you no matter what *anyone* says."

"I love you too."

They hurried back over to the command bunker and rode the elevator back down to the bottom floor. General Green was the first to see them. He had a very stern expression on his face. His eyes immediately went to Esther's, and as she looked into them, she almost stumbled and fell.

"Well…" General Green's deep baritone voice boomed out loudly. It seemed to echo throughout the entire room and into all of the hidden inner chambers. "I need to have a word with you, young lady."

That time, Esther knew she was just about to die. She knew her heart had already stopped beating in her chest. She also knew that every brain cell had suddenly seized up and stopped working too.

"Uh...yes, sir, Uncle, I mean, General, sir." As these words came tumbling out of her mouth her eyes suddenly filled with tears and she began wobbling on her feet.

Ezekiel reached out and put his arm around her.

General Green's heart suddenly went out to this most beautiful of all women. She looked so much like her mother, his little sister, who no longer even knew her own name or that of her daughter. "Oh, my darling, precious child. Please, do not take my stern voice as an indication of anything wrong. Please. I am very much in favor of this soon-to-be union of man and wife in God and man's eyes. Yes. I give my blessing. In fact, as you may or may not know, as your commanding officer, I am authorized under our laws to perform marriages. If the both of you were so inclined, I could marry you right now and you could later seek a civil marriage union, if you so desired, after this mess we are in is over."

They turned to look at each other. Part of them felt confusion, but the bigger part screamed out, "Let's do it!"

A huge smile larger than any he had ever before felt wrapped all of the way around General Green's head and, in fact, around his whole body. Colonel Jeremiah had already returned from getting the general's Bible, and the general was now holding it in his hand. He glanced down at it. Then he held it up for everyone to see.

"I asked Colonel Jeremiah to get my Bible and bring it to me because I want to read something out of it to all of you gathered in this bunker, but also to join Lieutenant Colonel Ezekiel Cohen and my beautiful niece, Major Esther Asher, in an unbreakable bond of marriage."

"Uh...Uncle...uh, General Green, I am not a major; I'm still a lieutenant," Esther quickly reminded the general.

"No, you're not. As of now, you have been promoted to major, and from this moment on, you will be my personal assistant and aide. You must be a major to be my assistant. You will assist Colonel Jeremiah in keeping me abreast of everything. But you have more than earned this promotion. Unfortunately, I have allowed this promotion to sit on my desk for over three months now. I have been very neglectful in doing so. Please forgive me, Major Asher."

Esther couldn't help herself. She suddenly broke out of Ezekiel's grasp and ran up to General Green. In the next moment, all military decorum and discipline went completely out the window as she stood on her tiptoes, put both her arms around the general's neck, and kissed him on his cheek. Then, she suddenly realized what she had done. She jumped back and came to a rigid attention with a quick salute coming from her right hand.

At first, General Green was taken aback for just a minute. But before Esther pulled away and came to attention, he quickly wrapped her up in his big, bearlike arms and gave her a huge hug. At the same time, everyone from the lowest ranking person in the huge room to the highest ranking began clapping and hooting and hollering. General Green raised his big body up to his full height and returned her salute with the best one he had ever given.

After that, he turned around and faced the entire audience in the room. "Ezekiel, get on the horn and get all of your men here on the double. I'm sure they want to be a part of this happy occasion."

It was the longest thirty minutes Esther or Ezekiel had ever lived until his men all arrived. But during that time, it reassured them that they were doing the right thing. He knew his parents and siblings would be angry, but they would get over it just as soon as they met Esther. Plus, with the storm clouds of the world's armies gathering against them, who knew when they would have another chance?

Shortly after Ezekiel's squadron arrived, General Green turned to address the entire group. By now, everyone except the most crucially needed analysts, planners, and strategists were present, including several of the cooks and aides.

"All of you here will be witnesses to this marriage that I truly believe with all of my heart to have been preordained and ordered by God Himself between Lieutenant Colonel Ezekiel Cohen and Major Esther Asher. If anyone has any reason to deny this union, let them speak now or forever hold their peace."

Without pausing, he gathered Ezekiel and Esther in front of him, opened the Bible to Genesis 2:24 and began reading, "'Therefore shall a man leave his father and his mother, and shall cleave unto his wife: and they shall be one flesh ...'"

He continued on for a while longer reading more scripture. Then, he pronounced them husband and wife. Ezekiel turned to Esther to seal their new relationship with a kiss. As he did, the entire room exploded into yelling, hugging, back-slapping, laughter, and congratulations.

In the meantime, Colonel Jeremiah had gone into the kitchen area of the bunker. He turned to the head cook and asked if he had any wine that he used to cook with. The cook had been standing in the hallway, watching the ceremony taking place. He had already been thinking about the same thing.

"You mean something like this, Colonel?" the cook asked as he reached over, opened a cupboard door, and pulled a bottle of Barkan Cabernet Sauvignon Reserve Kosher 2004 from the shelf. The grapes were grown and the wine fermented and bottled in Israel. Colonel Jeremiah was so happy that he could have kissed the cook. He was ecstatic that he didn't have to, somehow, some way turn water into wine. He didn't think he had that much righteousness inside of him.

"Perfect, my friend. Just perfect," the colonel said as he took the bottle from the cook. The cook quickly turned and hurried over to where the good crystal was kept. He reached in and brought two crystal wine glasses out.

The colonel took those from him and turned to go back into the room. He arrived at the same time as Ezekiel and Esther's lips were very slowly pulling apart. He walked up to the newly married Lieutenant Colonel and Major Cohen and declared that a toast was in order.

After that, the celebration went on for about fifteen minutes. Finally, though, the general was forced to once again hold up his hand and bring the room back under control. The little, red LEDs on the map of the world indicating the angry armies forming against them could no longer be ignored, even for such a joyous occasion.

"Everyone, please let me have all of your attention," he yelled. "A while ago, before Ezekiel went to get Esther and bring her over here, I asked him for his opinion about what we should do. He made some very astute observations and suggestions.

"By the way, Ezekiel," he said, "we took your suggestions and right now are in the process of beginning to put a plan into effect to be able to carry those out. But what you said about us basically keeping all of our troops inside of our borders and forming a protective front, that reminded me of something. So I asked Colonel Jeremiah to go get my Bible. I want to read something from it to all of you here."

He opened it to Genesis, chapter fifteen. "Gentlemen, this is the covenant God made with Abram." He began to read, "'After this, the word of the Lord came to Abram in a vision: "Fear not, Abram. I am thy shield, and thy exceeding great reward."

"'And Abram said, "Lord God, what wilt thou give me seeing I go childless and the steward of my house is this Eliezer of Damascus?" And Abram said, "To me thou hath given no seed, and lo, one born in my house is my heir."

"'And behold, the word of the Lord came unto him, saying, "This shall not be thine heir, but he that shall come forth out of your own bowels shall be thine heir."

"'And he brought him forth abroad, and said, "Look now toward heaven, and tell the stars, if thou be able to number them." And he said unto him, "So shall thy seed be." And he believed in the LORD; and he counted it to him for righteousness. And he said unto him, "I am the LORD that brought thee out of Ur of the Chaldeans to give thee this land to inherit it."

"'And he said, "LORD God, whereby shall I know that I shall inherit it?"

"'And he said unto him, "Take me an heifer of three years old, and a she goat of three years old, and a ram of three years old, and a turtledove, and a young pigeon." And he took unto him all these, and divided them in the midst, and laid each piece one against another: but the birds divided he not. And when the fowls came down upon the carcasses, Abram drove them away.

"'And when the sun was going down, a deep sleep fell upon Abram; and lo, an horror of great darkness fell upon him. Then the Lord said to him, "Know for certain that your descendants will be strangers in a country not their own, and they will be enslaved and mistreated four hundred years. But I will punish the nation they serve as slaves, and also that nation, whom they shall serve, will I judge: and afterward shall they come out with great substance. And thou shalt go to thy fathers in peace; thou shalt be buried in a good old age.

"'But in the fourth generation they shall come hither again: for the iniquity of the Amorites is not yet full.

"'And it came to pass, that, when the sun went down, and it was dark, behold a smoking furnace, and a burning lamp that passed between those pieces. In the same day the LORD made a covenant with Abram saying, "Unto thy seed have I given this land *from the river of Egypt to the great river, the Euphrates.*"'"

General Green continued. "Everyone, listen to me. Not once in our entire history have we possessed all of this area that God promised to us through Abraham, our forefather. The closest we ever came was when King David conquered much of Syria and also held a large area in what is now Lebanon in his hands.

"But I take this scripture to mean that we should consider all of Lebanon, Jordan, most of Syria north up to the Euphrates River, and eastward across much of Iraq until you again get to the Euphrates River, and down from there until it empties into the Persian Gulf as the land that God promised to Abraham. Then we need to go southward across the Sinai Peninsula to include all of Egypt down to the Nile River. This should also be considered as our rightful, God-given, declared homeland. So, what I am wondering is should we be ready to move many of our troops into these areas and occupy them to meet the onslaught of these armies coming against us?

"As you can see from the LED lights, the king of the south, which includes Sudan, Libya, and Egypt—and this is just as the Bible declares it would happen—are moving their armies into position to come against us. I ask, should we move against them now and, with God's help, defeat them for all time forevermore? As for the kings of the north, should we swarm through Hezbollah in Lebanon, strangle the life out of Syria, and move into Iraq to be prepared to meet the Russians at the great Euphrates River? I ask these questions to give you something to think about, not for you to give answers right now. If you can come up with some solid plans or ideas, please do not hesitate to speak up.

"As for your suggestion, Ezekiel that we take out the dams in Turkey, a crack squad of explosive experts will shortly be preparing to do that as we speak. They agree that if we take out the two upper-most dams on the river, that should be enough explosive waterpower to destroy every dam below it all of the way until it empties into the Persian Gulf. Of course, along with the dams, all bridges and roads crossing over the river will also be destroyed too. That should delay the combined armies for days and possibly even weeks, and it is certain to cause much confusion and angst on their part.

"Also, there are several steep mountain passes both in Turkey and in Syria that the Russians will have to come through. I have also ordered that we attempt to set explosives that will destroy these passes and anything in their paths. Hopefully, that will occur as their armies are passing through."

nside the private dining area of the White House, the president of the United States, Hussein Anwar was eating a plate full of eggs and hash-brown potatoes. The cook made sure never to serve bacon or even have any pork products inside of the White House. This was a late evening snack he sometimes enjoyed.

Across from him was the Israeli ambassador to the United States. Also present were two radical friends of the president, plus several of his so-called czars. All had big plates of steaming food in front of them. All, that is, except the Israeli ambassador. He was not invited to share in the meal. In fact, he was not even invited to sit down. He was made to stand incommunicado in front of the table for the first ten minutes after he came into the room. This was totally humiliating to him. He felt like a little child standing before the school principal about to be told whether or not he was going to get spanked for his misdeeds.

The meeting between the Ambassador and the president had been postponed from earlier because the president had spent much of the day on the phone with the Russian premier. Now, he was having to stand there while the president stuffed his face with food.

Finally, the president looked up at him. He still had a mouth full of food along with a bemused smirk on his face. He was thoroughly enjoying himself at the Israeli ambassador's humiliation. "So, Ambassador, it looks like your tiny, little, problem-causing country has finally bitten off more than it can chew. Huh?" He was laughing so hard that chunks of half-eaten food flew out of his mouth and landed on the table in front of him. He glanced down and saw the wet, slimy chunks splattered and began laughing even harder.

The Ambassador thought, *How in the world did this uncouth, unqualified, absolute fool ever get elected in this once great and wonderful country?*

Eventually, the president stopped his insane laughing. He slowly began lifting his head up until he was looking directly into the ambassador's eyes. Like a wisp of a magician's smoke screen rising into the air, an evil transparent apparition suddenly ascended up from the bowels of hell and entered into his mind and body. And in that same instant, the president transformed into the most evil and diabolic individual the ambassador had ever met.

"Ambassador," the president screamed, "I called you here to let you know that we, the United States, are not going to do anything to help you get out of this mess you deliberately started. I declare to you that if Israel is completely destroyed by my friends around the world, the better it will be for the rest of us left in the world.

"In fact, I have offered Russia and all of the rest of my Muslim friends throughout the Arab world who are willing to join in this *jihad* against you all of our assistance up to but not including our own military troops. We will give them everything they need to destroy you. That includes weapons, knowledge, intelligence, motivation, *everything*. I want your country and all of the rest of you Jews throughout the entire world to be totally destroyed once and for all!" he thundered.

At the same time this meeting was going on, another meeting was taking place. But no one was supposed to know about this one. It was supposed to be without the knowledge of the president or any of his allies and advisers, or even of their own aides. It consisted of the four joint chiefs of staff of the four different military forces of the United States, plus the head of the CIA.

It was taking place at a popular restaurant in Antietam, Maryland, outside the Washington, DC, metro area. The place was crowded to the walls with dinner patrons or ones staying late to enjoy after-dinner drinks. The other people in the restaurant could be heard talking about what the Israelis had done and where the world was heading next.

None of the military leaders were wearing uniforms. All were trying to blend in in case anyone noticed them. They had gotten together to discuss the ramifications a military coup against the president would bring.

They were aware about what had taken place in Iran and were very proud of what the Israelis had accomplished. The Israelis had stopped Iran from turning the Middle East into a nuclear holocaust.

"They should be praised and honored! But instead," General Curtis Rockford, the top military officer of the Marine Corps, declared, "the whole world has turned against them. Unfortunately, that also includes the United States government at this present time. At least that includes this present administration and his elitist cronies in the Congress."

Immediately after the Israelis had launched their raid, the far left liberal elitists of the American Congress were already screaming about the "outrageous criminal actions" the Israelis had committed. The elitists began crying for the prosecution of the entire government and the top military leaders of Israel. They wanted them all brought before the United Nations for public humiliation and condemnation and then taken before the World Court at The Hague for prosecution of crimes against humanity.

The elitists had stood up in the hallowed halls of Congress and declared that because of these "unthinkable crimes against humanity" the "criminal leaders of Israel" should all die in a public hanging or have their heads cut off by a guillotine! And it should be shown on worldwide television. But these five immensely powerful leaders of the United States knew that those deluded members of congress were the same ones who vehemently decried the death penalty for murderers and rapists and child molesters. They knew that these so-called representatives of the people believed those who actually deserved death were far more worthy of life than the leaders of the Jewish nation who had the courage to stop a psychopathic, insane madman from polluting the entire world's atmosphere with radio-active fallout. At least, in their deluded eyes and their mouths, the Israelis were guiltier than anyone else.

But because of the actions of the Israelis, riots and protests were taking place all over the United States. They began shortly after the foolish president's statements that joined in harmony with the liberal elitists' declarations in the Congress condemning the Israelis. These riots and protests were further inflamed by the leftist Hollywood crowd along with the skinhead crazies on the far right who hate Jews, Blacks, and everyone not like them.

The leaders knew they had to do something and do it quick or their country would soon disintegrate into complete chaos and anarchy. But another thing that was troubling to them was they knew that Israel was also a nuclear power. They also knew that Israel had the third most powerful air force in the world. Plus, they knew that Israel had something else on her side that was just unexplainable, especially to someone who didn't believe in the God of Abraham, Isaac, and Jacob.

These five men knew if they were to have any chance to save their own country, and thus the world, they had to act now. If they didn't act on their convictions, they knew that all of the demons of hell were soon going to break loose throughout the world.

General Isaac Woods, the head of the United States Army, leaned his head in close to be able to keep his voice from being heard by anyone nearby. "Gentlemen, I say it is imperative that we declare an immediate military coup. I say we need to arrest the president and all of his advisers and put them in custody in a secret location, possibly some CIA safe house. And at the same time, we need to institute martial law throughout the country until we can bring stability back to it."

The CIA Director, Mark Winston, glanced up at General Woods. "I know just the place. It's an underground facility with individual holding cells. It's where we keep and interrogate some of the more ... uh ... shall I say, *unsavory* characters we capture."

Admiral Adam Decker, the head of the United States Navy smiled at the *unsavory* description and then spoke up. "I agree with you, General Woods. This bunch of narcissistic, *unsavory* anti-Americans who are now in charge of our government has got to go. There's no other way. These people have brought the United States to the razor-sharp edge of oblivion. If we don't remove them, I declare we won't have a United States to call as our own country within the next few weeks."

All five men sat there, nodding their heads in agreement. They knew that if they did not make a move against their own country then what Admiral Decker had just said would be very true; they wouldn't have a country in a very short time. They also knew that Israel, their only real friend and ally in the Middle East, would almost certainly cease to exist if they didn't act. More importantly, they knew this would take place in just a short matter of days.

General David Benjamin, the Air Force chief of staff, spoke up. "Do you believe the country will go along with us? What about the national guard units; the police departments across the country; militias; in general, all of the people?"

General Rockford spoke up again. He was a very no-nonsense, very tough, old school leader originally from West Texas. In his southern drawl, he said, "Gentlemen, I don't give a rat's rear end what the people say and do. That goes for the national guard and all police departments too. We must do this. Our oaths that we all took say we will do whatever it takes to protect our country from all enemies, both foreign and *domestic*. If this batch of yahoos running our country right now is not a bunch of domestic enemies, then I don't know who is. These people are guilty of treason. That's what they are. My only concern is that when we issue the order for all of our units to act, how many of them will actually follow those orders without hesitation?"

"That's my concern too," General Woods declared. "We must have over fifty percent participation from our troops to be able to pull this off."

"I believe I can get several air squadrons flying over all of our major cities. Doing this in a show of maximum force will create enough of a diversion to allow your ground units to move in and occupy those cities. Of course, the most important one is DC," General Benjamin replied.

"I think then that we're all in agreement that this is what we have to do. The question is, when do we make our move?" General Woods asked.

"We have to move fast, so I propose we move tonight. That way, most people will be asleep, not even realizing anything is happening until they wake up tomorrow morning. I say we move against Washington, DC, at three o'clock tomorrow morning. That way, it will be midnight on the west coast," General Rockford quickly stated.

The leader of the CIA spoke up. "Men, this is a little off what we are discussing right now, but I believe it gives us an added incentive to do what is being proposed. Last night, we received an intelligence report that proves without a doubt that our president is a treasonous traitor against our country. We intercepted a phone call from the president's own private BlackBerry. You want to know who he was talking to? He was talking to Premier Anatoly Butin, the Russian leader. They were discussing about the president assuming a second-in-command role in a new *one-world government* that will be formed once Israel is destroyed. You see, gentlemen, Russia's main goal is not only to destroy Israel, but to destroy all of the Arabs too. Thereby, they would assume control of at least eighty-five percent of all of the oil in the world. In other words, if that were to happen, Russia would control the world. Men, we have dedicated our lives to the service of our country, let us—."

Kaboom!

He never had a chance to finish what he was saying. A car loaded with explosives parked at the curb just outside the building exploded. In less than the blink of an eye, the building where the supposedly secret meeting was taking place was turned into a fiery heap of rubble. There were no survivors. Fifty-seven innocent people died in the blast. "Collateral damage," is what the nation's headlines screamed the next morning.

At the same time, in the White House kitchen, the meeting with the Israeli ambassador was just ending. The president, with eyes as cold and sharp as black obsidian yet as hot as the fires of hell, stared straight into the face of the ambassador and said, "I want you and the entire Israeli diplomatic contingent out of my country. I want this to happen within the next twenty-four hours. Do I make myself clear, Mr. Ambassador?"

As the ambassador stared back into those cold, black eyes, he swore he could see actual flames of fire flickering in them. There was such evil in those eyes—in fact, there was such evil all over his face—that the ambassador suddenly felt chilled all the way down to his bones. He felt he was actually standing in the very presence of Satan himself.

ithin a short hour after receiving the words from the ambassador about his meeting with the president, the government of Israel found out about the car bombing that killed all four leaders of the four armed services of the United States, plus the death of the CIA director in the same bombing.

As General Green received the news, he said to the people in the bunker "We really are on our own now. We now have no hope other than God coming down and fighting to save us."

He turned to Ezekiel. "Ezekiel, I hate to do this because of your wedding, but duty must come first at a time like this. I want you and your squadron to make a couple of reconnaissance flights. I want half of your men to fly over into Iraq and see what is happening there. The others I want to fly down into Egypt and check out the situation there. Do not allow yourselves to be seen, and do not engage the enemy in any way at this time. Just look around, take some pictures, and return home safely. Okay? And make sure you stay above the radioactive fallout cloud!"

They all quickly snapped to attention, "Yes, sir. Consider it done, sir."

Ezekiel turned toward Esther and wrapped her in his arms and kissed her before running to catch the elevator door before it closed on him. On the way up, Ezekiel pointed to four of his men. "You guys come with me. Major Malachi, you take the others."

An hour later, all ten planes were heading toward their destinations. The weather was still terrible throughout the entire Middle East. A continuous cover of thick clouds was still covering all of the countries. In many places throughout the entire area, over twenty inches of rain had fallen in the last twenty-four hours. As Ezekiel gazed down with his infrared optical illumination unit and his ground mapping radar, he was able to see with those electronic eyes all of the flooding and devastation that was taking place. Looking at the devastation, he knew it was going to be very hard for the Russians and Arabs to move against Israel, at least until the storm passed and the ground dried some.

As he was watching the devastation fly by below, Ezekiel suddenly sat straight up in his seat. Without thinking, he broke radio silence and yelled over the squadron frequency, "Guys, do you hear that ... that ... that sound? It's like the sound of a beautiful trumpet or something."

All four of the other pilots quickly keyed their microphone switches two times to indicate that they heard it too. But none spoke over the radio.

Then, in a flash, in the twinkling of an eye, it happened so fast that Ezekiel and his men were not for sure they had actually seen it; a bright, almost blinding light burst forth directly out of the eastern sky and then disappeared just as quickly as it had appeared.

Ezekiel had no idea what had just happened. But in his gut, he knew it had been something very unusual and probably supernatural. All he knew was that he and his squadron needed to get back to Sharon Air Force Base as quickly as possible.

Inside of the command bunker, both General Green and Esther heard what sounded to them as the most beautiful trumpet ever played. They also saw a very bright and glorious light suddenly appear just as the final note from the trumpet was drifting away into eternity. Even deep inside of the bunker where they were, the glorious light was just as bright and intense as if they were standing right in front of it on the surface. And then, in less time than it takes to blink an eye, their bodies suddenly felt like a huge magnet was pulling on them. It was something that felt so strong, it was going to suddenly rip them right off the ground and fling them straight up through the bonds of the universe.

But before their feet actually left the ground, they both heard a voice speaking to them. It was not an audible voice they heard with their ears but was something they heard deep within them.

"You, Esther Cohen, and you, General Green, are part of my chosen remnant that must remain on the earth at this time. Because I love you so much and appreciate the stand you have taken with the type of lives you have lived in front of others as a witness for me, I desired to bring you to be with me at this time. But I need you and the other one hundred forty-four thousand people of Abraham's chosen family who have made me their Savior, their Lord of lords, and their soon-coming King, to be my witnesses to the rest of your countrymen during the next seven years of tribulation that is coming upon the world beginning today.

"Remember this though: you are mine, sealed with my sign on your foreheads. No man can harm you. No man can stop you. What you *say* in my name, I will do. What you *do* in my name, I will do. Speak my Word. Pray in my name. And most of all, do not fear, for I am with you always, until the end of the world."

Throughout every country, every region, every *place* on the face of the earth, the sound of a beautiful trumpet was heard by the ones who believed Jesus was their Savior and had made Him Lord over their lives. As the last note was fading away, a booming, mighty voice burst throughout all of the earth and the heavens above.

"Hear me. I am the voice of the archangel. I am declaring that the bridegroom has made his house ready for His bride. He desires to bring His bride home to be with him forever. All who have been washed in the blood of the Lamb who was slain for mankind are invited to come to the marriage supper of the Lamb. All who have been faithful and have oil in your lamps, come up hither."

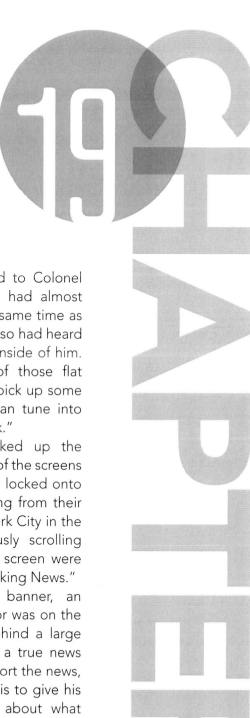

General Green turned to Colonel Jeremiah, who also had almost left the earth at the same time as Esther and he and also had heard the voice speaking inside of him. "Colonel, switch some of those flat screens to see if you can pick up some world news. See if you can tune into ONE World News Network."

Colonel Jeremiah picked up the remote that controlled six of the screens on the far wall. He quickly locked onto the ONE broadcast coming from their national studios in New York City in the United States. Continuously scrolling across the bottom of the screen were these words, "Urgent-Breaking News."

Behind the scrolling banner, an opinion news commentator was on the screen. He was sitting behind a large anchor desk. He was not a true news anchor whose job is to report the news, per se. But this man's job is to give his so-called expert opinion about what happened in the world on a daily basis.

Normally, his appearance would have been as close to perfect as possible. His makeup would have been done, his wrinkles smoothed, his hair perfectly coiffed, and he would have been dressed in an expensive, custom-tailored pinstriped suit with one of his trademark $1500 brightly colored silk ties on. But at that moment, he looked more like a dumpster diver who had just climbed out of a dirty dumpster scrounging for food behind a restaurant. He was still dressed in his custom-tailored suit, but it was wrinkled and stained from either sweat or he had spilled something on it. His shiny rainbow-colored tie was twisted and facing backward inside of his suit jacket, which was completely unbuttoned, and he had purposely pulled the tie knot loose to allow more room to breathe. His hair was a disaster, most of it sticking up and out at odd angles from him constantly running his hands through it. But most of all was the appearance of his face. It was pale, sunken, and ashen, almost like a death parlor. The expert opinion commentator was trying his best to speak. But he was so excited, frightened, and worried, plus every other emotion that a man can have, that the words he was trying to speak were very hurried and mumbled. They were tumbling out of his mouth in a jumbled mess of twos and threes all running together.

"*Pe*-pee-pep…people, we–we…don't know who, or wha-what has happened." He stopped. He couldn't go on. He turned his face away from the camera for a brief second and took several deep, cleansing breaths.

The reason for all of this was throughout the entire world, hundreds of millions of people had just suddenly vanished off the earth. They just vanished into what appeared to be nothing but thin air. And what was really scary and unnerving was that even in graveyards and mausoleums, many of the graves and canisters had burst open and the coffins and containers are overturned and splattered, but nothing was in any of them. The dead had disappeared too.

He turned back to the camera and tried to continue on. "Excuse me, but as I was trying to say, we don't know what has just happened all across the earth. But we are getting astounding reports coming in from everywhere telling us something completely strange and totally frightening has, or still is, taking place. People, these reports are saying that millions upon millions of people have just suddenly disappeared from off the face of this planet.

No one knows where they have gone, and it seems that no one saw or heard anything before they suddenly just left. I'm telling you, they just vanished right into thin air. At this moment, our phone lines are flooded with people frantically calling in to tell us that persons they were just speaking with suddenly disappeared from right in front of them. Right in the middle of conversations, they just vanished."

He stopped once more and turned his head to glance over at his producer, who was speaking into his earpiece. A brief second later, he turned back to the camera.

"My producer wants me to digress for a moment and pass this information on to you while I am still able to talk somewhat coherently. We are being asked by the police to please ask all of you who had someone disappear to please be patient. Their phone lines are flooded with calls. Plus, a lot of their own officers seem to be part of this vanishing. They have lost all contact with many of them. They are working as hard as they can, but right now, they're extremely shorthanded. Please be patient, and they will eventually get to you.

"Now, viewers, let me get back to what I was saying earlier. On top of everything else, we now have reports coming in that all of our freeways and toll ways, and even most of our major cross streets, have come to a complete stop. It seems that a tremendous number of major accidents have taken place on all of our main thoroughfares and on almost every street in the entire city. This has brought traffic to a complete standstill metrowide. I honestly can't tell you how many accidents have taken place. There are just too many to number them. I can tell you this much though. If I were you, I would not venture out and try to go anywhere. All you would do is just add to the unbelievable gridlock that is taking place in our city. So, stay home. Until the authorities can tell us what, when, where, and especially who is behind all of this. I hate to say this, ladies and gentlemen, but this has given me a major case of the heebie jeebies."

Once again, he paused, this time in an attempt to gather his rambling thoughts into some kind of an organized and coherent order. Finally, he pressed on.

"Let me throw this out to all of you who are fortunate to be able to view this program. I don't want to sound like some kind of conspiracy freak who populates late-night AM radio, but... do you... or might it be possible that our planet has just been visited by space aliens and that for some reason, they have stolen multitudes of people off the earth? Or maybe it could be that the earth has suddenly entered into some kind of a space-time warp, or a worm-hole, or even another dimension, or something else similar to those. You know, even Einstein predicted such things as these. I promise you I'm not trying to sound silly here, but science fiction stories and comic books such as Superman, and even Dick Tracy, have for years been spreading the gospel about what has just taken place.

"There is another possibility too, that this could possibly be ... well, I'm reluctant to even say this ... but as you know, our own government has been experimenting with hologram technology and even invisibility cloaks like in the *Harry Potter* movies... so, could it be possible that these things are responsible for these disappearances? Let's don't rule this out either. Maybe this is some kind of new technology that the Russians or Chinese have developed, sort of like a new form of virtual reality.

"I tell you, I just don't have any idea what is going on in our world right now. But I will tell you this much. I am extremely nervous and very, very frightened, and I am not afraid to be brutally honest with you and to admit this. But before I totally lose my composure, along with my entire mind and this evening's dinner, if you do have to go somewhere, use small residential side streets to wind around and hopefully get to where you're going. But, and this is the most important thing of all; keep looking up. Yes, keep looking up to see if something above you is about to snatch you too. You know, until we can find out what this is all about, it is better to be safe than sorry because you just might be the next one to disappear."

"People who are stuck in traffic right now are calling us on their cell phones, saying things like, 'All of a sudden, the car in front of me just went completely out of control and began smashing into everything around them. They just went crazy. It was the most bizarre thing I have ever seen. And when the cars finally stopped crashing—

they're empty. No one is in the cars. Whoever was driving the cars have just disappeared.'"

Again, his producer was speaking to him. With all of the weird happenings taking place in the world, news reports were coming in faster than they could keep up. Professionalism and order had gone out the door.

He slowly turned back to the camera. His face was even more sunken and ashen and his voice was at least an octave higher than it had been. Once again, he began stuttering with his voice quivering and breaking.

"People, I do not know what has happened, and maybe I shouldn't even be saying this...but maybe we really have been invaded by space aliens, and...and right now, they're trying to kill all of us. I'm not trying to be facetious here. I have never been more serious in my entire life.

"We have just gotten word that at least six passenger aircraft have crashed here in the United States since the beginning of these unknown disappearances. That's just here in the US. We have not received any word at this time about what is happening in other countries, but one must assume that the same terrible things have happened there and are still going on. I ask you, is it possible that space aliens are shooting them out of the sky? Or Russia or China? Or some other country who has developed some kind of super-secret weapons? I must admit that for the first time in my career as an expert opinion commentator, I just don't know what in the world has happened and I am not afraid to admit the fact that I am completely scared out of my wits.

"Several of the airplanes have crashed into residential areas. At this time, there is no word on any survivors. But my God, people, the death toll could very well be in the hundreds of thousands if airplanes have crashed into residential areas all over the world like here in the US!" he screamed. "I have to ask this again, do you think it really might be possible that space aliens have invaded our planet. If you will search your memory, this is something Hollywood has been trying to warn us about for years!" These words came blasting out of his mouth at the top of his voice as he completely lost his composure, along with his coherent mind.

The camera stayed on him for a few seconds as he began screaming unintelligible words and began throwing papers and pencils and anything else he could find into the air. The last thing it showed was him reaching up and grabbing big handfuls of his hair and pulling it out.

As the screen went dark, Colonel Jeremiah and General Green looked over at each other. Both were slowly shaking their heads from side to side in amazement and wonder. Their faces were full of bewilderment. But at the moment, both were too stunned to say anything.

When the screen came back live, a different opinion anchor was sitting behind the desk. But just like the last one, this opinion-giver looked extremely disheveled and very, very frightened.

"Wait … what's that?" he was asking someone off camera as he reached his hand up and cupped it over his ear. Eventually, he realized the camera had come on and he was now live on air. "Uh … oh … we're live. Sorry about that, but so many things have happened, or are still happening, that we are a bit ragged and out of sorts right now. I apologize and ask you to please bear with us as we all muddle our way through this extremely awful occurrence that has happened in our world.

"Wait … what's that?" he asked again as he once more cupped his hand over his ear. A moment later, he turned back to the camera. "Viewers, we're going to break away from our local coverage for a brief time and go to our network affiliate, ONE, which you know stands for *One World News Network*. It appears they have a lot more breaking news to inform us with. But please stay tuned. Hopefully, unless another sudden mass exodus from the earth suddenly takes place, we will all still be here and back on the air locally as soon as possible."

As he finished speaking, the screen went dark again for a brief moment as the switch was being completed. Finally, a very pretty woman reporter appeared. Her platinum blonde hair was cut short to accentuate the nice features of her face.

As soon as the red light on top of the camera came on, she began saying that she was broadcasting live from a communal farm in the valley of Megiddo, in Israel. It was impossible not to see the almost paralyzing fear emanating through her entire being.

"Hello," she said in a shaky and breaking voice. "My name is Katie Spitzer, and I have standing next to me a woman who says that she and her friend were out in the middle of their field, tending their crops of leeks, onions, garlic, and cucumbers, when all of a sudden, right in the middle of their conversation, her friend just disappeared. In case anyone might see her missing friend, let me give you a description of her. She is thirty-three years old; stands five feet two inches tall; weighs one hundred and nine pounds; and has long, brown hair and brown eyes.

"Here. I'll let her tell you about it. First of all, though, tell us your name," she said as she nervously placed the microphone in front of the girl's mouth. She was so nervous and her hand was shaking so badly that she almost hit the young woman in the mouth with it.

"Hello. My name is Leah Ishmael. And yes, it is just as this lady said. My best friend, whom I have known all of my life, just disappeared into thin air. We were born just two days apart in the same hospital, and our parents knew each other for a number of years before that. But yes, she just vanished. In fact, she was telling me that just last night, she had finally opened up her heart and had become a Messianic Jew. This means that she believes that the ancient Rabbi and prophet of old, Jesus, is the true Messiah. Yes, there are quite a few of the people who live—or, I should say, lived—here, at our commune, who are—I'm sorry, were—Messianic Jews.

"But as I was saying, my friend was telling me she has been listening for several years to a man on TV who had finally convinced her without a shadow of a doubt, that Jesus was the true Jewish Messiah. She said that after watching him again on TV last night, she had gotten down on her knees and asked Jesus, whom she called *the Christ*, to forgive her of her sins and unbelief and come live inside of her heart.

"My friend, who, by the way, is named, Rebecca Bloodworthy, had just finished telling me this. And then—*poof*—she's gone. Disappeared. I don't know where. But I am really frightened. And not only is my friend missing, but every one of the other people here who were also Messianic Jews are missing too. So this makes me very, very scared."

"Yes. I think we are all very scared," the lady reporter said as she moved the microphone back in front of her own mouth. It was still shaking so badly that it looked like a straw blowing in a hurricane.

"Ms. Ismael, could you tell us how many Messianic Jews disappeared from here?"

"Yes. I believe it is around one hundred and twenty men, women, and especially children who disappeared. I say especially the children because *all* of them disappeared. There are no children at all left except for some over the age of sixteen. It is just as the ancient prophet, Jeremiah, declared, 'In Rama was there a voice heard, lamentation, and weeping, and great mourning, Rachel weeping for her children, and would not be comforted, because they are not.' Ms. Spitzer, for sure, these words have come true today! Everywhere throughout Israel, there is much weeping for their missing children. It seems all of the children all over Israel have suddenly disappeared."

The reporter suddenly froze, not moving, staring straight into space. Huge tears welled up in her eyes and began flowing down her face. Her mouth began quivering as she began mumbling something incoherent.

"What? What did you say, Ms. Spitzer?"

"I said, I wonder if my own son is still here, or was he taken too? Excuse me. I need to call my husband." She dropped the microphone on the ground and hurriedly reached into her purse, searching for her cell phone. Finally, she found it and hit the speed dial to call her home.

Leah Ishmael stood there, watching not knowing what else to do. Katie Spitzer's hand that was holding the phone was shaking so badly that she could barely hold onto it. Even though the microphone had fallen to the ground, you could still hear the conversation.

"Mohammed, is Gerald there with you?"

"No. I thought you had picked him up and he was with you." Like a broken marble statue the very pretty young reporter began slowly sinking to the ground as the phone tumbled out of her hand. At the same time, an unearthly guttural noise blasted out of her throat in a bellowing, animalistic scream.

The camera had stayed on her all of this time. The cameraman was transfixed and didn't know what else to do. Finally, he realized he should shut it off.

Approximately thirty seconds passed before a switch was made to a reporter who was standing inside of what appeared to be a huge warehouse-type grocery outlet with very dim lighting. It appeared to be almost deserted except for a few workers standing near the reporter. The building was located in London, England, according to the scroll along the bottom of the TV screen.

The reporter suddenly looked up at the camera and began speaking. "Hello. My name is Martin Smith of ONE World News coming to you live from inside of a huge grocery co-op on the outskirts of London, England. It seems that at least eight of the employees of this large co-op have just suddenly disappeared within the last hour. I have here, standing next to me, some of the remaining employees to tell us their version of what happened.

"Sir, will you tell our viewers what happened here not too long ago?" he asked a burly, heavyset man. The man stood in excess of six feet tall and weighed at least two hundred and sixty pounds. He was wearing a thick, heavy, dark brown, plastic apron stained with what appeared to be dried blood all over it. It was looped over his neck, tied around his waist, and drooped down to cover his knees. On his feet were rubber boots. He appeared to be a butcher. The reporter put the microphone in front of the man's mouth.

"Yes. Or at least, I'll *try* to tell you what happened. I'm still trying to make sense of it myself though." The man's voice was shaking and trembling. It was also heavily tinged with a Liverpool accent that made it hard to understand.

*Or,* the reporter thought, *he's been hitting the bottle since this mess happened.*

"Well, again, I don't really know what happened, except they just disappeared."

"Who disappeared?" the reporter asked. "Try to be a little more specific if you can."

"They did, all of the other employees. We were in here, stocking the store, which is getting the shelves full in time for the doors to open to let the customers come in. And as we were doing this, some of us were kidding around with the ones who disappeared.

"You see, we always do that. All of the ones who vanished from here all claimed to be Christian believers who believed that Jesus Christ had saved them from all of their sins. They were always spouting this garbage to all of us. But some of the weaker-minded employees started to believe what these fools were always spouting. Those employees also disappeared too though. But we, my good drinking buddies you see here with me, well, we were always kidding these fools and making fun of them and their beliefs. You know, it was a fun thing to do."

"What do you mean, you kid them? Did you intimidate them or bully them?"

"Well, you know. We just kidded with them. We made fun of their beliefs. You know, things like we would purposely use the name ·of Jesus Christ as a curse word. And you know, most of those fools went to one of those holy roller types of churches. You know, where they speak in weird languages that don't make no sense, you know, the kind of church where they jump around and shout al-le-lu-ya. They raise their hands in the air and pray in loud voices. And some of them are always yelling, 'Amen,' or, 'Glory,' or, you know, stupid stuff like that.

"Well, we kind of made fun of this stuff by garbling our own speech like we were speaking in tongues and acting like we're puk-ing at the same time … and, you know, just stuff like that. Or we, you know, would roll around on the floor like we're having a spastic attack and yell, 'Jesus save me,' or, you know, just stuff like that. We never meant any harm by it. We were just trying to get them mad so we could laugh at them because they wouldn't be turning the other cheek, you know, like Christians are supposed to do."

"Did they ever get mad?"

"Sometimes they did. You could see it on their faces, but they would never say anything other than, 'Ralph'—that's my name, you know—'no matter what you say or do, I still love you, and Jesus still loves you, and I'm praying for you before it's too late for you to make a decision for Christ.'"

"So, listen. Tell us what happened. I think we have gotten a little sidetracked here," the reporter said.

"Well, like I said, we were kidding them, like we always do, and John the Baptist—that's what we call the one who is their leader—had just finished telling me that Jesus loves me. Then, as I let out a huge laugh, just like that, all of those fools just disappeared. Just vanished. *Poof. Gone.* All eight of them. We blinked our eyes, and they were gone. Right into thin air. Say, man, do you think that maybe space aliens got them? Maybe there really are Martians, huh? Anyway, I'm glad they're gone. Whoever it was that took these Christian fools off the earth, I'm very happy they did. And I hope they got every one of them in the entire world. I'm sick of people like them holier-than-thou types, you know."

Moving the microphone away from the employee's mouth and back in front of his own, the reporter said, "Well, there you have it. Now you know. It seems like we are getting reports like this from all over the world right now. Something extremely strange and maybe even supernatural has happened or is still happening. We just don't know. Personally, though, I don't believe it is Martians. But whatever this is and whoever is behind it sure are freaking out a lot of people, including yours truly.

"Also, I need to tell you this. There are reports coming into our headquarters in Brussels, Belgium, from all over the world about hundreds of airplanes that have recently crashed throughout the world because the pilots who were flying them disappeared from the cockpits. It really seems like the Bermuda Triangle has suddenly engulfed the entire world.

"Or maybe it could be that these pilots, and all of the other people who have also disappeared throughout the world, have suddenly passed into one of those magnetic vortices that the new age people are so wild about. Maybe some of those vortices have suddenly formed up inside of our atmosphere and are wrapping around the world, gobbling people up. Who knows? None of us really knows for sure what is happening right now. None of us.

"Also, people, I have just gotten notice that there are still many, many airplanes still flying in the air that are flying on auto-pilot only. There are no pilots in them anymore. So, it is almost a certainty that these planes will, in a very short period of time, be crashing to the earth too as they run out of fuel.

"Viewers, I don't know how else to say this, but it seems that our entire world has suddenly gone *crazy*. What is happening right now is just totally, completely, unbelievably bizarre. It is like we have suddenly entered into the real Twilight Zone.

"If it were up to me to give my own opinion about this—and thanks to my employers at ONE World News, I do have that right— I would have to say that the number of people who have vanished must be in the hundreds of millions worldwide. In fact, I would put the number at well over a billion people have disappeared.

"But as Ralph just said, out of his place of employment, it was only the holier-than-thou, so-called Christian people who disappeared. So, well, I ask, could it be possible that these so-called Jesus believers are the only ones to have disappeared worldwide? Is it even possible that there could have been that many so-called believers in the world? Due to the astronomical number of missing persons worldwide, I just don't believe there could have been anywhere near that many deluded or just plain stupid and ignorant people to have been on this earth.

"People, do *you* really think there could have been that many people in the world who actually believed in fairy tales like there being a god? And then of that god sending his own son to earth to be born in a miraculous, immaculate birth to be a sinless perfect human being?" He laughed. "I can't help it, folks. Even in a situation like we are in, I can't help but laugh at that.

"Plus, I would have to say that the number of deaths and injuries caused by these vanishings must be equally as large as the number who have disappeared. Due to the astronomical number of vehicles, trains, trucks, planes, subways, and ship accidents that have taken place since the beginning of this … this … whatever this is, the number has to be close to or exceeds the number who disappeared.

"So, viewers, do you really believe that if there really is a god, he would allow all of these needless deaths and injuries to occur? Well, in my opinion, there is no way a good god would do something like this. So, this has to be some kind of an evil occurrence that has come upon the world from someplace else, possibly from outer space.

"But let me tell you, no matter where it has come from or what has caused it, all of these strange and weird things are causing complete chaos to run unabated and rampant throughout the world. In many, many cities, riots have suddenly erupted and are completely destroying the cities. Millions of people are looting everything in sight. People are going absolutely wild. Total anarchy has or will soon be taking place over most of the world within a short time. These lawless looters are setting fires and smashing store windows and taking everything inside, whether it has any value or not.

"We are also getting reports that massive numbers of people are committing suicide all over the world right now. Some of them are screaming, 'The end of the world has come.' Many others are screaming something about a word called *rapture*, whatever that means. Most of the people who are using this word are running rampant throughout the streets, trying to find a church where the doors are open so they can rush to the altar or confession booths and try to get absolution. Millions of others are causing huge traffic jams as they are trying to flee the cities and run to the hills for some odd reason.

"Friends, the word *apocalypse* is being shouted all over," he yelled loudly into the microphone, "*Fear* and *anguish* are the bywords for today." He hesitated just briefly before continuing "Truly, viewers, our world has been turned completely upside down. All I can say is, God help us. And where are you when we need you, *if you even exist?*"

He paused again to catch his breath and to listen to his producer. Eventually, he said, "Viewers, it seems that if the news and opinions I have been giving you is not incredible enough, we have some even more astounding news coming from our bureau in Washington, DC. Without further delay, we are going to switch there right now. This is Martin Smith, ONE World News Network, coming to you live from London, England. And I must say, I really do hope to stay that way and to see you very soon in the near future. Now, to Washington."

As the switch was made, the camera panned onto the face of another very pretty female reporter. In a very high-pitched and excited voice, she began speaking. "Hello. This is Peggy Durham of ONE World News reporting to you live. I'm standing on the sidewalk on Pennsylvania Avenue directly in front of the White House in Washington, DC, and I have some incredible, almost *unbelievable* news to share with you."

Behind her, you could see what appeared to be thousands of people running wild and going completely crazy. People were screaming and cursing at everyone else. It didn't matter who. Cars were beeping and honking their horns. Other people were hanging out of windows of high-rise buildings, screaming obscenities at the people down on the streets. It looked as if full-fledged anarchy was rapidly taking over the nation's capital.

The pretty reporter stood there, trying her best to remain as professional as she could manage under the circumstances as she continued speaking. "Viewers, what I am about to tell you is of the utmost importance. You see, it seems that our government of the United States is right now without a leader at this time. *Yes.* That's right. Our president has suddenly disappeared too.

"His wife is still here. She has been seen inside of the living quarters of the White House, but she is completely distraught and incoherent. The reason is because her children are part of the ones missing. They were part of the original group of persons to go missing off our planet.

"But now, the president has vanished too, and no one seems to know where. He was seen shortly after the disappearances with his wife, trying apparently to calm her. But shortly after that, he disappeared too. We do know this much though. His chief of staff is also missing and assumed to be with the president."

She paused for a moment and held her hand over her ear to be able to hear whoever was speaking to her. A minute or two later, she continued, "Viewers, we have just learned that both the president and his chief of staff, Darwah Policy, were both seen approximately thirty to forty-five minutes after the initial vanishings occurred. Yes, the president and Mr. Policy were seen by some eyewitnesses right here on this block, Pennsylvania Avenue. They were seen getting into a private car together and then driving off to who knows where. The president did not tell anyone he was leaving the White House, and no one inside, including his wife, knows where he has gone. And what is really, really scary is that the president disappeared without the Marine escort who carries the football with him. For those who do not know what the football is, the football is the briefcase that has all of our nuclear launch codes in it that would allow us to defend ourselves if we were to come under attack."

She paused momentarily to take in a deep breath. Then, very loudly, she yelled, "People, I don't know what is going on in our world right now. But I, for one, am very, very scared and worried. We really are, at this moment, leaderless. We don't have anyone to tell us what to do or to calm us down. Has our president run away like a coward? Has he gotten so scared himself that he fled his office to go try to find someplace where he can be safe? Has he just left all of us behind to try to find out for ourselves what is happening? What would happen if someone like the Russians or Chinese were to attack us right now? We couldn't even retaliate."

As soon as those words left her mouth, her brave attempt at maintaining professionalism went out the window, and she broke down into deep, anguished sobs, and large tears began flowing freely out of her eyes and running down her cheeks. In a pitiful little sobbing voice, she eventually said, "We do not, I repeat, *do not*, have anyone in charge right now, and I'm afraid that we are about to see all *hell* burst loose at any moment."

Suddenly, in the background behind the reporter it seemed that all of the people suddenly began going even crazier. One old man came running into the picture and almost ran right over the top of the young reporter. As this happened, some unintended words suddenly began to flow out of her mouth.

"What the—?"

But just then, in that very instant before she was able to finish her curse, the last thing anyone watching on TV saw before their screens suddenly turned to white static snow was a brilliant, almost blindingly bright flash of light. And the last anyone heard was a bloodcurdling scream blasting the airwaves before it was suddenly cut off in mid scream. At that exact instant, a large jumbo jet that took off in Paris, France, with three hundred and seven souls on board, was supposed to be heading for Ronald Reagan Airport to land. But both the pilot and co-pilot were missing, along with several flight attendants and many of the passengers. The autopilot had been set to fly the plane to Washington, DC. But without anyone to take control, the plane began a gradual descent toward the ground. Unfortunately, that descent took them straight toward the White House. It hit the ground directly on the sidewalk on Pennsylvania Avenue in the exact spot the young reporter was standing. It bounced back into the air, still mostly intact, and flew straight into the huge building. In that instant, the plane and the entire White House exploded into a tremendous fireball of flying metal, wood, concrete, broken bodies, and debris.

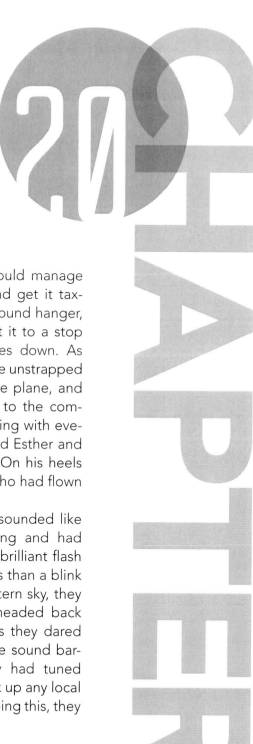

As soon as Ezekiel could manage to land his plane and get it taxied into the underground hanger, he hurriedly brought it to a stop and shut the engines down. As fast as he could manage, he unstrapped himself, climbed out of the plane, and began running back over to the command bunker. He was hoping with everything inside of him to find Esther and General Green still there. On his heels were the other four men who had flown in the mission with him.

After they heard what sounded like a beautiful trumpet playing and had seen an almost blindingly brilliant flash of light that flashed for less than a blink of an eye through the eastern sky, they had turned around and headed back toward the base as fast as they dared to go without breaking the sound barrier. Along the way, they had tuned their radio receivers to pick up any local news they could find. By doing this, they found out that millions and millions of people had just suddenly vanished off the face of the earth.

All five of them jumped inside the elevator to descend to the bunker. As soon as it came to a stop and the door opened, Ezekiel was the first one out.

"Esther!" he screamed at the top voice.

She hurried out from behind a bank of displays and then ran and jumped up into his arms. He reached around her waist, picked her up off the floor, and began spinning in circles with her.

"Oh, my darling, I thought you might have been part of those strange disappearances. I was so afraid." Warm tears suddenly swelled into his eyes and began trickling down his face.

"Oh, Ezekiel, yes, we almost were part of them, both my uncle and I and Colonel Jeremiah. We heard the trumpet of God, and then we saw a bright flash of light that signaled that the Savior of mankind was calling His bridegroom home to the marriage supper of the Lamb. Then we felt our feet beginning to lift off the floor. But just before that happened, we heard a voice, not in our ears but in our hearts. It told us that we are needed here in Israel, along with another hundred and forty-four thousand Israelites, until the seven years of tribulation written about in the book of Revelation are over. We are to be Jesus Christ's witnesses to our people to show them that He is the Messiah and that only through Him can salvation and eternal life come."

"Esther, I … all of us heard the trumpet and saw the light too. But none of us felt like we were going to be taken out of our planes. What has happened? Where have all of these millions of people gone? Who is behind this? And … what is all of this about the 'marriage supper of the Lamb'?"

"Ezekiel, and all of you other men too, listen to me. First of all, I truly believe that since all of you heard the trumpet and saw the light, God has placed His mark on all of you too, to keep you and to protect you. You see, that is what Jesus told us when He said we had to stay here. He said, 'I have placed my mark on you, and no man can harm you.' So, I believe that most of us here in this room right now are safe. Most everybody in here, after the rapture took place, immediately gave their hearts and lives to Jesus Christ, the Son of

God. Sure, there are still a few holdouts, but they'll come around. I'm positive of that."

"The *rapture*? What is that?" Ezekiel asked.

"That is what has taken place with the people who have disappeared. You see, Jesus Christ has raptured, or taken up, all of the people in the world who had asked Him to come and live in their hearts. Surely, there have been hundreds of millions who have gone to be with Him in heaven. We must rejoice for them. But we must also be prepared for what we are going to have to go through for the next seven years.

"You see—I'm speaking to all of you men here, all of you who are part of Ezekiel's squadron—the Bible declares that these next seven years are going to be the worst years that have ever taken place on this earth. In fact, it declares that if these years were not shortened to only seven years, then all of mankind would perish."

"Well, what do we need to do to make sure that we really are protected by the mark of God?" Billy Bartwaith asked.

"That's simple. Just ask Jesus to forgive you of every sin you have ever committed, and then invite Him to come and live inside of you. That's all there is to it. And if you will do that, an immediate change will come upon you. You will know, without a shadow of a doubt, that He lives inside of you. I can't explain it, but there will just be an understanding inside."

"Yes," Ezekiel said. "I had that knowing, that understanding, inside of me when we flew our first bombing missions against Iran. I had actually prayed for the first time in my life while on our way over there. I had prayed that God would protect and keep you, honey. And I heard—no, I didn't actually hear a voice; it was more like I *felt* a voice speaking to me on the inside. Then I just had this knowing inside of me that everything would be all right."

"Oh, Ezekiel. See? You have already heard the voice of God. That was Jesus speaking to you in your heart right then. He does have His hand on your life. Ask Him right now to forgive you and to come live in your heart. Do it now. All of you."

Every one, to the man, immediately sank down to his knees and began, in their own words and their own ways, to ask Jesus to forgive them and to come live in their hearts.

General Green was standing against a wall, watching his young, formerly timid and shy little niece take the initiative and lead five young Israeli heroes to salvation in Jesus Christ. He knew that if heaven wasn't already celebrating in the biggest party the universe had ever known, then they surely were now.

# CHAPTER 21

In a deep, hardened, nuclear blast-proof bunker secretly dug out and constructed over one hundred fifty feet directly below the Kremlin in Moscow, Russia, a meeting was taking place. The bunker was supposedly so secret that every construction worker and even the architects who drew up the plans were all assassinated shortly after it was completed during the bloody reign of Joseph Stalin.

The meeting was being conducted by Premier Anatoly Butin, the head of the Russian government. He was standing at the end of a long, rectangular conference table.

Five more men were attending the meeting. They were seated along the sides of the table. These men were the four leaders of the Russian military forces. Down the left side of the table from Premier Butin's perspective at the head of the table sat General Ivan Borokovsky, leader of the Russian army forces. Next to him sat Admiral Ilyich Murochev, leader of the Russian naval forces. Next to the admiral sat General Georgi Chekov, leader of the Russian air command. Finally, next to him sat General Boris Denkovsky, leader of the Russian nuclear missile forces. Across the table from the four men sat only one man, Vasili Gerokovich, a former head of the Soviet Union's KGB, now retired.

Behind the premier were several large flat-screen monitors. Three of the monitors were showing the status of their troops massing to get ready to move down through Georgia and from there on into Turkey. Other ones were showing their eastern flank troops that were getting ready to move down into Kazakhstan, and from there into Uzbekistan. Once those moves were completed, they would continue to move down through Turkmenistan on their way into Iran, where, once they arrived there, they would merge with their Arab allies for their final push into Israel.

Along another wall were other monitors showing the locations and status of their nuclear weapons. For the first time in their history, all of the lights were showing green, meaning they were all up and operational.

On the wall at the far end of the room, wrapping around to include the wall along the other side of the table, were several screens showing the alert status of most other major countries in the world, including the United States and China.

Those two countries were the only ones the premier was concerned about. They were the only two who could make him back down from his plan to totally destroy the Jews in Israel. And if they were to force him to back down, he would then be unable to complete the second part of his plan, which was the most important part of the whole operation.

No one else in the world knew that the premier had another part to his plan, except the other men in the bunker with him. The Jews were just a diversion. But now, because of the very fortunate act of the Jews' attack against Iran—which killed twenty-two Russian construction workers—they were the perfect excuse to allow Russia to move into the Middle East to retaliate against them. But the second, most important, part of his plan entailed the complete takeover of the entire Middle East after the destruction of the Jews. This part of the plan included the complete destruction of all of the Arab and Islamic nations too, or at least all of the people in those nations. It was his extreme desire to annihilate every one of Abraham's descendants, both Arabs and Jews. Without them, the world would finally be able to live in peace and harmony, and his plan was for him to rule over it.

Every man in the room knew that if they could accomplish this, Russia would then ascend to its rightful place in the world as the ruler of it. They would have a monopoly on most of the oil in the entire world and, thus, all other countries on the earth would have to bow down to them if they wanted to survive. They all knew that the world runs on oil. Without it, a country would very quickly dry up and die.

At that time, neither the United States nor China was doing anything to try to stop the Russians. Premier Butin had spent a lot of time on the phone with the leaders of both countries. He had been personally assured by the president of the United States that America would do nothing to stop Russia from ridding the earth of the Jews. In fact, as the president had said the word *Jews*, it sounded like he was spitting the word out of his mouth. The premier of China had a very happy, musical sound in his voice as he stated that the "Jewish problem" would finally be taken care of once and for all. He had declared that the world will be a much safer place once the Jews are gone from the earth.

But there was one other item that had been discussed between the American President and Premier Butin. The Russian premier had offered an olive branch to the president if he would stand by and do nothing, thus allowing Russia to destroy the Jews. He had secretly confided of his plan to also destroy the entire Arab and Islamic nations. He stressed to the president that if all of the evil-causing, trouble-making descendants of Abraham were finally, once and for all time, removed from the world, the remaining countries in the world would all come together in peaceful co-existence with love and harmony ruling over everything. So if the president would stand by and do nothing while Russia took the initiative and completed this unpleasant task, the president would then become second in command of the new, one-world ruling hierarchy under Premier Butin.

Premier Butin had no intention of really doing this. He had another, more evil and sinister plan that would take care of America and her gullible president.

*The man is a fool. All the fool has to do is just stay there doing nothing, and we'll do everything else to insure we rise to the top of humanity,* he thought to himself.

Premier Butin began to address the assembly. "My dear, faithful friends and brave, valiant comrades, I am glad all of you could come on such short notice. But what I am about to say to you is of the highest priority and is in the complete best interest of our great country, Russia.

"Gentlemen, I am not going to take up our time here by going over the obvious. As you can see from the monitors in the room, our military forces are on full alert and preparing for their deployments as planned. But time is short and of the complete essence with what all is happening in our world right now. So let me get right to the point of why I have called you here. I am sure, though, you probably all believe the reason is because of all of the people who have suddenly vanished from the earth."

The men glanced around at each other and then looked back at the premier while nodding their heads in agreement.

"Yes, well, part of the reason is exactly that. As you know, we have been monitoring reports from all over the world concerning these missing persons, and the tally of people missing is in the millions. Some reports are even saying that hundreds of millions are missing. In fact, we have heard that it has been estimated that up to twenty-five percent of the entire world's population has suddenly vanished. My friends, that is upward of one and one half billion people.

"We have even heard that there very well might be around forty-five million people from our own country who have suddenly disappeared. Also, we are right now searching but so far have been unable to locate over twenty members of our own parliament, and I am afraid that it appears very likely that they have vanished too.

"Gentlemen, comrades, yes, of course, these disappearances are very, very troubling. As of this time, we do not have any idea where all of these people have gone, nor do we have any idea who might be behind this. But my friends, I am not afraid. I have absolutely no fear.

And let me emphatically state that neither should any of you fear either. Not for one minute do I suspect that space aliens have suddenly appeared and kidnapped these people from off the earth. Not for even a second do I believe this. But you want to know something funny? We have heard from some sources that these disappearances have come about because of the actions of a so-called supernatural God." As these words came out of his mouth, he couldn't help himself and suddenly burst into a huge, belly-shaking laugh.

"Oh. Excuse me, gentleman. Excuse me. But I must ask you this: if a so-called God were to be behind this, do you think He would have left the premier of Russia behind?"

This time, an even louder bellow of laughter worked its way up from the bottom of his huge, inflated stomach and quickly traveled all of the way up until it exploded out of his throat, sounding like a jet fighter plane taking off on full afterburners. Big tears of bellicose amusement also swelled up in his eyes and began rolling down his cheeks.

Every man in the room was also consumed in riotous laughter and merriment. Several were bellowing so loud that they were probably even heard up on the surface of the earth. Others were leaning over the table and slamming their fists down on top of it. They also had huge tears of laughter running unabated down their faces. And all were yelling, "No, a so-called god would certainly not leave the premier of Russia behind."

This unabashed laughter went on for at least four minutes.

But finally, the premier began to gather his composure back and things began to settle down in the room. Finally, he began again. "Oh, my friends, we must stop this. I tell you, this meeting is of a very, very important nature. So, please forgive me for my lack of decorum. But, gentlemen, I must confess that I do not believe in a supernatural God. If there is such a thing as a so-called god, then surely the premier of Russia would be one too, wouldn't he? At least he would have to be equal to a god, yes?"

Once more, an unrestrained roar bellowed out of him that sounded just like a pack of hungry wolves howling at a full moon. And again, just as before, every man in the room began howling just like the premier was doing. Plus, every one of them had their heads bobbing up and down just like bobble-head dolls sitting in the back window of a 1968 Z-28 Camaro.

The laughter and merriment went on for several minutes. But finally, the premier began to regain his composure. But before beginning again, this time he took his time and slowly looked around the room at all of the men there. He wondered, *Will these men, all of whom I have known for many years, all of them my very good friends, have the inner courage and the wherewithal to do what I am about to ask of them? Will General Denkovsky, the head of the Russian nuclear missile forces, in particular, be courageous enough?*

Premier Butin once again continued, "Gentlemen, it is good medicine to have a good laugh every now and then, but as I said before, we have some very serious business I need to discuss with you. So, once more, I ask that you will please forgive me for my outbursts. But no, gentlemen, it's not these vanishings that I asked you to be here. What I have to say is of much more importance than even these things. So, please let me get started.

"Comrades, as all of you are aware, back during the so-called Cold War with the United States, we had two top secret plans. One of those plans is Jacob's Ladder. This is the one you gentlemen are getting ready to launch very shortly.

"As you know, Jacob's Ladder consists of us launching a full-scale frontal ground attack with over two and a half million of our troops against Israel. We knew that if we were to ever implement this plan, all of the Arab nations would quickly join forces with us, just like they are preparing to do now.

"But as you also remember, the real goal of this plan is to goad Israel into launching massive, preemptive strikes against all of the Arab countries first before we move our troops into them. That is the purpose for all of our posturing and our troop call-ups and such. We're hoping Israel will react now before we make any move and they will destroy these other nations.

"Hopefully, these strikes will be enough to totally destroy all of the loathsome Arab and Islamic people or to weaken them enough that we will only have mop-up duty to perform ourselves. And hopefully, Israel will be so preoccupied with those duties that she will leave herself vulnerable enough so we can march into her and totally destroy her. And from there, as you all know, we simply step over the top of all of the dead bodies and take over the entire Middle East. And from there, comrades, we become rulers of the world."

He stopped for a brief minute to catch his breath. He had gotten himself all very excited from just mentioning the possibilities that awaited them. Finally he continued.

"My faithful friends and comrades, as you remember, the only reason we never instituted Jacob's Ladder in the past is that we assumed it would lead to a full-scale nuclear war with the United States. And we knew if that were to happen, both of our countries would be totally and completely destroyed. Both countries would perish from the earth. But, gentlemen, we have also known all along that if one country could control all of the oil in the Middle East, that country would rule the world.

"We knew it would take some extraordinary turn of events for an opportunity to come along that would allow us to accomplish this plan. *Now* gentlemen, *now*, this extraordinary event has come along and presented us with this opportunity.

"Israel has made a fatal mistake by bombing Iran and destroying her nuclear capabilities. The entire world has turned against her. Even her only friend and protector, the United States, is not going to lift a finger to give assistance to her. America's president actually hates Israel. He hates the Jews, all of them. Even though the liberal Jews in the US played a huge part in getting him elected in the first place, he still hates them and wants them destroyed. His eye is on one thing only. He wants the world to be unified under one government and he wants to be the leader of it. That, my friends, just isn't going to happen. As soon as we take over the Middle East, we, Russia, will be the rulers of the world, not America, not their naive president, not anybody but Russia.

"My comrades, this is our destiny. It is Russia's destiny to rule the world. We should have been rulers of it all along. I tell you this. No one will ever laugh at Russia ever again. We will be kings. No, not kings; *we will be gods*, I say. Once we own the world, everyone will have to bow down and worship us or we'll simply cut off their supply of oil and then watch them shrivel up and die."

Talking about this possibility got the old premier too worked up and excited to carry on right then. Again, he had to wait a couple of minutes to get himself back under control. In his mind, he could see himself sitting on a huge, gold and ivory throne, holding a large, golden scepter in his right hand, and having all of the leaders and rulers of every country on earth coming and bowing before him and bringing him tribute. They would bring gifts and fruits from their countries and present them to him in the hope that he would keep allowing them to buy oil.

*Oh, but at what price they will have to pay for it,* he gleefully thought. His eyes were sparkling. His mouth was quivering. In fact, his entire body was shaking with an adrenaline-filled fever. But finally, he said, "My friends, there is another item I want to bring up for discussion. To preface this, let me state that what I am about to say is of the utmost, *utmost* importance.

"From all outward appearances right now, everything looks very good for us to accomplish our goals and for Jacob's Ladder to be a smashing success, if I may use a pun. But all it would take is for some other country to throw a wrench into our gears and all of our plans would quickly go down the drain. For example, if the United States were to change their minds and enter into the fray on the side of Israel, for us to go ahead and accomplish our goals, we would probably have to resort to nuclear weapons. And that, gentlemen, is something we do not want to do, at least not in the Middle East, where the oil is located. And this is something that is not all that farfetched. We have intelligence that the meeting the four chiefs of their military and the director of the CIA were having before being killed in that bombing was to discuss launching a military coup and disposing of this president and all of his cronies. If that had happened, without a doubt, the US would definitely step in and honor their treaties they have with Israel and try to stop us from reaching our goals.

"My friends, this is something we cannot possibly allow to happen. So, I want you to remember another top secret plan we had during the Cold War. That plan was named Burning Star. As you all well know, Burning Star was the code name for us to launch an all-out, full-blown, first-strike nuclear attack against the United States. Friends, comrades, valiant warriors, the United States is in a complete state of disarray right now. The four heads of their military branches have just been killed. Their president is fighting to keep his position without being overthrown and ousted. Their federal government is in such turmoil that it is in basically a complete lockup. Both political parties hate each other so much that no one is willing to work with the other. It does not matter in the least about what might be good for the country. All that matters is how best to keep their party and themselves in power or to regain power if they have lost it."

A hard knock suddenly resounded from the main door interrupting the premier. The premier had specifically said that he was not to be disturbed unless it was of the most extreme importance.

*This had better be that kind of importance,* he thought. "Come," he yelled.

In walked his top aide, Aleksei Sevoia was carrying a stack of papers in his hand.

"What is it, Aleksei? I specifically gave instructions to not be interrupted."

"I know, my premier. But I thought you might need these latest reports that have just come in."

"What are they? What do they say?"

"Well, Premier, several of them are pictures. They are showing the White House in the United States. Or, I must say, what is left of the White House."

The premier raised an eyebrow. His aide continued.

"You see, Premier, apparently, a jumbo airliner has crashed into the White House and completely destroyed it. We have heard reports that the president's wife and kids are missing. Actually, his kids were part of the original group of people who disappeared off the earth. But his wife, from all reports, was still in the White House when it was destroyed by the plane."

"What about their president? What has happened to him?"

"That we do not know as of this time. Apparently, he had left the White House with his chief of staff shortly before this happened. They left through an underground tunnel that runs from the White House out to Pennsylvania Avenue. This is the same tunnel several of their presidents have used in the past to break free from the bonds of their office—and from the arms of their wives—to go enjoy a little variety on the outside, if you catch my drift, sir."

"Yes, I understand. But as of this time, he is nowhere to be found?"

"That's correct, sir. But also, sir, this is very important. The reports also say that the marine guard who carries the football is not with him. The football is what they call the briefcase chained to the marine's wrist with their nuclear launch codes inside of it."

"Yes, yes! I know what they call it! But you're sure? He's not in possession of the football?" the premier asked incredulously.

"No, Premier. Not as far as we know. All we can ascertain at this time is that he and his chief of staff has disappeared together. But to where, we do not know."

The premier stood staring into space, trying to figure out what in the world was happening. *Is this going to throw a new wrench into our plans? . . . Well, whatever is going on, I cannot allow anything to happen to stop my plans!*

Finally, he said, "Okay. Thank you, Aleksei. One more item. Are these pictures taken from our satellites? Are our satellites working again?"

"Yes, sir. We just pulled them off."

"Okay. Again, you were correct, Aleksei. This is very important to me. Thank you very much."

As soon his aide left the room and closed the door, he again turned back toward the men around the table. But at the same time, he was glancing through the written reports and pictures he had been handed. After a couple of minutes, he looked back up at the men and continued.

"My friends, this is very, very good news," he proclaimed as he raised the reports and began waving them about in the air. "These show that the entire United States is in an almost-complete state of disarray. It is right now bordering on the teetering edge of anarchy.

"Yes, comrades, I said *anarchy*. Anarchy has, or will very soon, engulf their entire country. As it stands right now, there are so many of their police officers and other law enforcement personnel missing that the people are having virtually a free rein to run wild, rape, pillage, steal, and destroy everything they want. Lawlessness is abounding without restraint.

"Plus, paralyzing fear and intense panic has gripped their entire nation. People are running around everywhere in complete confusion, total dread and agonizing distress. Millions and millions of people in America vanished in the disappearances. Many more vanished from there than from our own country. These reports are telling us that up to fifty percent of their population has disappeared. *Fifty percent*, gentlemen. And on top of that, many more millions of their population have just been killed or injured because of all of the accidents that were caused by these disappearances.

"Gentlemen, this chaos has caused widespread uncontrolled rioting in the streets of every city in their entire country. Looters are everywhere. They're running rampant with a clear rein to do as they please. Entire cities are being destroyed. These looters have set so many fires, which are now completely burning out of control, that they can't be counted. In fact, in many cases, it appears that whole cities are in the process of burning down. Gentlemen, comrades, friends, America is burning down and being destroyed internally by her own citizens."

He paused and again looked around the room at each man. As he did, he paused on their faces and looked deeply into their eyes. He wanted to see directly into their souls if that was possible.

"Ah, my comrades, I am now going to tell you the full reason you were asked to come here today. I wanted you men to be here so we could speak face to face because I am about to present to you an option, an option that is going to shock you all of the way down to your inner core. But at the same time, it just might thrill you, as it opens a door for us to be rulers of the entire world.

"Comrades, listen to me very carefully. I want each of you to search your hearts right now. I want you to search the amount of courage and wherewithal you have inside of you. Then, I want each of you to tell me whether or not Russia should take its rightful place, it's destiny, as the ruler of the entire world. This is Russia's true destiny. Should we do this? Or do we bury our heads in the sand and ignore this great and fantastic opportunity that has surprisingly come our way?

"Gentlemen, without a doubt, we are going full scale and launching Jacob's Ladder. That much has already been decided and is in the process of happening right now. But what I am about to ask you will be the most important decision you have ever made in your lives. My friends, there is a great possibility that as we progress with Jacob's Ladder, our true intentions of taking over the entire Middle East and, thus, all of the oil there, will become known. In that case, I am sure that the United States will try to stop us if they are somehow able to regain control of their country. So, in case that scenario does arise, that leaves us with two choices. One, we go full scale with a nuclear attack against the United States at that time and pray we can destroy them before they can retaliate and destroy us too.

"Or two, we go ahead, right now, as soon as we possibly can, and launch Burning Star. If we take this option, I truly believe that with all that is going on in the United States, we could take them completely by surprise without them being able to launch any sort of a counter strike. As you just heard, it seems no one even knows where their president is. Plus, it is very probable that his wife was killed when that plane crashed into the White House. He is not going to be thinking about us. His entire mind will be elsewhere. And to top all of that off, he is no longer even in possession of the football. So if we were to launch against them at this time, they wouldn't even have the codes to retaliate against us. Gentlemen, this is another extraordinary opportunity that has been laid on our doorstep. So, as for me, I say we institute Burning Star as quickly as we can.

"And, comrades,"—he hurried on quickly before anyone could say anything—"it is of no matter even if they were to launch a few missiles back against us. Let me state this unequivocally. Our great country and proud nation is large enough and strong enough to be able to handle it. Think on this. With the United States out of the way, there are no other countries in the world that can stop us from claiming all of the oil in the Middle East as our own. So I am going to go around this room and ask each one of you what your opinion is and what you believe our course of action should be. General Borokovsky, please give me your decision first."

"Premier Butin, let me first state how much I value and respect you as a person. But also, I value and respect your wisdom even more. From what you have stated to us, I believe that you have already put much thought and wisdom into this. So if I have to make a decision right this minute, I say we should implement Burning Star immediately as soon as we can and destroy America."

"Fine. Good, General. I appreciate your kind words too. And yes, I have put much thought into this. But I will not make this decision on my own. That is why I have invited you leaders of our armed forces here today. We must decide as our country's leaders in what direction we are going to go. It must be a uniform one; no dissension among us. Admiral Murochev, you're next. Please give us your advice."

"I say we implement Burning Star and totally destroy the United States now. I say we do this if for no other reason than to let the rest of the world know what will be in store for them if they dare question us or try to stop us from taking our rightful place in history as gods of the earth."

Premier Butin said, "Good! Good! General Chekov, give us your decision."

"Gentlemen, I say launch now, for us and for Mother Russia."

"Great. Great. So far, gentlemen, we are in perfect agreement. Let me now go to General Boris Denkovsky. You are the one who will give the orders to actually launch our missiles. You are the esteemed soldier, the great leader. And you are the great keeper of the flame, the great Burning Stars that will rain down all over the United States and send that entire, retched, immoral country straight into the flaming lake of fire that she belongs in. So tell me, General, what is your decision? And also, do we still have the capability to completely destroy America?"

"Yes, my premier. Yes to both of your questions. We have both the capability and the *desire* to totally and completely destroy the United States many, many times over. Let me assure you that I will send so many Burning Stars against her that not a single one of her cities will be left inhabitable in that grossly arrogant and decadent land of hers. Her entire country will become a vast wasteland, a huge lake of molten fire. Our devastation to her will make the Grand Canyon in Arizona look like a tiny paper cut dotting her landscape. I say *do it* for Mother Russia and for our *destiny* so we can be gods."

Premier Butin sat at the head of the table with a huge smile plastered across his face. Never in his life had he been this happy. Traces of happy, joyful tears were misting over his eyes. Then, he bowed his head in deep appreciation to all of them and said, "Thank you, my dearest friends and closest comrades. Thank you. Thank you. Thank you."

Then he added, "Gentlemen, I will not ask General Gerokovich's vote or advice. I am already aware of it. In fact, we have the great general here to thank for suggesting all of this to me. It was he. It was his great foresight and deep love for our great country to bring this to my attention. Gentlemen, I say we drink a toast, a toast to General Gerokovich, a toast to our destiny, and a toast to the most important thing of all; a toast to our great country, Russia."

With that, Premier Butin reached under the edge of the table and pushed a hidden button. Within mere seconds, the door into the room quickly swung open.

An army corporal exquisitely dressed in his finest full dress uniform walked into the room and quickly came to full attention. He glanced at the premier. "Sir?" he asked.

"My young friend, will you kindly get us all some glasses and pour each of us a double shot of some great Russian vodka? We want to share a toast to our great country, Russia."

The young corporal nodded his head toward the premier then quickly walked over to a cabinet built into a section of the wall. He reached in and took several glasses and put them on a serving tray. He then walked over and put a glass in front of each man. Then, opening a new bottle of the best vodka made in Russia, he slowly moved around the table until he had filled each glass at least three quarters of the way full. When he was finished, he looked at the premier.

"Sir, anything else the premier wishes?"

"Yes, my young friend, there is. Give yourself a glass and join us in this toast."

"Sir?" he asked quizzically, looking completely startled at the same time.

"Join us, young man, I say. Today, you are just a young man. But tomorrow, or very soon thereafter, you will no longer be just a young man. I say with my full authority as Russia's premier that you will soon be a god."

"To Mother Russia."

"To our *destiny*."

"To being rulers of the *world*."

"To beings *gods* over all of the earth."

On and on it went, toast after toast after toast. Joy and happiness combined with a large amount of vodka were flowing freely. Eventually though, with his speech slurring, Premier Butin began to speak once again.

"Comrades, we could go on celebrating like this for a long time, yes? But now is not really the time for us to do this. We should do all of our celebrating after we destroy America; after we destroy the worthless Jews and the equally worthless Arabs; after we take the oil; and finally, after we become rulers of the world. So you see, we have much work still to accomplish first. And we need to get started immediately. Do you not agree? So tell me this. How soon can we expect to accomplish our missions? Tell me, how prepared are our nuclear missile troops and, for that matter, our missiles themselves?

"I am sure you are all aware that time is of the complete essence. We cannot allow the fervor of the hatred being thrown at the Jews the whole world over to dissipate. We cannot allow America time to straighten out either. In my opinion, we must be ready within forty-eight hours at the very most to launch our missiles against them and to begin our march southward toward Israel. So now, I am asking all of you, comrades, can we do this? Can we accomplish our missions in this timeframe?"

General Denkovsky, supreme commander of Russia's nuclear missile forces and keeper of the flame, spoke up. "We will be ready, my Premier. Within forty-eight hours, I give you my personal word and guarantee that we will send hundreds of our Burning Stars onto America's cities, infrastructure, and military installations. We will totally and completely obliterate her out of existence. We will destroy her, along with all of North America. I give you my word and my guarantee concerning this part of our plans.

General Borokovsky, supreme commander of the Russian army forces, spoke up. "Comrades, let me assure you, I can have our troops ready and poised to go within this forty-eight-hour time frame that General Denkovsky stated. We will be fully armed and fully prepared to conquer. Our entire military is already on full-alert status, so it is a simple enough task for us to move them into position for what will soon be the greatest land attack that has ever occurred in the history of the world."

As the general finished speaking, a shudder fluttered up and down the old premier's body. He was absolutely thrilled at the prospects waiting ahead of them, but at the same time, he was trembling with fear of what the possible consequences from their nuclear attack could bring. But he hid those emotions well as he said, "Okay, comrades? Are there any more comments. No? Then, I say, to our *destiny.*"

In one voice, all loudly replied, "To our destiny."

# CHAPTER 22

In Israel, Emanuel Ben Joseph, the premier of Israel, was standing behind his desk inside of his eighth-floor office suite. He was facing the large picture window that took up almost the entire outer wall. But his eyes weren't really seeing anything. They were glazed over, just like his mental state. But at the same time, a feeling of awe, wonder, and bewilderment was deeply ingrained on his rugged features.

He was slowly shaking his head from side to side. In the trancelike state he was in, he was not aware of the people hurrying to and fro down on the streets below. Nor was he aware of the so-called storm of the century that was still raging on uninterrupted. His mind was totally consumed about the strange disappearances that had taken place throughout the entire world.

In a way though, he knew that his country was partially blessed because Israel was one of the few countries in the world that did not have an overly large group of people disappear.

Yes, they had some, but the majority of the population was still intact, he knew.

But what was really so disturbing to him were the reports saying that the only ones missing were all members of the Christian faith.

Was Jesus really the Messiah? Was He really the Christ?

The whole world had been turned upside down, and most of it was in complete anarchy and turmoil. "I don't know. I don't know. I just don't know," he mumbled to himself.

He didn't notice two strange-looking men who were silently standing behind him on the front side of his desk. He slowly began to turn around and sit down. But out of the corner of his eye, he suddenly caught sight of the two men. An immense terrifying fear instantly slammed into him with the force of a sledgehammer, and he jumped straight backward and crashed hard into the huge, tempered glass window.

"Who are you, and how did you get in here?" he bellowed.

One of the men very gently but firmly replied, "Premier Emanuel Ben Joseph, please do not be afraid. El Shaddai, the Almighty God of Israel, has sent us here to be with you."

"What? What are you saying? How did you get in here? Tell me before I call security."

"Premier Emanuel Ben Joseph, do not call security. It will do you no good even if you do call them. So please, sit down. Just sit down and calm down please. If you will be so kind as to let us speak with you for a few minutes, we will explain everything completely to your satisfaction, I am sure," the same man said.

Because of the gentle tone and kind yet rugged and strong features of the two men, the premier reluctantly pulled his chair up behind him and slowly sat down, facing them. But he never once took his eyes off their faces for even a second. He also placed his hand on top of the intercom button that if he were to push it, would immediately bring several of Israel's top security men running into the room.

*But how did these men get past my security people in the first place?*

Also, he wondered if his secretary, Lynn Goodman, was all right.

But even though he had managed to sit down, he was still shaking like a dead leaf blowing in the howling wind outside. The two

EZEKIEL'S WAR

strange-looking men sat down in the two chairs directly in front of the premier's desk, making themselves as comfortable as possible as they looked pleasantly toward the premier with friendly smiles on their faces.

The premier did not smile back. "Okay." He managed to croak out, "What is it you want?" But at the same time, he couldn't help but think, *These two men are the strangest, oddest-looking men I have ever seen.* "Wait. Before you answer that, tell me, what are those clothes you are wearing? Burlap sacks? Monk robes? I mean, if I did not know better, I would say that you two look just like Moses and Elijah."

Both men's jaws dropped wide open. They turned and looked at each other in amazement as good, hearty laughs bellowed up out of them. Then the man who had not yet spoken began to speak.

"Ah. Premier Emanuel Ben Joseph, this is going to be easier than we had anticipated. Yes. God is so good. He is already speaking to your heart, and we thank Him because you are listening. If you will allow me, sir, please let me introduce my colleague and myself to you. Premier Emanuel Ben Joseph, this is Elijah, and I am Moses."

They both suddenly stood up out of their seats and began leaning over the large, elegant desk while extending their hands toward the premier. But in a blur faster than the human eye could follow, the premier instinctively placed both of his hands against the back edge of his desk and, with a mighty shove, sent himself flying backward. He and his large, expensive chair flew straight back and crashed so hard into the big plate glass window that if it had not been made out of bulletproof, tempered glass, he would have crashed right through it and fallen all eight stories down to the street below.

The sudden fear that immediately surged through him caused the blood to drain out of his head. He was completely stunned. Totally speechless from what he had just heard. To have two men just suddenly appear in your office out of thin air, and then, on top of that, to have them suddenly introduce themselves to you as Moses and Elijah ... well, it was just too, too much.

"Wh-wha-what did you say? I mean, di-did-did I hear you correctly? Tell me ... tell me again who you are." He was stuttering and

167

stammering as a red-hot, deepening pain rapidly began to converge into the center of his chest.

Moses and Elijah both saw the premier's distress. "Oh, Premier Emanuel Ben Joseph, we mean you no harm. Please, do not be afraid. We have come here to help you, not to harm you," Elijah said.

The premier was shaking even more than he was before, and his face was rapidly taking on the pallor of death! He felt that at any moment, he was going to have a massive coronary. At the moment, he couldn't speak or even able to move. He just sat there, shaking all over and staring wide-eyed incredulously at the two men.

Finally, after a couple of extremely tense, nervous minutes had passed, he was finally able to gather enough strength to yell in a hoarse whisper, "What do you want with me?"

Premier Ben Joseph was absolutely certain the earth had somehow entered into some kind of a time-warp dimension that allowed people to come and go at will into other places and time periods.

*That's what all of these strange occurrences have to be,* he thought. *That's the only thing it can be. All of the people who are missing have just gone into some other time period, and that's why Moses and Elijah are here with me now.*

He sat back and violently shook his head, trying to clear his mind from these irrational thoughts. He knew they couldn't be true. But as he opened his eyes, Moses and Elijah were still sitting in front of him.

Moses and Elijah saw the mental torment the premier was going through and they were very concerned about him. They looked at each other and then back toward the premier.

Moses said, "Premier, first of all, before we say or do anything else, we are going to pray for you. My dear man, you look like you are about to die of a massive heart attack, and we want God to spare your life. We do not believe it is your time to go right now. So please, bear with us for just one moment."

"Our holy, heavenly Father, we ask in the precious, holy name of Jesus, your Son and our righteous Messiah, that you will immediately strengthen our dear Premier Emanuel Ben Joseph right this moment. Yes, we ask for you to give him extraordinary strength and also brave courage.

"We ask that the scales that are on his eyes will be removed and that the heart of stone that is inside of him will be replaced with the heart of God. We also ask that his ears will be opened to receive your words of truth. Again, we ask this in the precious, blood-bought Name of the Lamb, Jesus, our Lord and Christ."

They opened their eyes and looked at the premier. Normal coloring was already returning back into his face. The trembling and shaking were rapidly diminishing, and the throbbing veins in his neck began to settle back down and return to normal. Without a doubt, you could see God was working wonders on the man and helping him calm down. While this was happening, Moses and Elijah sat there patiently waiting until God finished His work.

A minute later, Elijah began to speak once again. "Premier Emanuel Ben Joseph, we are so sorry to have frightened you like that. We are. But truly, we have not come here to do you any harm. We have come here to save you and our country Israel from certain doom. Yes, many bad things are soon to come about, and some of them are to happen within a short matter of days or even hours. We have come here to get you prepared for these things. God has sent us to show you and all of the people of Israel how He, El Shaddai, the Almighty God, will fight for His people. Yes and how the Almighty will bring the victory.

"Then, my dear man, after you see with your own eyes how God will fight and deliver you, it will be our extreme pleasure to go throughout the whole country of Israel for the next three and one half years and tell the entire nation that Jesus, the ancient prophet of old that they called the Nazarene, was the Messiah. It will be our duty and our pleasure to convince the people of Israel to turn from their wicked ways and accept Jesus as their eternal Lord, Savior, and soon-coming King.

"Now, just to prove to you that we are who we say we are, please take a look out your window. Go ahead. Look. What do you see? You see a mighty downpour of rain, yes? Not even a speck of blue sky anywhere to be found, is there? You're in the very middle of a storm that weather forecasters are calling the storm of the century. Now, Premier Emanuel Ben Joseph, I am going to command it to stop raining, and this downpour of rain will immediately cease, and the gale force winds will stop altogether, and within a blink of an eye following that, a clear, blue sky will instantly appear."

Just barely loud enough to be heard, the premier quietly muttered, "This I have to see."

"Oh, Jesus our Savior and God our Father, I ask that you will immediately stop this rain that has been pouring down on Israel to prove that you are the true God and that Jesus is the true Messiah, God's Son. Do it now, we ask, and do not leave a single cloud in the sky as a sign to this unbelieving man and nation."

Before Elijah's words had even faded out of the room, the huge drops of rain that had been falling stopped. The loud, clattering noise against the office window ceased instantly. Then, in less than a blink of an eye, every cloud in the entire sky instantly disappeared and a bright, blue sky with a brilliant yellow sun suddenly appeared, along with a gorgeous rainbow that sparkled with every color in earth and in heaven.

Down on the street below, the people were totally stunned. A moment before, they had been getting drenched. But then, they blinked their eyes and the enormous storm had completely disappeared as if by magic. Now they were staring in complete surprise into a brilliantly shining, beautiful yellow sun flashing its intense golden rays into an even more beautiful, sparkling, totally clear blue sky. It was the last thing any of the people of Israel would have ever expected.

The people stopped running and slowly began staring up into the beautiful blue sky. Their loud, startled voices began floating all of the way up and seeping through the window into the premier's office.

"What is happening in our *world*?" was heard above the rest. "First, millions of people just suddenly disappear into thin air, and now, look at this; a downpour of drenching rain has been falling on us without stop for the last day, but in less than a blink of an eye, there are absolutely no clouds at all in the sky. What is going on? Oh, God, please help us."

The people's faces were indelibly twisted in complete astonishment and total wonderment.

"How in God's name can a totally clear, blue sky suddenly appear when just a second ago, we were in the midst of the storm of the century?" they wondered.

But at that moment, they had no idea that God's name was the exact reason why it had stopped raining.

After watching the furious, drenching downpour instantly stop and suddenly turn into a clear sky for a few minutes, the premier slowly turned back around toward the two men. Again, his face had become an ashen gray color and had taken on a transparent appearance. Also, he could once more feel his blood pressure beginning to skyrocket at the same time sharp pains began shooting through his chest again. He reached up and placed his hand over his heart while he managed to find just enough of his voice to loudly blurt out, "Okay. Tell me, who are you? Really, just who are you?"

Moses spoke up this time. "My dear Premier Emanuel Ben Joseph, we are who we say we are, Moses and Elijah. But begging your pardon, sir, please excuse me for just one moment." Glancing over at Elijah, he said, "My brother, maybe we should turn the faucet on again, yes? Our dear fellow Jews down below came prepared today for rain, and I am afraid they are being scared completely out of their entire wits by these miracles."

Elijah nodded his head in agreement. He said to Moses, "Yes, Moses, you're right; a good soaking is just what these people need to wash the blinders off them." He looked up toward heaven and mumbled a quick prayer. Instantly, like turning off a light, the bright daytime sky was again filled with thick, black clouds releasing their drenching downpours onto all of the people of Israel.

The premier quickly spun around in his chair to look outside. For several seconds, he stared in complete shock and astonishment. *Who are these men that have power even over the elements?*

As he turned back to face the men, he tilted his eyes upward; and said, "My God, please help us all."

"Yes. Yes. That's the spirit," Elijah blurted out while slapping his knee in exuberance. "Yes, our God will help us all if we will just ask Him."

The premier was sitting there dumbfounded, not knowing what else to do or even what to say. After a moment, he slowly slumped forward in his chair, leaned out, and placed both of his hands palms down on top of his desk and finally blurted out, "Okay. I give up. Maybe you are who you say you are. But why have you come? And what is it that you want?"

"Premier Emanuel Ben Joseph, we thank you. Yes, God has now revealed it to your heart that we are who we say we are, and now you have believed," Moses said. "Now, if you will allow us to take a portion of your time, we will tell you the whole story."

"Listen. Take all of the time you want. I give up," he resignedly replied.

"Thank you, Premier Emanuel Ben Joseph. Yes. Thank you. First of all, sir, your country—excuse me, I should say *our* country—is about to come under a major attack. If you have access to a Bible, you will find this prophesied in the book of Ezekiel, chapters thirty-eight and thirty-nine. Yes, this battle that is about to take place was described in perfect detail by our dear brother and fellow prophet Ezekiel."

"That's strange. What a coincidence," the premier interrupted. "The battles we have already been in have been led by a very brave man named Ezekiel, Lieutenant Colonel Ezekiel Cohen, to be exact."

"Yes, we are very aware of that. We believe that God, in His eternal providence, purposely put Ezekiel Cohen in this place at this time for this particular mission. Yes, Ezekiel Cohen embodies the same bravery, determination, and trustworthiness that our dear brother and fellow prophet Ezekiel embodied many, many years ago. God has put him in this place because God can trust him.

"But let me get back to what our brother and fellow prophet, Ezekiel, wrote almost two thousand six hundred years ago. You see, under the anointing and inspiration of the Holy Spirit, he wrote down the exact order of things that are going to take place here in Israel in the next few days and weeks. He wrote this prophecy just for this day you are living in right now. And let me just say this in passing: our dear brother Ezekiel was not at all happy when he was not chosen to come back with us so he could once again preach this news. Ah, but God has other plans, and we must not question God."

Moses suddenly stopped for a moment to consider something. "Premier, I know this might be too much to ask of you, but it would be so helpful. May I ask if you would have access to a Bible? I know that you do not believe in the New Covenant as of this time, but I really could use a complete Bible for everything I am going to show and teach you during the next several days. Many of those things will be found in the book of Matthew and others in the book of Revelation."

The premier sat straight up in his chair, and twisted his face into a stunned mask. Then, with complete incredulity and astonishment in his voice, he exclaimed, "A *Bible*? You ask me if I have a Bible, my... whoever you are. It is your turn to know just who I am. If you have not figured it out yet, well, let me tell you, I am *Jewish*. That is J-E-W-I-S-H, *Jew-ish*." He laughed. "And you want me to bring you a complete Bible. Oh I tell you, that is a good one."

Nonplussed in the least, Moses continued on without missing a beat. "Yes... well, tell me anyway, my dear fellow, do you have access to one? And if you do, would you please be so kind as to get it for us?"

"I don't have the faintest idea if a *Bible* would be lying about somewhere. Here. Let me ring my secretary; she might know where a Bible can be found. She is good at finding things." Still laughing, he reached over and pushed the intercom button on his phone.

"Yes?" a female voice on the other end said.

"Lynn, I need your help. If you can, would you find a complete Christian Bible for me and then bring it in to my office?"

"A Bible?" she exclaimed. "I mean, I'm sorry, sir, but did you say *a Christian Bible?*"

"Yes, Lynn, a Christian Bible. If you could locate one for me, would you please be so kind as to bring it to my office as soon as possible? It would be greatly appreciated."

As they were waiting, Moses looked at the premier and said, "Excuse me once more, Premier Emanuel Ben Joseph, but may I please trouble you for one more favor? If I may, would you happen to have a glass of water that I could get from you? And possibly, Elijah would like one also. I must say, it has been a rather long journey for both of us."

The premier nodded his head as he stood and began walking over to a built-in bar and entertainment area along one wall of his office. He reached into a cupboard and pulled two glasses out and began filling them with water. But a funny thought struck him. He turned around and looked at Moses and said, "I would say so. Tell me, how long of a journey has it been? For you, Moses, I would have to say at least a three to four-thousand-year journey. Am I correct?"

Moses instantly began roaring with laughter that rattled the entire office. "Oh my, dear premier, that is a good one. Yes, indeed, a three to four-thousand-year journey. Ah. That is good. I will have to remember that one," he roared again as tears of amusement filled his eyes.

While they were all laughing and enjoying themselves, a soft knock came on the door.

"Come in," the premier yelled.

Lynn Goodman, longtime secretary and semi-permanent fixture in the premier's office, opened the door and came sauntering into the room, holding a Bible in her hand. On her face was a look of confusion. She couldn't understand just what the premier would want with a Christian Bible.

But she stopped as she suddenly noticed the two very strange-looking men who happened to be in the premier's office with the premier. The shock of seeing them made her jump about two feet straight up into the air while letting out a screeching scream that came dangerously close to piercing the eardrums of all present. The Bible went flying out of her hand. It shot straight out in a flying arch; bounced once off the ceiling; and then flew over and smashed against the farthest wall, where it finally fell with a crash down onto the floor.

While this was happening, she began returning awkwardly back to earth from her quick trip to the moon and back. But as soon as her feet barely touched the floor, she lost her balance and went stumbling straight backward about four steps, until she suddenly crashed hard into the wall, right next to the door. As her eyes slowly began to stop bouncing up and down and to come back into a semblance of focus, she managed to bellow out, "Who … who are you? And how did you get in here?"

Elijah and Moses instantly stood up and began to extend their hands out to her as they moved toward her. As they did, she drew her hands up against her chin and squeezed her arms in so tightly against her body that it almost cut off her breathing.

"Lynn." The premier was smiling as he called her name. "Lynn, let me introduce you to both of these men. This man on your left is Elijah, and the man on your right is Moses."

But before he could even get Moses's name out of his mouth, Lynn's eyes rolled back up into her head and she began sliding slowly down the wall to the floor, where she fell crumpled into a ball like a soft ragdoll.

"Oh my." Moses exclaimed in a very concerned manner.

But Elijah almost disgustedly began shaking his head from side to side and mumbling under his breath, "Why couldn't you have made that wicked Jezebel to be this afraid of me?" he walked over to where Lynn was lying crumpled on the floor. He then reached down and took her by the hand. "My dear lady," he said, "stand up. You are all right."

She opened her eyes and gazed up at him. Her face was plastered with a combination of fear and shock. But she slowly began to climb back up.

Elijah held her hand and helped her back onto her feet until she was finally able to regain her balance. Then he said, "See, my dear lady? You have nothing to fear."

"Yes … well … uh … tell me, how did you get in here? I have not once, for even a second, left my desk. I never saw the two of you pass by and enter into the premier's office."

"My good lady, there are certain things that God allows to happen that are beyond the comprehension of humans. For one, how we got into the premier's office is one of those. But let me assure you, only good will come from our being here."

While Elijah was speaking with Lynn, Moses walked over and picked up the Bible. He bent down and gently and lovingly gathered the Word of God off the floor and turned it over and around, checking it for any damage. Then, he mumbled, "Lord, I ask you to not hold this attempt at destroying your Words of Truth against this dear lady. If you will remember, I too, once threw your Word down and tried to destroy it. Oh, Lord, we thank you for your loving-kindness and for your forgiveness."

At the same time, Elijah was gently trying to usher Lynn out of the room. But as soon as they got to the door and she was just about to exit through it, she suddenly turned around and said, "May I ask one more question? Uh…what are those clothes you are wearing? Are they burlap sacks?"

Elijah smiled. "No, Lynn. These are not burlap sacks. These are what used to be called sackcloth garments. They were worn when major problems or sudden destruction were soon to come on God's people. That is why we are wearing them now," he said as he was finally able to walk her out of the door and close it gently behind her.

In the meantime, Moses had opened the Bible to Ezekiel chapter thirty-eight and had handed it to the premier. He then told him to read both chapters thirty-eight and thirty-nine. The premier had his head buried in the Bible and was now doing just that.

Moses and Elijah sat back down and waited for the premier to finish reading. Moses reached out and picked up the glass of water the premier had placed on his desk. He gingerly brought the glass up in front of his face and peered into it. Elijah sat there, watching him, wondering what he was doing. Moses then touched the glass to his mouth and then quickly took a full drink, draining the entire glass.

As he slowly brought the glass away from his mouth, he let out a small laugh and then turned to Elijah and said, "Yes, my dear brother, I have waited for more than three thousand years to enjoy this fine water from God's Holy Land. As you may recall, I never had the opportunity to enjoy this water before. My journey came to an end on top of a mountain overlooking this Holy Land. Yes. This is my first time. And let me tell you this, it is very good." Again, a good, hearty laugh bellowed out of him.

Elijah joined in the laughter and then picked up his own glass and took a large drink. As he returned the half empty glass to the coaster on the desk, he turned to look at Moses and laughingly declared, "Yes, my dear brother, I might not have waited as long as you for this fine water, but I have waited too long as it is. *Yes,* it is mighty fine. It truly is God's *holy water.*"

After that, they sat there with the joy of the Lord flooding through them, basking in the enjoyment of each other's company, sipping God's holy water and hoping that the premier would not take all day to read just two chapters.

Finally, after a little over thirty minutes had interminably ticked off a large antique wall clock hanging above the bar and entertainment area in the office. Premier Ben Joseph finally finished reading the two chapters. Then as he gingerly laid the Bible down onto the desk in front of him, he slowly lifted his head and stared at the farthest wall in the room. His eyes had a faraway glassy look in them. seeing everything at once but seeing nothing at all at the same time. Again, his face had become gray, ashen, almost transparent in appearance. Also, both of his hands that were lying on the desk in front of him were noticeably trembling even though he was making an unconscious effort to keep them from it. After a good minute or two had gone by, he slowly turned his face to stare at the two strange men sitting in front of him. His eyes were those of a haunted, terrified man. His mind was racing in a thousand different directions at once. But finally, he found enough of his voice and began to speak.

"Okay, Moses and Elijah, you came here to tell me that we are going to be attacked by the Russians and . . . only God knows who else? What can we do? I mean, we are vastly outnumbered, outgunned, outmanned, out-everything. Listen. If these words that were written well over a thousand years ago are true and are for us here right now in our time, then only God can help us."

"Yes, and He will," Elijah enthusiastically yelled back to him. Then in a lower, calmer voice, he continued, "Yes, He will, Premier Ben Joseph. That is one of the reasons why we have come."

"So tell me, what should we do?" the premier asked. "We must find a way to get prepared. . . . Excuse me while I call General Green, the commander over our armed forces,"

"Yes," Moses said. "You must get General Green notified, and also all of your troops. But actually, Premier Emanuel Ben Joseph, General Green is already prepared. You see, General Green is, and has been for many, many years, in constant contact with our Lord and Savior, Jesus Christ. And God is even now speaking to him and telling him what must be done.

"But these things must be done in a hurry. Premier Emanuel Ben Joseph, your men will be standing against an army with a vastly overwhelming disparity in size to yours. In fact, you will be outnumbered at least *one hundred thousand* to one. But God has allowed it to be this way so that He can prove to you and to your fellow countrymen that *He* will fight for you. He will do this to show you and the whole world His glory."

"But what should we do? Should we attack all of them first, or what? Do we allow them to come all of the way here, or should we fire on them now to try to stop their advance?"

"No, my Premier. If you tried to stop them now, you would not succeed. They will come up against Israel just like a *storm cloud*, exactly like it says there in the Holy Book. But when they get here, it will be just like it says; they will fall in the valleys of Israel. Yes, Magog and all of his vast hordes will be destroyed within the boundaries of this Holy Land of God's that God promised to give to Abraham and his descendants. And then following that, all of Israel's children will have fuel to burn for the next seven years—just as it says there—from all of the spoils you will gather from these enemies of God.

"Oh, my dear Premier Emanuel Ben Joseph, this is a great day for you to be alive and to see God's glory. I see the fear in your eyes but do not be afraid. God is with you. And let me tell you, after Israel has watched God fight for her, not one person in Israel should ever deny God again. The Children of Israel are God's chosen, beloved people. So, let God do the fighting and let Him receive the Glory," Moses exclaimed.

For several more minutes, Premier Ben Joseph sat there, staring unblinking at both of them. Wild thoughts of the total annihilation of the Jewish people that he had been elected to lead and to *protect* were racing through his mind. But with the presence of two wild-looking strange men sitting calmly and unconcerned in his office, he also felt a brief foray of hope slip into his consciousness, too. He was a highly decorated combat veteran of the Six-Day War that took place in 1967, and against vastly overwhelming odds at that time, they had defeated a numerically superior coalition of Arab armies in only six days.

All of the top army officers, including him, knew that God had helped them that time. *I mean, it had to be God. There was just no other way,* he thought. *But my precious God, this is different... this is the Russians; the second most powerful country in the world... plus all of the Arab countries will unite with them and again come against us.*

Also, according to the words written in the Bible, there are several other countries that will be joining with them that he didn't know who they were. The Bible called them Put, Cush, and Togarmar. Even though the Bible did not tell him who these ancient countries were, he would find out very quickly.

Finally, he puckered up his lips and allowed a loud sigh to whistle through them. At the same time, he sat back in his chair and stared intently at these two very strange men for another full minute before saying, "Let me just say this. You two had better really be who you say you are. And may *God help us.*"

"Yes, He will. He certainly will," Elijah shouted. "Premier Emanuel Ben Joseph, have you wondered why we have continued to call you by your full name, Emanuel Ben Joseph?"

"Yes, that has crossed my mind," he replied. "You have used it a lot!"

"Premier Emanuel Ben Joseph, do you know what your name means? Your name, Emanuel, means, 'God is with us.' Yes, that is why we call you Emanuel Ben Joseph and why we must continue to call you by that name. Every time we say your name, we let Satan and all of his demon hordes know that God is with us. God is with us. God is with us. That is why we believe God has placed you in charge of His people for this very occasion because of your name."

The premier's brain was already too rattled and confused to respond to that. He just looked intently at the two men for a long time, allowing everything to soak in. But then, he suddenly thought of something else. "Let me ask you one more thing. What does it mean there in chapter thirty-nine, verse six, where it says, 'I will send fire on Magog and on those who live in safety in the coastlands, and they will know that I am the Lord.' Russia doesn't really occupy 'coastlands' as such, unless you count the frozen coastline in Siberia. So who are the 'coastlands?'"

Elijah replied, "Unfortunately, those 'coastlands' that are written about in the Word of God happen to be your former friends in what is called the United States of America. The continental United States has been enormously blessed with the bountifulness of *three* coastlines along her spacious borders. These coastlands are what has helped her to become the world's greatest power up to this time in history. But even as we speak right this moment, Russia is preparing to bring fire and brimstone and burning sulfur down onto the entire country of America. And let me say this to you with my deepest regards. America will be destroyed. But I must also add, do not be alarmed or feel sorry for her. God has finally passed divine judgment on America.

"Now that Jesus has snatched away the people who believed in Him from off the earth to be with Him in heaven for the next seven years, the dispensation of unmitigated, underserved grace to mankind has finally come to an end. It is now time for God's judgment. Yes, God has passed His judgment on America for many, many reasons.

"One of the reasons is because of the grievous sexual sins that were committed by many of her previous immoral and unrepentant leaders. These leaders were placed in their high positions to be examples for the populace, but instead of being good and righteous examples, they have actually committed disgusting acts of cheap fornication and blatant adultery in the very center of her government under the accepting, approving eyes of her people. These immoral leaders have set examples that have led America down a steep, slippery slope of immorality. And the unrepentant people who are now left in America have willfully accepted and given their tacit approval of this sinful behavior by the continuing popularity of these former leaders. My dear Premier, do not be deceived. God has not approved, nor has He accepted these sins.

"Premier Emanuel Ben Joseph, in addition to these sins, God has also passed judgment on America for the millions of liters of innocent blood that she is constantly spilling on a daily basis. This judgment is for all of the precious unstained pure blood that has poured out of the little innocent children who have been sacrificed in the demonic name of *choice*. Premier, that demonic demon that has come up from the very darkest pits of hell named *choice*, has gotten falling down staggering drunk from the blood of more innocent babies than all other mass murderers who have ever lived, including Hitler and Stalin, combined.

"Yes, God has passed judgment. The blood of those millions of little innocent babies who are slain on a yearly unstoppable basis before they were ever able to see and enjoy the light of day has reached the ears and even the nostrils of God. And just like Abel's innocent blood cried out to God for vengeance from the dirt where it lay, these little babies' innocent blood also cries out to God every day and every night from the dirty drains and filthy sewers that it has flowed down. My brother, there has been so much of that precious innocent blood spilled that it has actually painted the walls of the sewers *red*. This choice that has caused all of this bloodshed is no different and, in fact, is the very same thing as was done in ancient times when heathen people sacrificed their own children on the altars of false gods. It is the same thing, infant sacrifice.

"The only difference between then and now is that back then, the god they sacrificed their innocent babies to was named Molech. Now, the god they sacrifice these infants to is named *choice*. But, again, it is still the same, *infant sacrifice*. While these precious little infants should have been feeling warm, snug, and secure inside of their loving mother's womb, they have had their precious little bodies ripped out and pulled apart because their supposedly loving mother made a *choice* to kill them before they could ever be born.

"Oh yes, my brother, it is time for judgment. Yes, America will pay dearly for all of her sins. God has also passed judgment on her for her filth and totally open immorality that she wears with such keen smugness and even with pride. In her depravity and utter vulgarity, she has completely lost her ability to even be ashamed or embarrassed. With a pleasing look and smug amusement on her face, she lifts her skirt and exposes her nakedness to the world as she exports her pornographic filth without any embarrassment or remorse.

"Yes, God has passed judgment on America. But lastly, Premier Emmanuel Ben Joseph, God has passed final judgment on her because she has turned her back on you, God's chosen people. The holy Word of God plainly declares that 'whoever blesses God's people, God will also bless. But whoever harms God's people, God will send judgment against.' The present ruler of that country has openly turned his back on you and convinced the majority of the rest of the people to do the same.

"So, I declare to you in less than two days' time, the blood of the innocents, the filth, the adulteries, the uncountable number of murders, the turning their back on you, and all else that she is guilty of, will be burned up in the wrath of God. I declare this to the world. Stand and see the glory of God," Elijah thundered in the same voice as the one he used when he called fire down from heaven that burned and consumed all of the priests of the false god Baal many years before.

"Oh, Premier Emanuel Ben Joseph, God is a good God. He is faithful and true; kind and loving; and most of all, forgiving. But the despicable, putrid smell of tainted *sin* has reached high into the heavens, all of the way up to Him, and it has finally aroused His wrath and fury. There has been *no* asking of forgiveness or showings of sorrow. So now, it is time for judgment.

"Yes, America will fall. But I declare to you that she will not be the only one to do so. You see, my brother, God has passed judgment on the entire world. *All* nations and countries are being judged right now, and all of them will succumb in the near future. In fact, even as I speak, a man who carries the *name of destruction* is almost here. This ungodly man who proudly wears the mantle of Satan will subdue and rule the nations of this world with an iron fist. His rule will be a yoke of iron, and in his trail will follow the spilled blood of many more millions of people. At this very moment, the scene is being set, and he is rising to the top.

"Premier Emanuel Ben Joseph, the days ahead that are coming upon the earth will be the worst days mankind has ever experienced. In fact, our precious Savior is quoted in Matthew chapter twenty-four, beginning in verse twenty-one—turn to it, sir, if you will, and follow along. 'There shall be great tribulation, such as was not since the beginning of the world to this time, no, nor ever shall be. And except those days should be shortened, there should no flesh be saved: but for the elect's sake those days shall be shortened.'

"Yes, my dear brother, those days that are written in God's Holy Word and were spoken by God's own Son, Jesus Christ, are here upon us now. But let me assure you, God is in control. While all of this calamity is going on, also what will be happening during these dark days that are ahead of us will come the greatest turning and coming back to the Almighty God that has ever been in the history of the world. You will see with your own eyes the mighty works and miracles that our God will perform.

"But, my precious man, let me assure you of this, unless *you* open your eyes and your heart to receive them, you will suffer the same consequence that will befall the man of perdition after he has run his course. Turn your heart to God. I say, repent. And then, see the wonders of His Majesty."

# CHAPTER 23

Three days later, another meeting was taking place. In Brussels, Belgium, ten high-ranking diplomats of the European Economic Development Commission were involved in a hastily called emergency conference. They had all arrived within the past thirty minutes on very short notice and were now already involved in very serious discussions.

The meeting they were attending was being held in a very rich and elegantly adorned conference room that is located inside of the headquarters building of the European Economic Development Commission, or EEDC, as it was sometimes called. At the moment, nine of the men were sitting in very comfortably appointed, dark, leather-upholstered chairs around a long, rectangular, dark red, cherry wood conference table.

The one remaining man, who happened to be the highest-ranking diplomat attending the meeting, Mr. Angel Abaddon, whose title was undersecretary of foreign affairs of the EEDC was standing at the far end of the table and had the floor speaking. Mr. Abaddon was a very charismatic, handsome, well-educated, and well-versed man who had an extreme air of superior confidence about himself and who, just by his imposing presence and being, commanded complete attention as he spoke.

All eyes and the attention of all there were raptly focused and attuned to him. "Gentlemen, I am sure that you are well aware of the devastating surprise nuclear missile attack that Russia launched against the United States just a few hours ago. And I am also sure that you are just as utterly shocked and totally dismayed about this as I am. I can hardly begin to express myself of just how evil this attack was. It was a calculatingly cowardly act committed by deranged, demonic criminals who are in charge of the Russian government. There are no other ways to describe it. And as you are well aware, it has totally shocked and completely dismayed what is left of the entire civilized world.

"Gentlemen, not only has it shocked and dismayed the entire world, but I say that it has brought our entire human civilization to the very brink of total disaster. It has brought all of us to the razor-sharp edge of the civilized cliff with one foot already teetering over the precipice." He emphasized this point by slamming his fist down hard onto the table.

Then, with even more extreme dismay in his voice, he continued, "I don't know if you have had a chance to see any of these yet, but reports have been coming in to us within the past hour that are saying that now, India and Pakistan are engaged in extremely heavy fighting. All-out war has broken out between those two countries as well. But fortunately, as of this time, there are no reports of their nuclear weapons having yet been used in that conflict. But gentlemen, let me ask this; since Russia has deliberately slammed wide open the previously closed and sacred doors of nuclear warfare, how much longer do you think it will be before those demonic, devastating weapons of mass destruction are brought to the surface and will be used against each other over there? Oh, my friends, I am afraid it will not be long."

He briefly paused just long enough for his words to sink in and for the people in the room to hopefully grasp the full import of what Russia's criminal actions have brought. He then continued.

"Gentlemen, this unthinkable crime that Russia has committed is, at this very moment, filling the earth's atmosphere with extreme amounts of deadly radiation. It also is causing enormous spikes of electromagnetic impulses to shoot wildly about. Because of this, I am afraid that most of our satellites and communications equipment is fluctuating wildly in our ability to use them. We do not know how much longer things will be as they are. We are only able to intermittently pick up signals and to receive pictures, but if India and Pakistan bring their nuclear weapons to bear against each other, from all of that added radiation and electromagnetic impulses those will also bring, it might be weeks before we are fully operational and completely back on line.

"Oh. One more thing I almost forgot. As we speak right now, North and South Korea have also begun battling each other all along the demilitarized zone that has historically separated those two countries. And as all of you know, both of those countries are nuclear powers. Gentlemen, I am so afraid if something is not done quickly to stop this bloodshed and carnage throughout the world … well, my friends, we just might not have a world for much longer, at least one that would be habitable for human beings.

"But if you will, please allow me to get back to the destruction of the United States. The preliminary reports and pictures we have been able to receive are saying that it has become a virtual wasteland, a country completely devastated and totally destroyed. Gentlemen, with all due regrets, let me emphasize, very few survivors are anticipated, and none have yet to be confirmed. And if there do happen to be a few survivors, I am afraid that it will not be long before the awful radioactive fallout will eliminate even those unfortunate souls.

"From what we have been able to gather so far, it appears that Russia used massive numbers of high explosive thermonuclear weapons of mass destruction against every military target located throughout all of North America. In addition to those, it has been confirmed that Russia also used high explosive nuclear weapons against every other US military installation America had located around the world in other countries. *Every other military installation*, I say. Russia has not only violated the sovereignty of the United States but many other sovereign nations of our world, as well. My friends, by these unthinkable, despotic, criminal actions, Russia has also, knowingly and without any signs of a bereaved conscious, brought grievous death and destruction to many other innocent civilized peoples around the world.

"By her actions, Russia did not want to just wound the United States; she wanted to totally destroy the United States, no matter where the United States had people located. And from the appearance of all things, I would say she has admirably accomplished her goals.

"But, in all of these despotic actions Russia has committed, there is one thing that is confusing. It appears that Russia decided, for some unknown reason, to spare the larger cities in North America from destruction. Instead of destroying them with the same type of high explosive thermonuclear weapons, she instead used her neutron bombs on the civilian population of those cities. These bombs, as you know, kill by emitting tremendous doses of high-energy radiation. Russia used high explosive nuclear weapons against military targets but neutron bombs against the civilian population.

"Why? Why did she do that, I ask? Does she want to eventually move part of her own population over to North America and then occupy their cities? What was her thinking in doing this?

"My friends, from what little data we have been able to gather from our satellites so far, entire cities are still standing and appear to be completely normal in every aspect in the pictures. But let me emphasize that these cities have become virtual ghost lands. The buildings and structures in these cities are standing tall and straight, other than the damage that was done to them by the anarchy and rioting that had been occurring over the past couple of days. But let me say this with all sincerity and deepest regrets. Already, gentlemen, the nauseating stench of rancid death is permeating these cities from one end of the city to the other end of it, as the entire populations of these places have died.

"Now, my faithful colleagues, in addition to the terrible news I have just given, I have even more extremely troublesome news to report to you. I am so sorry to say that New York City is one of these cities where it appears that the entire population is dead. As you all know, all of our top diplomats of this EEDC just happened to be in New York at that exact time for a world conference meeting with most of the world's leaders at the United Nations. They were meeting to discuss the mass disappearances of so many millions of the earth's inhabitants. They were there when this surprise attack took place.

"Oh, my dear friends, it is completely unfortunate that not a single one of our leaders or diplomats have survived. Nor have any of the other world leaders who were at the conference. They are all dead too. Yes, this is a very sad day, indeed, in the entire history of mankind. But this also has created a very serious problem that needs our immediately attention. And this is why you have been called here on such short notice. As it stands, we are leaderless. And, gentlemen, without the benefits of a faithful, strong, courageous, and qualified leader in our ranks. We have no one that is able to stand up and face the Russians. No one, I say.

"Gentlemen, with America having been destroyed, there is no other single country on earth that can stand up to Russia by herself. I say, not a single other country can stand up to her. But let me make myself very clear and precise on this point here. I say, *we can*. Yes. We can—*if* we were to combine our strengths, our militaries, our governments, in fact, all of our peoples, and unite together under a single leader and a single government. We can stop Russia and make her pay dearly for her actions.

"Now, I must tell you the very latest disturbing news that we have just received while you were in transit to our meeting. I do not believe you may be aware of these new developments that are happening concerning Russia. But let me issue a most severe warning. Russia is not finished with her criminal actions. No. Her hunger and thirst for more innocent blood is still raging strong and unsatisfied.

"Gentlemen, within the last hour, it has been confirmed that Russia is massing a tremendous number of her troops along her southern borders. And without a doubt, it appears very convincingly that she is preparing to march southward down into the Middle East. Gentlemen, if Russia is allowed to move into the Middle East, I guarantee you that she will turn against her Arab friends and allies. I guarantee you"—he again slammed his fist down hard onto the table for emphasis—"that her entire plan of madness is so that she can control all of the oil in the Middle East.

"Now, gentlemen, *if* we allow that to happen, I want you to know that Russia will rule the world. Did you understand what I just said? Russia will rule the world," he screamed. "My friends, we need to do something about this. What *we* need to do is to stand up to her and stop her. There is no one else who can do this. Do you think that maybe China can? Let me ask, what does she have to offer? Two hundred million men in uniform, maybe, but what good does that do against the might of Russia's nuclear arsenal?

"Nothing!" he yelled. "And let me state this. In no way whatsoever did Russia use up her inventory of nuclear weapons in these strikes. No. She still has in her supply closet enough nuclear weapons to totally destroy every living soul on this planet many, many times over.

"My fellow leaders, let me say this again. We can stop Russia. We can. But we cannot stop her if we are leaderless. I, for one, believe that Russia plotted and timed this dastardly attack against the United States to purposely coincide with the meeting of our top diplomats along with all of the other world leaders in New York. I believe that she was well aware of the fact that she could chop our heads off, so to speak, if she launched her attack at this time. It was either that or it was an absolutely, phenomenally, and amazing set of supernaturally uncanny coincidences.

"Now, gentlemen, I also believe that Russia thinks that we, along with the rest of the world, will now simply wallow in self-despair and cower in fear to her. Well, I have one word to say: never. No, my friends, I say never. Never give up. Never surrender. And never bow."

He stopped speaking and began to look intently into the eyes of each man sitting around the table. His own eyes appeared to be glowing with actual fire in them. They also had a glassy, surreal, almost spooky look. But there was one thing that was for sure: there was absolutely no fear in them. And that was what each man wanted desperately to see.

He began to speak again. "My friends, we need to do a few things right away. First of all, we need to choose a leader. Under normal circumstances, this would be a rather simple matter. But under these circumstances that we find ourselves we need to choose someone who is very unique and unusual. We need someone who is not afraid, someone who will show absolutely no fear, someone who has the courage and strength and boldness to stand up tall and strong to the Russians, and someone who is willing to work together to unite our countries together.

"Gentlemen, I do not want to get ahead of myself here or to break normal protocol, but let me say this with all sincerity and meaning: *I* want to be your leader. Look at me," he yelled. "See that I am not afraid. I have no fear whatsoever. And I will unite our countries in an airtight fist of iron."

He again briefly paused before continuing. "Gentlemen, if I were to be elected as your leader, I would bring every resource that our respective governments combined can muster against Russia and her allies and would literally wipe them off the map. Due to her supreme arrogance and the extremely sinful actions against humankind that she has exhibited, Russia no longer deserves to exist on our planet.

"So if you have the courage to elect me as your leader, I will call *fire* down from heaven on her. I will cause the earth to open up and swallow her as she moves into the Middle East. I will cause her own troops to turn against and kill each other within her own ranks. Gentlemen, I will completely destroy her."

This last and final statement was made with Angel Abaddon slamming both of his fists so hard and loud down onto the table that everyone immediately jumped up out of their seats like they had been shot out of a cannon. After a brief awkward moment of silence, loud handclapping and even louder shouts of agreement and approval swept through the men.

"Yes. Yes."

Ernesto Terzanokolis, the representative from Greece, quickly grabbed the floor. "Gentlemen, if *I* may, let me say that I agree with everything Mr. Abaddon has just said. *Everything!* In fact, I say it is time that we declare martial law in our own countries. I say we unite under one leader, one flag, one military, and one government. And I nominate Mr. Angel Abaddon to be this man to lead us."

At that point, everyone immediately either seconded the nomination or voted to confirm Angel Abaddon as their new leader. Again, a lot of hand shaking and back slapping began to take place. Also, a sudden sense of hope and a strong feeling of overriding power began to emanate inside of the room.

Angel Abaddon turned to the men, "My faithful friends and new partners, we need to conduct a little more business before everyone returns to their own country and declares martial law. What is it, you say? Well, we need to give a new title to your new leader."

It took a while amid much discussion, but it was finally decided that His Supreme Highness, Excellency Abaddon, Supreme Leader of the new, United Confederation of Nations would be the title given. Everyone wanted it to be a very powerful statement, powerful enough to limit any dissension at all within their own countries.

# CHAPTER 24

Premier Butin was very pleased and in a wonderfully joyful mood. At the moment, he was sitting in a large, overstuffed executive leather chair. He had extended his legs straight out and had placed his feet up on top of his desk. In his right hand was a large, hand-rolled Cuban cigar and a tall, half-empty glass of vodka was sitting on a tray next to his desk. All of this was in an underground nuclear blast-proof executive office suite situated well below the Kremlin. Joining him in his happiness and celebration was General Boris Denkovsky, the keeper of the flame, the head of Russia's nuclear deterrent forces; the man who had just unleashed the fires of hell on the United States of America..

"My dear general," the Premier began, "let me be the first to congratulate you on the wonderful success of Burning Star. What a magnificent accomplishment you have completed. I am so very proud of you, as is our entire great country."

He paused to clink glasses with the general in a celebratory toast before continuing, "General, let me ask you. Do you happen to remember a few years back when one of the United States' former presidents called us the *evil empire*? Yes? Good. He called us an evil empire and then had the audacity to declare that his policies had turned us into a third-world country. He declared that they had brought us to our knees. He actually had the astonishing gall to declare that they had brought our wonderful Russia down and had turned her into a third-world country.

"Well, my general, I believe the tables have been turned around. Yes? You, my dear man, have brought *that* evil empire to her knees. *No.* I say, you have cut her off at her knees. *No.* Not even that much is left of her. In fact, my dear general, I believe we could actually say she no longer has any knees at all, does she? My friend, my comrade, my compatriot, I say she no longer has any *body* left at all. She is dead. Kaput. Finished. My congratulations, my friend. Yes. Yes. My congratulations.

"And now, if only our second plan, Jacob's Ladder, will meet with similar success. Actually, if it does even half as well as Burning Star has for us, my dear friend, we might have to make you and the rest of my generals *kings* over all of the different countries of the world. Yes. Kings. Yes. Yes."

Clearly, the old premier was completely enjoying himself without an ounce of regret, remorse, or humility to be seen.

They refilled their drinks, then the premier continued. "General, at oh-three-hundred hours, Moscow time, the order will be given for our troops to begin their advance to the south. I was just thinking though. Maybe you can remember how some of Hitler's troops used to be called stormtroopers during World War II? Well, let me just say, they haven't seen anything yet. Let me declare that there will be so many of our troops advancing southward that they will cover the ground like a storm cloud. Yes, our troops will not be called storm troopers but a storm *cloud*.

"I say, let no one get in our way or try to stop us. We will consume everything and everyone who might dare to stand in our way, if any might have the audacity or be foolish enough to do so. Yes, our troops are ready, willing, and raring to go. And they will. They will at oh-three-hundred hours tomorrow. At that time, our troops will begin to move southward down into Turkey and then on into Lebanon, Syria, and Jordan. Within twenty-four to thirty-six hours, comrade, we should have enough of our troops in place to fill the entire north and eastern border of Israel. And behind us, to our east, will be Iraq and Iran chomping at the bit.

"Let me also tell you, my friend, Turkey has decided to join us in our invasion. A very smart and astute move on her part, I shall say. Right now, even as we speak, we have many of our troops and divisions already moving into her. By tomorrow afternoon, we should have a combined force of our troops, Turkey, Lebanese, Syrians, and Jordanians, of over three and one half million men. And, General, not long after that, they should be fully in position and massed on Israel's borders, ready to storm on into Israel. And in addition to these countries, Egypt and Libya and even Sudan from the south are joining in our cause to destroy the Jews. They are massing to come up from the south to destroy Israel from that side. Oh yes, General, tomorrow will be a great, great, day.

"Can you just picture it, General? Can you picture this in your mind? Israel will wake up tomorrow morning as usual. But all of a sudden, she will see herself surrounded by millions of soldiers from a vast multitude of countries. Not just the Arabs this time, whom Israel has defeated so many times in the past. But a great cloud of troops from many nations will envelope her. Everywhere she looks, she will be surrounded.

"Can you imagine the terrible face of fear she will instantly feel as all of her blood suddenly turns to ice and begins running cold? What must it be like to know that your entire country, along with every living person in it, will be dead in just a few short hours, totally annihilated?" He said this with a laugh.

"Oh, absolutely wonderful for us, my General. Wonderful for us. Yes, she will wake up and see on her northern border Turkey, Lebanon, and our own great troops who will be poised and ready to devour her. With great fear and trembling, she will then turn her head to look on her eastern border. There, she will see Syria, Jordan, and Saudi Arabia. Plus, Iran and Iraq will also be staring and growling at her behind them. Then, with her heart almost ready to give up and quit, she will turn south and look in that direction. There, Egypt, Sudan, and Libya will be showing their teeth and snarling.

"But, General, within hours of her waking up, if she is not already frightened to death by then, she will not only see all of those countries ready to attack her, but she will be seeing the enormous strength and infinite might and power of her absolute worst nightmare, our mighty Russia, armed to the teeth and ready to totally annihilate her.

"Picture this in your mind, General. Israel will awaken tomorrow morning and will walk outside. She will look up at the sky. Suddenly, she will notice that dark, evil storm clouds are covering the entire sky and are approaching fast. With paralyzing fear filling her every part, while keeping one eye on the storm, she will slowly turn around and look in all directions. And as she does that, she will immediately come to the realization that she is doomed, doomed. There is no hope at all.

"She is trapped. And without her protector, the United States, to help her, all hope and help will be gone because, my friend, her only avenue of escape would be if her *God* were to split the Mediterranean Sea in half for her.. And do you think He will or could do that? The Mediterranean Sea is not some small, little water outlet that supposedly their God once split for them before down in Egypt to lead them to safety. No. I say, she is doomed, doomed, doomed.

"But we must not be too anxious in our zeal to kill the Jews. We still base part of our plan in the hope that Israel will see us coming while watching all of her Arab enemies massing against her at the same time. Then, our hope and desire is that she will launch a preemptive strike against all of them before they can get fully prepared and before our troops move in to take our positions. If they do that, it will be very unfortunate for the Arabs but very, very fortunate for us. It will either destroy the Arabs completely or, at the very least, severely cripple them. If all of that should go according to our plan, my general, we will waltz right on in and destroy every remaining Jew on the face of this earth, plus all of the remaining Arabs too. Then, my friend, we will claim the victor's prize, which is, of course, ruler of the world.

"Ah, but in the grand scheme of things, it does not really matter. If we mighty, glorious Russian gods have to do all of the dirty work ourselves, and wipe the earth clear of all of the Arabs. While at the same time, my friend, we will go ahead and complete the job that Hitler attempted to do and wipe the earth clear of every Jew also. Do you agree, my general?"

With exploding enthusiasm, the general replied, "Oh yes, my Premier. Oh yes. Let us wipe the earth clear of all of Abraham's children. In fact, let us wipe the earth clear of everyone who does not carry pure Russian blood."

"Oh, my friend, you do have grand ideas, don't you? Yes, well, that would be nice, but we have to be careful what we say or do. There are some in our own ranks who are not pure, white Russian, including your own premier. But let me say this. I like your exuberance. I will say that."

A loud knock came on the premier's door. The premier looked up at the general and then over at the door. "What can it be now? I've again given specific orders to not be disturbed unless it was of the most extreme importance. This had better be good. Come," he yelled.

An aide quickly walked in. "I'm sorry to disturb you, Premier, but we have just received some very important information that needs your immediate attention."

"What is it?" The premier asked disgustedly. But the aide didn't say anything and glanced over at the general. The premier noticed his hesitation and said, "You can say anything you want. There are no secrets here between the general and myself."

"Yes, sir. Sir, we have just received reports that a private civilian jet aircraft is rapidly approaching our border. We have made contact with what we assume is the pilot. He says he wants to fly directly to Moscow. He says he has onboard with him both the President of the United States, Hussein Anwar and his chief of staff. He is requesting permission to proceed and land, Premier."

For a moment, the premier was stunned. "The president of the US?" he asked incredulously. "On a civilian aircraft? Why is he not on Air Force One?"

"Yes, sir, the president of the United States. As to why he is not on Air Force One, maybe it was destroyed before he could get on it."

He sat there for a moment, shaking his head, wondering what in Hades the president was doing flying to Russia. *Also, how had the naive fool escaped? We have just totally destroyed the entire North American continent.* He looked up to his aide and said, "Send up four of our best pilots and planes to escort it. And, Ivan, you tell the pilots that if that plane varies even by a fraction of an inch from its flight plan, shoot it down. And as soon as they land, have the GBU bring them here to me. I'll find out what all of this is about. Also, make sure there are no weapons of any sort. Even take away any fingernail clippers. Oh, and thank you very much, Ivan Nororovski. You were correct in interrupting my meeting for this."

"Yes, sir. Thank you, sir!" the aide replied and backed quickly out of the room to go issue the premier's orders.

t 6:00 a.m. Jerusalem time, Moses and Elijah were in the command bunker located at Sharon Air Force Base. The base is located south of the Valley of Megiddo, and near their northern border with Syria and Lebanon. With them in the bunker were Premier Emanuel Ben Joseph, along with General Green and his full staff, plus Ezekiel, Esther, and Ezekiel's squadron pilots.

All of them were nervously standing around a long table centered in the middle of the command center; all, that is, except Moses and Elijah. In the middle of the table lay a ten-foot-long rectangular map. Israel was located in the center of it. It also showed all of the Arab and Muslim nations that surround her on every side. Standing on the map were little figurine soldiers that represented every division of the Israeli military juggernaut and where the divisions were presently located. It also had hundreds of little figurines of the Arab and Muslim armies that were gathering against them.

The air inside of the bunker was thick with tension. All day long, Israeli reconnaissance flights and satellite images had been showing that Russia was in the process of massing multitudes of troops and equipment on her southern border. Other pictures taken a little later were showing these troops moving on down into Turkey while others were showing many more hundreds of thousands massing to come down through Iran and then on toward Israel.

This news could only mean one thing. After Moses had gotten Premier Ben Joseph to read both chapters thirty-eight and thirty-nine of the book of Ezekiel, it left no doubt to what Gog's intentions were. Especially now, after what Russia had just done to the United States, they knew that Russia's thirst for human blood would not be satisfied until she had completely destroyed every living person inside of Israel.

Every man in the room was praying that God's Word was true. *If His Word is true, they knew they had nothing to fear.*

*But... yes, that small, little, three-letter word, b–u–t is sometimes the largest word in the whole world,* Premier Ben Joseph ruefully thought to himself.

Elijah decided that he was going to try to ease the thick tension and to try to bring a degree of renewed courage and faith to the men. "Gentlemen, if you will allow me, I would like to speak to you for a few minutes. I want to try to instill faith into you. Yes, faith. That is the key word. You must believe and have faith.

"Our Lord and Savior, Jesus Christ, I know that some of you do not believe in Him yet, but you will. Give it time and you will. Anyway, our Lord, Jesus Christ, once said in Matthew chapter seventeen, verse twenty, and I quote, 'If you have faith only as small as a mustard seed, you can say to this mountain, be thou removed and be thou cast into the sea. And it will be done.'

"Oh, my dear brothers, if you will only believe in the Lord your God, this very night will be the beginning of Israel's greatest victory in her entire history. Have faith, my brothers. Have faith."

His speech brought a few small smiles to some of their faces, but their reactions were not at all what he wanted or had expected. He wanted to see people going Pentecostal with hands raised toward heaven and with shouts of, "Alleluia," echoing loudly throughout the room. He wanted to see victory dances. He wanted to hear voices of triumph being shouted. He wanted to see faith in action.

But all he got were a few small, nervous smiles and courteous sideways glances. Elijah was very familiar with what trying to have faith in your heart is all about. When he was faced with what looked like certain death when Jezebel was going to kill him, well, it is sometimes just so hard to believe and have faith. So, he looked over at Moses and said, "Moses, unlike me, you, my brother, have been in a somewhat similar situation as this. Why don't you tell these men what it was like to be staring at a far superior army that had you surrounded, just like we are? It also was vastly more numerous than your valiant band of slaves. At least it was much more numerous than of the brave army of fighting men you had with you, which, if I remember correctly, your entire army only had a grand total of two, which were Joshua and Caleb, beside yourself.

"Moses, this powerful army you were up against was brandishing the best weapons known to man at that time while the deadly weapons your army of Joshua, Caleb, and yourself had to fight the mighty Egyptian army with consisted of only shepherds' staffs. Is this not correct? And all the while, at the same time, your backs were pushed up against the Red Sea with nowhere to run or hide. Am I correct in my analysis so far, Moses?"

Moses leaned his head back and let his eyes roll upward. A big smile began wrapping itself across his face as the memories came flooding back into his mind. He then slowly began shaking his head up and down. "Yes, my brother, you are correct in all of your analysis."

"My fellow brethren, I think Moses might have been feeling very, very similar to what you are feeling right now. Tell them, Moses. Tell them of your great adventure to Egypt and then back again."

Moses turned to Elijah and said with a big grin on his face, "It will be my pure pleasure, my brother. As you already know and have experienced on many other occasions in conversations we have had in heaven, I just love telling my old war stories."

He reached out and picked up the Bible that was lying beside him and opened it to Exodus chapter three.

"My brothers, let me read something to you. This is where God was telling me He was going to send me back to Egypt to rescue our people from under the punishing and cruel practices of Pharaoh. And let me tell you without hesitation, I was filled with dreadful fear just like some of you are tonight, and I did not want to go. So, I argued with God. I said, 'Who am I that I should go unto Pharaoh and that I should bring forth the children of Israel out of Egypt?'

"And God replied to me, 'Certainly, I will be with thee.' My brothers, God was with me. Did you hear what I said? God was with me. Yes, He told me that He would be with me. Men, nothing else mattered. God was there with me.

"Can't you see it? Oh, El Shaddai, Almighty God, I ask you to open these men's eyes. These men, our brothers, open their eyes to see you and to hear you speaking to them right now. Let them know that you are with them here tonight and they have nothing to fear but unbelief.

I am sorry, brothers, but I sometimes get a little emotional when the old memories are stirred up and aroused. But as I was saying, God told me He would be with me. Well, at the time, that was not a real big assurance to me. Kind of what you're feeling right now, I suppose. All you have right now are God's words, just like what I had at the time; nothing but words. And like you, I wanted something else, something more from God than just hearing His voice and listening to His Words. So, God said to me, 'And this shall be a token unto thee, that I have sent thee: When thou hast brought forth the people out of Egypt, ye shall serve God upon this mountain.'

"Well, gentlemen, if you will allow, let me start at the very beginning. You see, all of this was kind of new to me. This all began for me one day when I was minding my own business, just shepherding my father-in-law's herds out beside a large mountain in the Sinai desert. Yes, I was a goat herder, and I enjoyed a good, comfortable life because of it. But as I said, I was just minding my own business, thinking about my upcoming eightieth birthday and the party my wife was going to throw for me when, all of a sudden, I saw something extraordinary. I saw a bush that was on fire. But, my brothers, something drastically weird was going on. You see, the bush was not being consumed by the fire, and because of that, I was very amazed and extremely curious about it. So I began to walk over to get closer to it so I could see better. As I did, something else began to happen, a really truly frightening thing. You see, this flaming, fiery bush began to speak to me.

"Oh, boy. Now, let me ask you something. Have you or anyone you have heard of ever had a conversation with a flaming bush before?"

A low voice in the back of the group trying to break the extreme tension said, "Maybe Laura has."

Moses stopped and hesitated for a moment, "Laura? Oh. Laura Bush, you mean. Yes, well, as you say, she might have had many conversations with a flaming *Bush* before George stopped drinking that firewater he used to consume in great quantities. Yes! That is good.

"But getting back to what I was saying, maybe now you can see how I felt as this flaming bush began speaking to me, yes? Let me tell you, when the flaming bush first began to speak with me, I immediately thought I might have consumed some very bad mushrooms or maybe eaten the wrong kind of cactus buds. You know, things like this do not happen every day. Am I correct?

"But as I was saying, this flaming bush began to speak to me. It told me to take my shoes off because I was standing on holy ground. Well, let me tell you, that was not much of a problem at all. If I do say so myself, I moved pretty well for an eighty-year-old man right then. In fact, I do not recall ever moving any faster in my entire life up to that time, so it was not really much of a problem to get my shoes off. You see, when the bush had first begun to speak to me, it had scared me so badly that I had already instantly jumped about three quarters of the way out of my sandals. So, to undo the remaining one quarter left hanging on my feet was not a problem at all.

"Now, my brothers, let me be very candid and straightforward with you and tell you this. I was very, very frightened. There are no other ways to put this. I was scared. But suddenly, as I stood there, trembling all over, something else amazing began to happen. You see, it finally began to sink in to me, and I began to realize that I was not really having a conversation with a flaming bush after all. No. What was really happening was I was having a conversation with God. I mean, God was speaking with me. How wonderful is that? Who am I that God should speak with me?

"But then, shortly after I began to realize that it was God who was speaking with me, I began to feel something else. I began to feel

His love for me. No, He did not say at that time that He loved me, but I could feel it. Also, I could feel another thing. I could feel power surrounding me. Let me tell you, it was an awesome, unimaginable, extraordinary power. It was power that was greater than any power in the entire universe. Oh, and another was holiness. Oh, let me also tell you that I knew that I was ... well, let me just say this and quickly move on. I knew that I needed to quickly change my ways. You see, this was God's presence I was standing in, and I knew that I stunk like a slimy snake for lack of a better word.

"After I knew that it was God who was speaking to me, I knew that I had better listen up real good. So when God told me to go to Egypt and bring our people out of there, I had a pretty good feeling inside of me that it could be done. But I was not for sure that I was the correct person to do the job though. In my mind, I could think of several people who were more qualified than I was. Actually, any-one else, in my way of thinking, would have been better. So I argued with God to try to get Him to change His mind and to choose someone else.

"Now, my brothers, let me stop here and tell you something right now that will save you a lot of trouble in your life. Take my advice and don't do that. Don't argue with God. Just believe me. Take my word for it and you will be very happy that you did, okay?

"I quickly realized how futile it was to argue with God. Actually, He kind of convinced me of that rather quickly. You see, I made God so angry by arguing with Him that He put me on death row for a few minutes. Now, my brothers, you know what I mean about don't argue with God, don't you? Well, let me tell you, after being placed on death row, even if it was only for just a few minutes, I was extremely happy to change my mind and agree with Him that He probably knew better than I did what was best for me.

"So now, I knew that I had to go to Egypt. I had no other choice. But since I had to go to Egypt, I wanted some kind of assurances from God that He was going to protect me through this whole ordeal down there. You see, there was a warrant out for my arrest in Egypt for murder. If you remember, I had once killed an Egyptian. He deserved it, but that's another story for another day.

"So, anyway, in my way of thinking, I had come to the conclusion that I was kind of stuck between a rock and a hard place. If I went to Egypt, Pharaoh would probably arrest me and then kill me by burning all of my skin off with boiling oil one inch at a time. But if I didn't go to Egypt, God was going to kill me. So, let me ask you, which one would you have chosen?

"My brothers, this was a no-brainer. Yes, I chose God. I figured that I at least had a chance with Him. But I still wanted some kind of assurances that I would be safe. I wanted God to show me some of His awesome power that I had felt. I mean, we are not talking about just anyone here. We are talking about God. I said God, the all-powerful creator of the world and everything in it.

"So, I wanted God to give me some assurances that consisted of a few demonstrations of His power. You know, like blowing the top off a mountain would do. Something like that. I was not greedy. I would accept any demonstration of His power that consisted of a volcano, an earthquake, a hurricane … oh, that was the one I really wanted, a hurricane in the middle of the Sinai desert. Yes, that would have convinced me rather quickly.

"But now, let me get to the point of my story. My brothers, God did not do any of those things for me. He did not give me any demonstrations of His power whatsoever. All He did was give me a bunch of His words, just like you have here tonight. Well, because this was all I had, let me tell you, I was kind of discouraged, just like you are. I can tell you with all honesty that I was in the same boat then as you are tonight. But, my brothers, with nothing else but God's words to go with me, I eventually left on my journey and started going toward Egypt. And as I was walking in that direction, everything God had told me kept running over and over in my mind.

"Then, suddenly, it hit me. Yes, I saw the light. God had told me, 'And this shall be a token unto thee, that I have sent thee: When thou hast brought forth the people out of Egypt, ye shall serve God upon this mountain.' Don't you see, brothers? Are your eyes so covered that you can't see? God told me that I would be worshiping Him on the mountain with the burning bush *after* I had returned from Egypt. So, this meant that Pharaoh could not harm me. It meant that I was coming back.

"Oh, don't you see? At that moment, I realized what the words God had said to me were really saying. Then, all it took was for me to believe his words, and after that, everything turned out just marvelous. Oh yes. Oh yes. You see. You see. Oh, thank you, Jesus, my Lord."

Right then, every man inside of the huge military bunker began to weep. There were some thirty men all together congregated in the room. All of them were battle-hardened Israeli combat veterans who were proud, strong, and courageous, and all of them had tears running down their faces like little children.

"Yes. You see, brothers, you don't need anything else here tonight for God to prove Himself to you. You have His words, and that is all you need. If God said it, that settles it. Oh, praise You, my God. Praise You, my Savior. Praise You, my Redeemer. Praise You, my Protector. Praise You, my Provider. Praise You."

# CHAPTER 26

fter being elected and while Russia was still in the process of moving her troops southward, His Supreme Highness, Excellency Angel Abaddon, supreme leader of the new, United Confederation of Nations, sent out an urgent message to every nation and country on earth. His message was:

> We request with all urgency for you to attend a meeting of the most critical kind. The meeting will be held in the amphitheater at the headquarters of what used to be called the European Economic Development Commission. The commission has now been renamed the United Confederation of Nations. The meeting will begin at 8:00 a.m. April 15. We ask you to please send the highest-ranking official from your country. If at all

possible, we ask that the actual leaders of each country attend. Again, we repeat, this message is of the *utmost urgency*.

On the day mentioned, his Supreme Highness, Excellency Abaddon was standing before an assembly of over two hundred leaders or delegates from every country of the world. In his hand was a long pointer. He was using it to show places of interest of what was being shown on a large screen behind him.

"My fellow leaders, these pictures you are looking at were taken by our satellites. What these pictures are showing is the tremendous destruction that has befallen the United States of America." At that, he almost spit the next words out of his mouth. "The destruction and devastation brought about by the criminally deranged barbarians who are in charge of the country of Russia. This attack, my fellow leaders, was a dastardly and cowardly crime committed against a totally unsuspecting country.

"With all of the strange disappearances and other calamities that have recently taken place, the United States was completely defenseless. As you probably are aware, many of her top leaders were part of the disappearances. Plus, the four leaders of their military and the head of their CIA were killed in a terrorist bombing attack shortly before these disappearances began. Those things, plus the fact that their president and his chief of staff have also disappeared had left the United States totally unaware of what Russia was about to do.

"Inside of America, anarchy was running wild and unabated because many of her law enforcement personnel were missing. Plus, massive numbers of her military personnel were also missing. This is why I say that America was taken by complete surprise. As you might know, the United States did not return even one missile toward the cowardly barbarians. Not one.

"Also, at the same time of the missile attack on America, Russia's navy, using tactical nuclear weapons, attacked every American ship and submarine and naval base that she had. And at the same time those attacks were being carried out, the Russian air force was launching tactical nuclear weapons against every American army and air force base located in the different countries around the world. I am sure many of those attacks happened in some of your countries as well.

"My fellow leaders, do not be deceived. This was a well-planned attack that was not designed to just cripple or wound the United States. This was an attack that was meant to completely destroy America. And leaders of the world, let me assure you, Russia accomplished her goal of total devastation."

Every person in the room looked on in complete horror as the pictures slowly rotated on the screen. Nothing in the history of humankind had ever come close to the carnage they were seeing. Millions of people were lying dead. An entire country completely laid to waste, along with what appeared to be her entire population suddenly and tragically dead.

His Highness briefly turned the screen off and then turned to face his audience and said, "Ladies and gentlemen, if you think these pictures you have just seen were awful, let me explicitly warn that the next pictures you are going to view are not for the timid of heart or for the weak of stomach. I must warn you of that. Some of you might get very nauseous from seeing the images. If you do, under your seats are some bags. These are for you to use if you feel like you must. But I insist that you use the bags. I do not want a single person leaving this room. You must see what I am about to show you. Do I have your complete approval?"

A low rumble ensued as everyone in the room murmured an approval. At that, His Highness flipped a switch and the screen came back on. But before he started rolling through the pictures, he began to tell them some more.

"The pictures you are about to see are live pictures. Yes, pictures that are being broadcast even as I speak. Because Russia used neutron bombs on America's cities, the infrastructure of these cities pretty much remain just as they were before the attack, except all of the people from those cities are now lying dead in their homes, places of business, the streets, and the gutters. But because of the neutron bombs that were used, America's electricity, her phones, her water supplies, and her TV stations are all still intact and operating normally. This means that whatever was showing on the televisions at the time of the attack are still being broadcast and will continue to broadcast because no one is alive to turn them off.

"Now, what I am going to show you first is a picture of Tracy Boric, the number one news anchor for their Continental Broadcasting News. Most of you know who this woman is or, excuse me, was. This program was their top-rated newscast."

At that, he flipped a switch and the screen switched to show Tracy Boric sitting in a nicely upholstered leather chair behind her news desk. She was smartly dressed in a custom-tailored women's suit. At first glance, she looked perfectly normal. Except after His Highness zoomed in for a closer examination, you could see that only the left side of her face appeared to be normal. It appeared that she was staring straight ahead out of her left eye. But the entire right side of her head had received a full dose of the intense radiation that had been released from the bomb that had exploded only one quarter of a mile directly above their studio.

From the bottom of her right jaw up to the top of her head, the skin had been completely burned or melted away. Much of the skin appeared to be of a gluelike substance and was hanging down in large strips from the jaw bone, which was now almost completely exposed. What was most horrifying to look at though was much of the skin that was hanging off the jaw appeared to be liquefied. It was even slowly dripping off in little liquefied droplets, like a very slowly dripping water faucet. Where the right eye used to be was an opening filled with what looked like a smashed purple grape or chewed-up black olive. Where the nose used to be was completely open, other than you could see whatever it is that the human body has in it behind a person's face. Her tongue had slipped through the opening of her jaw on the right side of her face, and it was swollen to more than six times its normal size. It actually looked like a giant rubber balloon ready to burst. The blood that had been inside of her head had fallen out of it, not flowed or dripped but fallen out in huge gobs, and it left stained streaks of red on the pure whiteness of her exposed facial bones. Without a doubt, the world-famous news personality they were accustomed to seeing had turned into one of the most horrific, chillingly monstrous scenes many of them had ever before witnessed. It tragically looked like a Frankenstein experiment gone horribly wrong.

As the picture was being shown, many of the people in the auditorium reached under their seats and grabbed the bags. All over the vast hall could be heard the sounds of vomiting and painful moaning. His Highness did not stop though. He had a point to make. From there, he began to show more and more pictures of grossly deformed or partially melted, bloated up, dead human beings, with all of them looking like the skin on their bodies had just turned to liquid and begun to fall off in long, bloody rivers of red.

By the time His Highness had shown the last picture, only four or five persons out of the full complement of people sitting in the room had not reached for the bags. But to His Highness's pleasure, the pictures had the exact effect he had hoped and planned for.

He began to speak once again, but this time, in a soft, caring, fatherly tone of voice. "I am so sorry that you had to sit through this and see what you have just seen. But I felt it was so important for you to see with your own eyes the absolute carnage and human grief that the Russians have perpetrated against civilized humanity. My friends, what they have done is almost beyond the scope of human belief and reasoning. Yes, if you combine what the Russians have done, along with the grief and carnage that has been created in our world due to the strange disappearances and uncountable injuries and deaths that occurred from all of the accidents that ensued from those, it truly does stretch the sanity of our beings to their fullest limit.

"My friends, these are drastic days, strange days, days in which we are not sure if there will ever be another one to follow the one we live in now. That is why these drastic days call for drastic measures. Now my friends, I am going to show you a few more pictures—"

But before he could finish the sentence, a loud roar of, "No. No," reverberated throughout the room.

His Highness was momentarily taken by surprise, but he quickly regained his composure. "No, no, my friends. Oh no. The next pictures are not the same as you have just witnessed. We have all seen enough of those. Am I correct? But let me warn you. The next ones you are going to see could very well soon turn into those."

He again flipped the switch, and the screen lit up. "Now, ladies and gentlemen, let me emphatically state that the Russian barbarians who have committed these awful atrocities against America are not yet finished. No. Their hunger and thirst for human blood is still raging unabated and unsatisfied. Leaders, watch closely now as I show you her next victims."

He pushed the button on the switch and began showing satellite pictures of Russia's massive troop buildup in Turkey and along her southern border. "Yes, leaders, look closely. From these pictures, it is very clear what Russia's next target is. It is the oil in the Middle East."

This time, he paused for a full thirty seconds before continuing, "Must I tell you what that would mean if Russia is allowed to accomplish her mission?"

He paused once more, letting people think about what he had just said. Finally, he continued.

"If, I repeat, *if* Russia is allowed to accomplish her goal, you and you and you and you and you"—he was pointing his finger at the delegates in the room—"will all become her slaves. She will rule over you. Yes, Russia will rule the world if that were to happen. Now, you have already seen how bloody, brutal, and heartless those barbarians are. So let me ask you, do you want to live under her control as slaves?"

The entire room exploded in a thunderous, "No. No. No."

"Good. Neither do I. Leaders, as I said earlier, drastic days call for drastic measures. Two days ago, in a conference meeting room inside of this same building, every member of this organization—which, up to then, had been called the European Economic Development Commission—decided no longer to be just an economic alliance of nations.

"No. We decided to become something much more powerful, something much more magnificent, something much more united. Yes. We decided to unite as one *country*. And we decided to unite under a new name, the United Confederation of Nations. Yes, leaders, we decided to unite. And we voted to unite under one flag, one military, one government, and one leader."

At that moment, the applause was almost deafening.

Finally, he was able to continue. "My friends, I must tell you that I consider it an extreme honor to have been chosen as that leader."

At that, the applause was even more deafening.

Eventually, though, he was able to continue.

"Now, let me tell you what a leader is and what a leader does. First of all, a leader is one who is fearless, not afraid of anyone or anything, not even the Russians. And the world we are living in at this moment is a very fearful world to some."

That brought a small stifled laugh from around the room.

"Secondly, a leader is one who can take control of a situation and bring it to a satisfactory conclusion. Thirdly, a leader is one who is honest and fair and generous. He is loving and kind to his subjects. My friends, I could go on and on, but the point I am trying to make is this. We, all of us in this room, every nation and country here, need to unite as one nation. No," he screamed. "Not *need* to unite; we *must* unite if we are going to survive!"

This last action brought loud shouts of cheers and yells of, "Yes. Yes. Unite. Unite." The cheering went on for several minutes.

Finally, they began to settle down enough for His Highness to continue.

"My friends, I would be extremely humbled and greatly honored if you would dare to follow what has already been started by our United Confederation of Nations and would choose me to be your leader too."

Again, cheers and shouts of, "Yes," filled the room.

"Oh, thank you. Thank you. Let me state, I am so honored and grateful. I am truly humbled by this. Yes. Thank you. Well, now that we are united as one world, I believe that we should take action to stop the Russians. Do you agree?"

Again, loud shouts of, "Destroy them! Kill them!" erupted all over the convention.

"This is good, again. Well, I need to do something else first. I need to appoint a liaison to help me coordinate and unite your country's governments into our new one here. And I know just the man to accomplish this monumental task for me. He is my good friend and fellow co-worker, Performa Magor-Missabib. I need to tell you that Mr. Magor-Missabib's name means, 'fear on every side.' In fact, his name is found in the Bible in Jeremiah twenty, verse three. My friends, I guarantee Mr. Magor-Missabib will bring honor to his name against the Russians. Would you please agree to allow Mr. Magor-Missabib to become second in command?"

Again, shouts of confirmation filled the cavernous room.

"All right. This is so great. I am so proud to be standing here in front of all of you, my distinguished fellow leaders. Thank you so much, again. But now, back to the Russians. We need to unite our militaries as quickly as we can. This is the first step. Mr. Magor-Missabib will coordinate that with your governments as quickly as possible. But please, allow Mr. Magor-Missabib to contact you. He will bring every country onboard and in line in an orderly fashion.

"Now, that might take some time, and I am not sure we have that much time. The Russians could make their move any day. So, what I am going to do in the meantime is I am going to call fire, brimstone, hail, rain, and earthquakes of *biblical* proportions down on top of them and completely destroy them. I am going to cause them all to turn against and kill each other. I am going to completely destroy all of those diabolical armies until not one person is left alive. You will see. You will see."

# CHAPTER 27

Very early in the morning, a loud crackle of static electricity came from a short-wave radio sitting on a table in the room. Every man in the Israeli command bunker sat up and came to full attention. Due to the electromagnetic waves still running rampant throughout the earth's atmosphere that were caused by Russia's nuclear attack on the United States, the radio kept breaking up.

Finally though, a voice from a forward observer located near the topmost dam on the Euphrates River inside of Turkey was able to break through enough to be understood. He was part of a group of six specially trained demolition experts clandestinely sent to destroy the dam and the one below it, hoping to flood the land and slow the advance of the massive storm cloud of troops moving against them.

"The Russians are on the move. I repeat, the Russians are coming. The Russians are coming. Do you copy?"

Upon hearing that, Premier Ben Joseph loudly cried out, "Moses, Elijah, tell us what we should do! Tell us and we will obey."

Moses spoke up. "First of all, tell all of your people up there to fall back and join up with us here. Then, as soon as they get here, my Premier, you and all of Israel will begin to see the glory of God as he fulfills his word."

"You mean fall back without blowing the dams?"

"Yes. Tell them to make their way back here as soon as they possibly can. By sending these men outside of your own borders, you have stepped into the shoes of God and have tried to usurp His authority. God wants to fight your battles! God wants the glory to show the entire world that He is *God!* He wants to prove to the world that the imitator who has caused terrible destruction and death upon the earth ever since man fell from grace is no longer the god of earth and mankind! So yes, get all of your men, wherever they might be, back inside the borders of Israel as quickly as possible.

# CHAPTER 28

By the middle of the morning the following day, in Baghdad, in Damascus, in Amman, in Tehran, in Cairo, in Tripoli—in fact, in every Arab and Islamic country surrounding Israel, the shouts of joy and the dances of victory could be heard and seen. Their Russian friends were coming to help them to completely destroy Israel. "Finally, after thousands of years, all of the worthless scum descended from Isaac are going to die!" they shouted.

In Baghdad, Iraq, a man by the name of Mohammad Immad—more accurately labeled the "mad executioner"—had recently ascended to become the sole ruler of Iraq. He had accomplished this in a very bloody and violent coup not too long after the Americans had pulled out of the country. He had taken the place of his good friend and mentor, Saddam Hussein, and was determined to rule the country in a fist tighter than Saddam had ever dreamed of doing. For the last several years before this, he had been in hiding in Syria until he felt safe enough and confident enough to return and launch his successful coup.

For all of those wasted years he had been cooped up in Syria, Hussein Immad had been itching almost uncontrollably for a war with Israel. He was consumed with so much hatred for the "filthy pig Jews", as he called them, that it totally consumed him. He wanted this war so that once and for all, they could totally destroy them and rid the whole earth of the worthless scum.

Ever since he had assumed power—which had resulted in the deaths of over sixty thousand Iraqis—he had dedicated himself to following completely in the footsteps of Saddam, only crueler. And just like Saddam had done, he also was calling for a *jihad* (holy war) against Israel throughout the entire Arab world. In fact, he had continued the efforts of Saddam to form "a Jerusalem army," whose sole objective was to recapture Jerusalem for the Arabs.

"And now, praise be to Allah and his prophet, Muhammad—may all blessings be upon him—by the extraordinary kindness and extreme generosity of my friends from the far north, the Russians, I am finally going to get my wish. Now, all of the worthless, despicable Jews in Israel are going to die," he yelled.

But at that particular moment, he was far from being prepared to go up against Israel. The surprising but completely welcomed offer of attack by the Russians had not given him much time to get prepared and organized. At that moment, his ragtag troops were still in the process of being assembled into their proper divisions and correct units. And things were not moving anywhere near as quickly as he desired.

In his almost overwhelming anxiety to kill the Jews, being behind in organizing his army had put him in a very foul mood. And as what usually happens when he gets in these kind of moods, he began screaming, and cursing, and threatening to kill everyone in his sight. He even pulled his pistol out and was waving it all around,.

But within a few minutes the executioner's favorite unit called and reported they were online and almost ready to go. At that his whole demeanor changed dramatically. He went from a raving maniac to a benevolent father figure in less time than it takes to say, "I'm sorry." To all of his people, this phenomenon was so amazing, how their leader could instantly go from being Satan incarnate to being a benevolent god in just the blink of an eye.

The executioner connected to the call from his favorite unit, which happened to be his long-range missile launcher units—the ones the Americans never found because they had been smuggled across the border into Syria, along with him—reported that they were only about fifteen minutes away from being completely prepared and ready to go.

He had eighteen missiles left in his inventory. His only regret was that not all of them were carrying biological or chemical warheads. He wanted so badly to see, and watch, and laugh as the biological and chemical reactions from these weapons would begin to eat, and rot, and totally destroy all of the flesh on the Jews' bodies as they just stood there. These diabolical agents would actually eat all of the skin right off a person within a mere matter of minutes, and he wanted so much to watch and enjoy every minute of it. All but two of his missiles had these warheads. Unfortunately, the other two only carried high explosive warheads instead.

Now, in his great anxiety, thrill, and enjoyment, he ordered these units to get ready to launch as soon as they came fully online. Without getting Russian approval or giving them any notice of his intentions, he determined that he was going to be the first to attack and kill the worthless Jews. With that in mind, he ordered that nine of the missiles be targeted toward Jerusalem and the other nine to target Tel Aviv.

I will be the first to attack, and I will destroy the two most important cities in Israel. Then, my Russian benefactors will see how great and wonderful I really am, and they might just allow me to occupy and rule over what little might remain of that worthless country, he thought.

The fifteen minutes slowly expired, and the units finally completed their targeting procedures. They were lined up and reported that they were ready to go. Immad was barely able to contain his excitement. His joy was almost bursting at the seams. He knew this was going to be his greatest crowning moment. By some kind of a miracle, he had risen to become his own people's great leader, benefactor, savior, and protector. After this, he would be the great leader of the entire Arab world by being the first to bring burning, blazing death to the Zionist pigs in Israel.

Suddenly, he worked up a huge wad of saliva and then spit the thick mucus out of his mouth and down onto the ground. "Oh. I hate even saying the word Israel. Soon, though, there will be nothing left of Sarah's children. They will all be gone. They will all be dead. But there will be great spoils left for Hagar's family to reap. Great spoils," he screamed.

Immad picked up the radio. "My brothers, this is a great day and a great moment for our great country. This is the day we have been waiting for many thousands of years to finally arrive, the day when Isaac's descendants will be no more, the day when every last Jew in Israel will die. Today, we will extract our revenge for Abraham's awful mistake by sending our mother, Hagar, and her son, Ishmael, into the desert to die. Yes, today, we will finally claim our rightful inheritance from Isaac's descendants that should have been ours all along. So, my great and mighty warriors, fire. Yes, fire your missiles. Kill the Jews!" he screamed.

# CHAPTER 29

At that precise moment, Russia was engaged in the lengthy and extremely complicated process of moving her troops into Syria and on into Jordan before attacking Israel. They were very disappointed that Israel had not yet launched any preemptive strikes against the Arabs. And from the way things were looking, they were going to not only have to destroy Israel but also have to destroy all of the Arabs too.

But from the very beginning phases of moving their troops into these Arab countries, it had been almost a complete disaster. Russia was trying to move over two million of her own soldiers and integrate them into a coalition force with the Arab militaries. Unfortunately, they were in the unorganized and chaotic process of trying to assemble this huge contingent behind the totally confused and disorganized armies of Syria, Jordan, and Saudi Arabia. Plus, they were trying to assemble more of their troops with the equally disorganized and confused armies of Iraq and Iran.

Russia had convinced Syria, Jordan, and Saudi Arabia that they had the right to be the first ones to destroy Israel and that was why she was moving in behind them, for their support and to guarantee their success.

"Why should you allow Russia to steal your glory? This is the day you have been waiting for thousands of years to get here, so you reap the glory. You deserve it," the Russians said.

In actuality, her main goal was to trap the Arab armies between Israel and her own. Russia had to do this because for some unknown reason, the cowardly Jews had not yet launched preemptive attacks against the Arabs like Russia had been counting on. Jacob's Ladder had called for the Jews to attack and destroy the Arabs to assure Russia of success. Since that hadn't happened Russia was forced into the position of having to attack the Arabs from behind while Israel was killing them in the front.

Russia knew the Jews would eventually be forced to attack the Arabs once they crossed the border and invaded Israel. That is, unless Israel was just going to capitulate and allow itself to be slaughtered, but they knew that was not even a possibility. They knew the Jews were the most determined and hardened group of people in the entire world. No way would they lie down and allow themselves to be slaughtered. The commanders of the Russian forces were very concerned whether or not they would be able to kill all of the Arabs. For the life of them, they just could not figure out why Israel had not yet attacked.

"What are they waiting for? Come on out and fight like men. Don't be hiding behind your old women's skirts."

These were things they were saying amongst themselves.

"Are they waiting for their so-called supernatural God to save them? Well, we serve the god of the Russian premier. Only our god can save them. They should be on their knees, begging the god of the Russian premier to let them live and not die."

In Israel, one of the small outlying radar stations near the Jordanian border suddenly began to detect something on their screens. Eventually, they were able to count eighteen missiles heading their way. Apparently, they had been launched from Iraq.

"It appears that nine are targeted toward Jerusalem and the other nine toward Tel Aviv," they called in.

In the command bunker, the word was received.

"Men, it has started, but do not be afraid. Now with your own eyes you will see how God will fight for you!" Elijah shouted.

"What should we do, Elijah?" General Green, Supreme Commander of Israel's army, nervously asked. Even though he had been a believer in Jesus Christ for several years, he could not help but be very nervous. Everywhere Israel looked, they were surrounded by millions of enemy troops.

"General, continue standing still for the moment. Yes. Stand still and you will see the hand of God at work," Elijah replied.

In Syria, Saudi Arabia, and Jordan, with the confusion and disorganization of such massive troop movements in process, no one knew, nor even noticed, that the executioner had launched his missiles. Due to the extreme electromagnetic impulses in the atmosphere, none of their radar or detection units from any of the countries were working at that time. But at that exact moment, high above the ground, eighteen missiles that Iraq had originally purchased from Russia over twelve years before were screaming toward their targets.

But, suddenly, something totally unexpected went drastically wrong with the guidance systems on all but two of the missiles. Maybe it was caused by the electromagnetic impulses that were wildly fluctuating in the atmosphere. Or maybe it was caused by the hand of God because of the earnest prayers of two righteous, godly men standing in a bunker many miles away. But sixteen of the deadly missiles somehow retargeted themselves to fall way short of their desired destination. The other two carrying the high explosive warheads continued on their way toward Jerusalem. Twelve minutes later, those two hit.

But what they hit and totally and completely destroyed was the very last thing the Arab and Islamic people would have ever believed could happen. They hit and completely and totally destroyed the Dome of the Rock, the third holiest site in all of Islam and sacred to most Arabs.

But shortly before this happened, all sixteen of the other missiles that were carrying the chemical and biological agents fell directly on top of the Russian troops in both Syria, Jordan, and Saudi Arabia. And as they hit, uncontrollable chaos and absolute panic broke out in their ranks.

"Who is shooting at us? Where did that come from? What was that?" shouts from everywhere were screaming through the air.

Within seconds, everywhere their skin was exposed to the air, huge clusters began turning a brilliant bright red like the color of a fire truck. Shortly after that, the skin began liquefying into some kind of jellylike substance. In seconds after that, it began falling off their bodies in huge chunks and clusters.

In complete horror and terror, the soldiers that had been hit with these chemical agents stood and watched as their own bodies began to be eaten up and falling apart before they crumpled to the ground, dead. In that short time period, agonizingly loud, tormented, and terrorized screaming echoed throughout the entire Russian ranks. At first, it started out slow but rapidly began echoing ever louder across the entire land as the Russian soldiers were being consumed alive by diabolical agents that only demonic minds could have conjured up.

As all of this was happening, and because of the huge localized gathering of millions of troops and equipment all located in close proximity to each other, more than a million soldiers were eaten alive.

In addition to this calamity, uncontrollable panic, chaos, and confusion ensued throughout all of the remaining soldiers. What was left of the remaining Russian troops grabbed their weapons and began firing on everyone. It didn't matter to them who they were shooting at. They were just determined they were going to take someone with them before they died.

The Arab troops being fired on by the Russians grabbed their weapons and began to fire back. Within a short period of time, from the eastern border of Israel all of the way to the eastern border of Iran, everyone had turned on each other, and suddenly, everyone was killing everyone else. In actuality, though, no one had any idea what they were doing other than firing their weapons and killing, and that was all that mattered to them.

The Russian troops in Turkey heard over intermittent radio contact about the surprise chemical and biological attack that was taking place in Syria, Jordan, and Saudi Arabia. They began assembling the best they could and as fast as they could. Then, in a very haphazard manner, they began moving southward toward Israel. Within a few hours, millions of troops began crossing the border of Turkey, but as these Russian and Turkish armies were hurriedly moving into this area, it suddenly began to rain again. But this was not just any rain; hard, drenching, pouring rain began falling. Within minutes, the rain suddenly turned into a downpour of such intensity that it was impossible to even see more than a few feet in any direction. In fact, the rain was so intense that it was almost like solid sheets of hard liquid falling from the sky.

Along with the rain, the mild, pleasant breeze that had been blowing suddenly picked up such speed and strength that it immediately turned into a howling, revolving dervish of such intensity that most of the rain was being driven sideways, straight into the troops and equipment. The wind was so strong that it picked up several of the troop carriers and other types of vehicles and began flinging them through the air, destroying the equipment and killing all of the personnel onboard.

This driving, intense rain and howling dervish wind was bad enough by itself, but what was really worrisome, bothersome, and especially frightening to these armies was the fact that this tremendous rain and hurricane strength wind were coming out of the most beautiful, sunlit, bright blue sky anyone had ever seen. It was totally barren without any clouds in it at all.

It was not long after the dreadful sheets of rain began falling that the vast combined armies became completely bogged down in the mud and slush. This was after the lead elements had advanced into some long, narrow valleys that were situated in-between some very steep, mountainous areas. The units in the front of the columns were forced to come to a complete halt while the units following behind quickly bunched up behind them. Because of the mountainous terrain and steep, narrow, zigzagging roads they were trying to maneuver on, they immediately found themselves in a very treacherous situation. There were not any places to turn around or any other possible routes of escape to take at the moment. They were completely, totally stuck. It was the worst traffic jam in the history of mankind.

But then, in addition to the tremendous sheets of rain that were pouring down on them, it suddenly began to hail. But this was not just any hail. These were huge chunks of ice that suddenly began to fall out of the sky. Many of the chunks weighed over one hundred pounds and were at least the size of basketballs. And as these huge chunks of ice fell, hundreds of thousands of soldiers were immediately killed. In addition to that, many more millions of dollars of their supplies and equipment were damaged and destroyed. All of the damage and destruction done to their equipment and the vast multitudes of deaths made it even more impossible to move or evacuate anywhere. This vast multitude of troops and equipment was stuck, permanently.

But still while all of this calamity was going on, just in case this was not bad enough, God's hand moved once more and the cataclysm happened, something totally unexpected, something of such magnitude that it was almost unimaginable. A massive, earthquake erupted. From the tallest mountains to the lowest valleys throughout the entire Middle East, including Turkey to the north and the countries of North Africa that were coming against Israel from the south, all began violently shaking. All of this drastically added to the terrorizing fear, the total confusion, and the unabated panic that had erupted throughout all of the combined invading armies. Because of this, it caused even more widespread killing and destruction of each other. Plus, in many places throughout the area where there seemed to be large concentrations of troops, the earth suddenly split wide open and swallowed multitudes of these enemies of God.

Eventually, in a very short period of time, the Russian, Syrian, Jordanian, and Saudi Arabian armies just about totally destroyed each other. For the invading armies stuck in valleys between the mountains; huge rocks; boulders; and, in some cases, entire sections of mountains collapsed and fell down on top of them. For the ones coming up from the south, the earthquake made the earth open up and swallow the majority of them.

There was nowhere to run and nowhere to hide. There was nothing else they could do other than stand in fear and watch as the hand of God snuffed out their very existence.

# CHAPTER 30

is Supreme Highness, Excellency Abaddon, was sitting in his newly appointed and very richly adorned new office that he personally called his *throne room*. Performa Magor-Missabib was sitting on the sofa facing His Highness. They were discussing the complex issues of combining most of the world's governments into one.

A soft knock came on the door.

"Come," His Highness called out. His secretary walked into the room holding several stacks of papers in her hand. "Your Supreme Highness, Excellency Abaddon, look at all of these faxes and messages that are pouring in. They are all saying things like, 'Your predictions all came true, just as you declared,' or, 'Everything you said was like a prophecy; they have all come true,' or the best ones of all, and there are a lot of these: 'You are not a mortal; you are a god. You have done just as you stated. We have united under a god.'"

A huge smile wrapped across his face, extending from ear to ear. He leaned back in his chair, reached up with his arms and placed his hands behind his head locking them together. He looked back at his secretary and then said, "God, huh? They called me a god? Yeah. I like that."

After his secretary walked out, he turned to face Performa Magor-Missabib again. "Do you know what reports she's talking about? I haven't been monitoring any news reports for the last day."

"No, your Highness, with all of this other pressing business of uniting the world into one, I haven't been able to watch any news reports either. But let me turn the television on and we'll see what's going on."

He got up from his chair and walked over to the TV. It was already tuned to ONE World News. The reporter was going over all of the destruction that had just recently taken place throughout the entire Middle East. She was talking about how the earth had suddenly opened up and swallowed hundreds of thousands of soldiers from the combined armies of Sudan, Libya, and Egypt.

From there, she moved on to how hurricane-strength wind, hard-driving rain, and huge hailstones had suddenly developed over Israel, Syria, Lebanon, and even up in Turkey, which had caused the deaths and destruction of the entire combined forces of the Russian and Turkish armies.

She spoke about how Iraq had launched eighteen missiles, supposedly against Tel Aviv and Jerusalem, but how all of them had gone off target. She mentioned how sixteen of them had fallen directly on top of the Russian troops and how all of those missiles had carried either chemical or biological agents. She spoke of how those agents had caused the flesh on the soldier's bodies to liquefy and fall off them and how, shortly after that, the combined armies all turned against each other and began killing each other, and about how the other two missiles had totally and completely destroyed the Dome of the Rock mosque in Jerusalem.

The only item she failed to mention that His Highness had mentioned in his speech as he accepted the leadership of the world was the part about "bringing fire down from heaven on Russia."

# CHAPTER 31

At the time of Russia's surprise nuclear missile attack on the United States, one lone American submarine was slowly cruising under the solid sheets of ice that cover the North Pole. This was the one and only sub, or ship for that matter, that the Russian navy had lost track of before their attack. The last reports Russia had gathered on this sub was that it was in dry-dock, undergoing major renovations. The reports had said it would be out of service for at least another six months.

In actuality, the sub that appeared to be in dry-dock and undergoing major work was simply a plywood mockup. The Americans always kept a mockup ready whenever they wanted to try to escape the detection of Russian satellite spying. But almost one month earlier, when they had pulled the mockup into dry-dock, the real American sub had silently sailed under the thick, solid ice of the North Pole.

During the entire time they had been under the ice, the American sub had no ability to communicate with anyone. They were in their own, little, private world. But the mission they were on was to make sure no eyes or ears were watching them. Their orders were to cruise under the ice, wait there for thirty days to ensure they no longer were in danger of detection from Russia or China, and then sail just south of Greenland to do their own cat-and-mouse game of monitoring of Russian subs and ships.

It had been twenty-six days that they had been hiding under the ice. At this time, the captain of the sub was filled with overwhelming fear and anxiety. His insides felt like they were being gnawed away by ravenous, hungry animals, and he hadn't slept at all in several days. He wanted to speak with someone—anyone; it didn't matter— who could explain to him where four of his crewmen had suddenly disappeared to. They had just suddenly disappeared into thin air right off his ship, vanished. One of them had even disappeared while the captain was speaking with him. The captain had just blinked his eyes, and—poof—the crewman had disappeared.

It would be a tremendous breach of naval policy for him to break communications silence. He knew that for sure. For the entire six months that this operation was supposed to last, they were ordered to adhere to complete communications silence. But he was mystified; worried; and most of all, very, very scared. As soon as he could, whatever it would take, even if it meant court marshal and dishonorable discharge from his beloved navy, he was going to talk with someone.

Of course, he would not be foolish. His first attempts would be on the top-secret, scrambled channels that could make it appear that his transmissions were coming from somewhere else in the world and from some other ship. They called it the ventriloquist's channel. But if those attempts failed for any reason, he was prepared to bring the sub to the surface and stand on top of the deck and scream at the top of his voice, "Someone, anyone, tell me what is going on."

After the disappearances, it took four more of the longest days any of the crew had ever experienced to traverse the dangerous remaining route. Every one of them was as worried and scared as the captain. In fact, when the disappearances had first occurred, there was almost a mutiny on board. Many of the crew had wanted to surface immediately, even if it meant it would have destroyed the sub by trying to rise up through tons and tons of solid ice. The captain was only able to save the ship and them by finally convincing them they had to wait until they could get clear of the solid sheets.

The four remaining days that it took to clear the ice passed ever so slowly. But finally, the sub sailed past the last remaining piece of continuous, solid ice and emerged into the deep, cold, black waters of the Arctic Ocean. Within just mere minutes of that, the commander ordered the sub to come up to periscope depth.

This also was against policy. But he was almost dying of anxiety to see what was out there. He didn't know what to expect. His instincts, in fact, everything inside of him was telling him that the earth had suddenly been visited by aliens. No matter what, though, even if an ugly, scary-looking alien climbed on and peered back down through the periscope at him, he was going to take a look and also get some quick coded communications sent off.

As the sub came up and reached periscope depth, this was also the level where he could safely send out the communications buoys that would float to the surface and would allow them to receive and transmit messages while the sub remained underwater. But immediately upon the buoys reaching the surface, they suddenly began receiving urgent, top secret coded communiqués that were being sent to him from the ARC channel.

At this, the captain almost had a heart attack. He knew right then that something very, very bad had gone wrong in the world. *You don't get messages from ARC unless it is the end of the world,* he knew. "Man, something has gone wrong. Something terribly, terribly *bad* has gone wrong," he yelled to no one in particular.

The communiqués were coming to him on the top-secret, Automatic Response Channel (ARC) from one of the United States' top-secret military satellites floating twenty-two thousand miles above the earth. But the ARC channel was only to be used as a last-ditch effort of communications if every other form had been destroyed.

An example would be if the United States were to come under a surprise nuclear attack and had lost all other means of communications, then ARC would begin transmitting continuous coded messages. This was an automatic backup system in case the codes for the nuclear missiles had been lost or destroyed, or like the president of the United States fleeing the country and leaving the football behind. ARC had a backup copy and would continue to send out these messages until some ship, some aircraft, or something responded to them. Then, once the satellite received a response, it would automatically lock onto the position of whoever had responded. After that, within seconds, it would begin transmitting all of the codes that were necessary to respond to the attack. In other words, the launch codes and targets for all of the nuclear missiles he was carrying on his ship would be transmitted to it.

ARC worked by tracking all incoming missiles from where they had been launched. It would then calculate and determine how best to respond to those targets. After that, it would send those coordinates and the missile launch codes to the vessel that had confirmed its earlier responses. In this case, the last remaining American submarine, the *Phoenix*.

His thoughts were going crazy. *The ARC is a last resort means of communication. You get a message from ARC, it means only one thing: launch your missiles. Man, either aliens have kidnapped the entire world and we are the only ones left, or all hell has broken out in the world.* And at the moment, he didn't know which scenario he preferred best. *The world has gone completely mad and totally insane,* he knew. He also knew that whatever had snatched his men from his submarine probably had snatched a lot more people from land, maybe all of them. Now, not only was he consumed with terror in every pore of his body because of his men disappearing, but apparently, the aliens that took his men had destroyed the United States too. That could be the only reason he was being ordered to fire his missiles. It had almost brought him to the point of complete hysteria and total insanity.

The communiqués continued to come in to his ship. There were five of them altogether. As fast as they would come in, his men were working on decoding them as quickly as possible. After the first one had been decoded, though, every man in the area became as pale as a sheet and felt like they were going to faint.

"My God, we're being ordered to fire our missiles. The unthinkable has happened. The unimaginable has happened. This is just totally, completely unbelievable," slipped out of the captain's mouth.

After that, the remaining messages were the codes needed to unlock the missiles and to set the final targets.

At that point, the captain was completely stunned and confused. *How come the targets are all for countries that used to be in the old Soviet Union? Did the aliens land there and take over? Have they made Russia their launching pad? Or have those countries developed some kind of a new super weapon that can snatch people away and make them disappear from even on submarines under the North Pole?* he wondered.

The men in the control room began to function in an almost robotic manner as they were completing the work needed to be done to launch. Everyone had gone through so much training for this moment that they went through the motions automatically. No one wanted to *think* about what they were doing.

Within a few short hours, the sub finally reached the point called for in the messages for them to launch their missiles with the greatest accuracy. Upon arriving there, they hurriedly locked in the final codes. Within minutes of that, one by one, the keys were simultaneously turned in the launch boxes that set the missiles flying toward their targets.

The commander knew that his sub, by itself, carried much more explosive firepower than all of the combined bombs, rockets, bullets, etc., from all of the armies from every nation that were expended during the six years World War II had raged on in the world. In fact, one single nuclear missile by itself carried at least one full year's worth of explosive power; such was the almost unimaginable power of thermonuclear hydrogen weapons. So the combined destruction that all twenty-four of his missiles, along with all of their multiple warheads, would be enough to completely destroy Russia. It would be just like fire and brimstone falling out of the sky and burning the entire nation to smithereens. But missiles had also come from other countries that formerly were part of the old Soviet Union, and some of his missiles were targeted for there also.

As soon as all of his missiles had been launched and there was no turning back now, the captain couldn't help but wonder if he was shooting at aliens or human beings.

*What if it was not aliens who have taken my men? What if, right now, I have just launched my missiles against the former Soviet Union?* "Oh, God, please forgive me," he cried.

He quickly did the math in his head. If his missiles hit their intended targets, and there was no doubt they should, anywhere from 500 million up to one billion people or more could very likely die. And he was totally and completely responsible for that.

Not long after the missiles had been launched and were on their way, the captain walked into his stateroom. In his confused and tormented mind, he was thinking, *four men on my boat suddenly disappeared into thin air without a trace or explanation. Also, there is a distinct possibility that aliens have landed and destroyed the United States, or I've just become the largest mass-murderer in the history of mankind.* It was just too much. In a drawer next to his bed, he kept a military-issued .45-caliber pistol. Shortly thereafter, *kaboom!* echoed throughout the ship.

At the time of the invasion by Russia and all of her allies, Moses and Elijah had stayed inside of the command bunker with Premier Emanuel Ben Joseph and the rest of the military leaders of Israel. Moses's speech had built faith and trust into the men's spirits. They began to believe that if God's Word had been true for Moses back then, surely His Word would be true for them now. Moses kept proclaiming the Words of God: "I change not. I am the same Yesterday, Today, and Forever."

As the invasion by Russia and her allies began—who Elijah said was the Gog Ezekiel had written about in his book—Moses and Elijah told the men to stand still and let God fight for them.

"Just stand still and watch!" they shouted.

So for the first several hours of the invasion, all of them stood and watched in complete awe and wonderment as the hand of God moved and destroyed His enemies.

Yes, God fought the battle against the Russians and their Arab allies and destroyed them completely. There was absolutely no other explanation. And because of it, all Israel stood in awe and wonderment. At that time, not one person in all of Israel was found who would deny God. Not all turned to Him, but no one denied Him.

Eventually, Moses turned to the military commanders and told them, "You have seen the hand of God at work. There is no denying it. Now, you go and put the final destruction on all of the other countries who have come up against you and God will give you the complete victory. Do not leave a single one of your enemies alive. Cleanse the land of this demonic invasion."

In just a matter of a few hours, God delivered all of the surrounding countries who had dared to come against Israel into Israel's hand. There were great shouts of victory throughout the entire land.

Moses then told the leaders, "Go now. Occupy the land that God originally promised to give to Abraham, all of the land that was promised to him. Not once have you ever lived in *all* of the land that God gave to you. But now, it is yours. God has delivered it to you."

Moses and Elijah turned to Emanuel Ben Joseph and said, "Come with us, Emanuel. God is with you, Ben Joseph. We want to take you to a place where something extraordinary happened approximately two thousand years ago."

A little later on, while riding in an army command vehicle and on the way to where they wanted to take him, Moses handed Premier Ben Joseph the Bible. He said, "Premier, turn in the Bible to Matthew, chapter seventeen, beginning with verse one, and read through verse eight."

"'And after six days Jesus taketh Peter, James, and John his brother, and bringeth them up into an high mountain apart, And was transfigured before them: and his face did shine as the sun, and his raiment was white as the light. And behold, there appeared unto them Moses and Elias talking with him,'" he read.

The premier glanced over at Moses and Elijah and said, "So, this isn't your first trip back here, I see. Do you do this often, come back from the dead, so to speak?"

Elijah replied, "No. This is only the second time for us. But after we leave this time—and let us tell you, our leaving will be something spectacular that everyone in the entire world will see—we will come back one more final time three and a half years later. Then, at that time, we will spend a thousand years on this earth with Jesus Christ as He reigns as Lord and King over the entire world."

The premier smiled and turned back to reading the Bible out loud. "'Then answered Peter, and said unto Jesus, "Lord, it is good for us to be here: if thou wilt, let us make here three tabernacles; one for thee, and one for Moses, and one for Elias." While he yet spake, behold, a bright cloud overshadowed them: and behold a voice out of the cloud, which said, "This is my beloved Son, in whom I am well pleased; hear ye him." And when the disciples heard it, they fell on their face, and were sore afraid. And Jesus came and touched them, and said, "Arise, and be not afraid." And when they had lifted up their eyes, they saw no man, save Jesus only.'"

Taking a very deep breath, the premier exclaimed, "So, you are telling me, from my reading of this scripture, that you two appeared to Jesus and His disciples because He was the Messiah. And what you want to convince me of is that this Jesus was the true, real Messiah. Am I right so far? Yes? Good. So, if you … uh … you know what? I've just seen too much stuff with my own eyes come true from what you two have already said to *not* believe. If you tell me that Jesus, the old prophet, was the Christ, I believe."

"Ah. God is really with *you* now, *Emanuel* Ben Joseph," Moses proclaimed. "God has revealed this to your heart. Now, ask Jesus, the true Christ, to come and live inside of you. His Word declares, in Revelation chapter three, beginning in verse twenty, 'Behold, I stand at the door and knock: if any man hear my voice, and open the door I will come in to him, and will sup with him, and he with me.'

"Premier Ben Joseph, do you want to answer the knocking on your heart's door right now? You hear Him knocking. In your heart right now, you feel emptiness inside of it, don't you? That emptiness is there because no one is living inside of it. It's empty. Jesus Christ wants to move in and take up residence. He says, 'I will come in.' Premier Ben Joseph, if you will allow Him to come into your heart, it will never be empty again."

"Yes, I do want to. But how … what do I say … or do?"

Repeat this simple little prayer after me, my dear man. 'Jesus, I recognize that you are the Christ, God's own Son, the true savior and forgiver of all sins. I stand before you, knowing that I am missing something in my life, because of the hole I feel in my heart right now. There is emptiness inside there. But there is also a longing for it to be filled. I believe that the emptiness I am feeling is because I do not know you personally, Jesus. Now, I would like to get to know you. Yes, I will answer the door and let you come in. You said that you would. So please do."

"Ah, Premier Ben Joseph, Jesus Christ has come in. Yes, it is all over your face. I see the grin just about ready to burst from ear to ear. My brother, you are really a true brother now, a brother in Christ. Welcome to the real family of God."

remier Butin and the rest of his top generals and military advisers had all come out of hiding from under the Kremlin. They had spent only a little more than twenty-four hours in the nuclear blast-proof bunker. They no longer felt like they had anything to fear. They knew that they had completely annihilated and destroyed the United States of America.

Also in the room was the president of the United States, Hussein Anwar and his chief of staff, Darwah Policy. They were sitting in chairs with their hands cuffed in front of them and shackles on their feet.

After their civilian plane landed in Moscow, the premier had them brought in before him and his generals like Roman Caesars had done to their captured kings and nobles. As far as the premier was concerned, these two men were spoils of war.

He turned to the president and asked, "Why did you leave your country and come here? What made you leave your wife there to die while you and your henchman escaped?"

Hussein Anwar stared right into the eyes of the premier. Finally, he spoke. "You promised me I would be second in command in the new one world order."

"So, you fled your country, leaving it in the dire straits it was in, and came here?"

"Premier Butin, I do not care at all about the United States. My goal in life is to be ruler or co-ruler of the entire world; not just one country but all countries."

"But what about your wife? How could you just leave her behind?"

"My wife was too distraught to listen to me after our children disappeared. I had no choice but to leave her behind. I told her I was coming here. I told her I would soon be co-ruler of the world with you. But I couldn't reason with her. All she did was lie on the floor on her face, screaming to God to forgive her of her sins and take her to heaven to be with our kids. I couldn't make her understand anything. So, I left her there. It's her fault she's now dead. But I have heard that there are hundreds, or even thousands, of beautiful, lonely Russian women looking for a real man. Well, that's me. I'm here."

The premier sat staring at this conceited, narcissistic fool with disgust. Finally, he turned his face away and called for a guard to come in. Immediately, a big, burly Russian hurried into the room.

"Igor, take this … this … *fool* and his demonic sidekick lapdog and throw them into the dungeons of Lubyanka Prison. I never want to see their faces again. Is that understood?"

"Yes, my premier. Of course, my premier."

An evil-looking snarl began curling around Igor's lips while his eyes began to sparkle with anticipation of what the premier was giving him permission to do. *It will be just like the old days, when it was said that whoever enters into Lubyanka Prison never comes out alive.* Igor knew the dungeons were where the government-trained assassins still practice their skills on the prisoners.

As soon as Igor had ushered both men out of the room, the premier turned his attention back to his generals. But neither they nor he were in any mood for celebration. Nor were they enjoying themselves in the least. In fact, they were all in a very grim mood. Jacob's

Ladder, their operation into the Middle East, was going extremely bad for them. They could not understand why. How could something seemingly so simple like annihilating and destroying a nation as small as Israel be causing them so much trouble? They had just destroyed a country at least a hundred times larger in size and many, many, many times more powerful. So, how could they themselves be getting defeated and possibly even destroyed by a country like Israel?

"Our men are falling like dead flies down there," the premier cried.

Everything was falling apart. It wasn't just one section or area of their operation that was going bad, but the entire operation was blowing up in their faces. In Jordan, in Syria, in Turkey, in Iraq, in Iran, everywhere. All of the troubles and problems they were having had their concentration and attention focused solely down there. It was just so unbelievable just how bad their luck had turned.

"The timing, to be stuck in the middle of mountainous passes and deep ravines at the exact time of an enormous earthquake was unbelievable. What could the odds have been for that to have happened and to have happened at the very worst possible site you could imagine? And this was not just any earthquake; this one was huge. It was one of the largest that would ever be recorded. Any place else and their men would have had a chance. But no, they had to be stuck in the mountains and valleys of Israel. Then, when the earthquake had hit, all of those mountains began to crumble and eventually collapsed down on top of their entire army. It had completely destroyed them. All of this is just totally, completely, unbelievable!" the premier yelled.

"The last reports we've received, and these are several hours old, said that between the combined armies, an estimated three million men have been killed. And on top of that, how could it be possible like what had happened in Syria and Jordan. How could allies and merging armies begin to go crazy and begin to kill each other? This, too, is unbelievable. All of what's happening is almost beyond the scope of understanding."

All they could do was shake their heads in wonderment and disbelief. The estimated number of dead in Syria, Jordan, and Saudi Arabia were at least ten to fifteen million. That number included all of the combined armies and the civilians that had been killed too. But nonetheless, it was still a staggering figure.

Now, they were receiving reports that Israel had finally launched counterattacks against certain countries, and the Jews were holding nothing back. These attacks were including tactical nuclear weapons. In some cases, though, they had discarded the tactical weapons and had used the full-blown, multi-megaton nuclear weapons they had developed.

From the last reports that had been received, Lebanon, Libya, Sudan, and Egypt were all but destroyed. At least there was not enough left of them to even form a battalion of infantry. Israel had also launched massive attacks against Turkey. It was assumed that those attacks must have just about destroyed that country completely because they had long since ceased receiving any reports from there at all.

Finally, a strong suspicion had been aroused by his generals and top military advisers that the chemical and biological missiles that had hit their men in Syria and Jordan must have come from either that madman in Iran or Hussein Immad in Baghdad. They all knew of Immad's enthusiasm and constant desire to fight the Jews. So, based on nothing else but these suspicions, they had ordered all of their units that they could still muster to break off from the fighting they were in and to move against Iraq and Iran. It did not matter to them which country had actually fired the missiles. They were going to get even no matter what. In their angry zeal and determination to get revenge, they were determined to completely destroy both countries.

In a certain way, though, they were hoping it had been Immad that had launched the missiles. Even if he had not been stupid enough to have fired his missiles, they had put up with the executioner long enough. His name even described him perfectly: Immad ("I'm *mad*.")

In addition to sending a huge number of ground troops toward Iran and Iraq, they also launched massive air attacks against both countries. This was being done even as they spoke. It did not matter to them that massive numbers of civilians were being killed in each country. In fact, they were targeting the cities and villages on purpose.

They were going to punish and destroy the executioner and his coun-
terparts in Iran completely. And they would not be satisfied until both
countries were barren wastelands unfit for human habitation.

In what was totally amazing to them, too, was the fact that this
particular operation was the only success they were having anywhere.
In fact, they were doing an excellent job of destroying Iran and Iraq.
The reports were that almost every city, town, village, and military
location in both countries had been completely demolished. The last
report they had received from one of their communication specialists, who was, by now, located deep in the heart of Iraq and who was
trying his best to maintain a sense of humor, even if it was warped,
had told them that as of that moment, there were not enough people
left in either country combined to even put on a decent camel race.

Yes, they had suffered massive losses in this operation too. But
it had been worth it. In the final analysis, though, this action would
have to be called a draw. What they were unaware of at that time
was that they had lost almost all of their aircraft and almost all of
their ground forces had also been completely destroyed.

The total death toll was staggering throughout the entire area of
the Middle East, Northern Africa, and Turkey. If one were to stop
and try to determine all of the total dead altogether, a guess as good
as anybody's would be anywhere from 50 to 100 *million* people now
lay dead or dying.

"Where could it have all gone wrong? *Where?* It is almost
like something supernatural has taken over and is destroying us,"
they complained.

The old premier and his men did not know what to do. They still
had almost a million more troops still stuck inside Israel near a valley called Megiddo. They needed to find a way to get those troops
out one way or the other. If they could not get them out and pulled
back from where they were bogged down and stuck, because of all
of the rain and hail, it was just a matter of time before that whole
army would die too. If that were to happen, every man in the room
knew that it would be over for Russia. Russia would cease to exist.
Any country on earth would be able to waltz right in and set up rule
over her. They knew there was only one hope they had left. They had

to somehow, some way, pull back and regroup. And at the moment, that was looking impossible.

The heavy rain that had been coming down for a long time, still out of a beautiful blue and cloudless sky, had turned into raging floods. These floods were pouring down off the sides of the mountains and hills in huge, massive, almost solid walls of water and mud. In a short matter of time, they hit the men and equipment that were bogged down near Megiddo. None had a chance. At least one million men lost their lives in a matter of a few minutes. After that, nothing but huge piles of dead, drowned bodies and muddy, mangled equipment were all that remained of the once-mighty Russian army.

The old premier spoke up. "Comrades, I just don't understand this. We defeat and totally annihilate the greatest, most powerful nation that has ever existed on the face of this earth, America, without suffering even one causality. No, not even one causality. And now, look at this. Almost all of our military has been killed or destroyed. I don't know, because I am an atheist, but to me, I would have to say that it is almost like we are up against a supernatural supreme bei—"

The premier never had a chance to finish his sentence. At that exact instant, an American multi-megaton nuclear warhead five-thousand times more powerful than the ones dropped on Japan during World War II exploded one mile above the city of Moscow. Every man and woman in the entire Moscow metropolitan area instantly ceased to exist. Within a short number of minutes after that, almost the entire country of Russia followed suit. Within mere minutes of that, most of the neighboring countries that had once been a part of the old Soviet Union also ceased to exist.

It would later be determined that only approximately one sixth of the original population of the entire former Soviet Union was still alive. But it would forever be impossible to determine the total number of people who had died worldwide. The number would have to include the people who had died in the massive accidents and calamities that were caused by the disappearances. And of that, how many people disappeared instead of dying? But they were still gone.

The best estimate anyone ever came up with was that at least one quarter of the entire world's population had died. That estimated total was one and a half billion people. Plus, the number of people who had suddenly disappeared was estimated to be anywhere from 600 million to one billion persons.

But no matter what figures might have been used, it was simply safe to say that out of the world's original population of seven billion people before the disappearances began, less than four billion remained on earth. At least one third of the world's population was no more.

When Elijah had declared to the leaders of Israel inside of the command bunker, "You have seen the hand of God at work. There is no denying it. Now, you go and put the final destruction on all of the other countries who have come up against you and God will give you the complete victory," Lieutenant Colonel Ezekiel Cohen had quickly taken Esther into his arms and kissed her passionately. Then, he and the rest of his squadron had hurried over to their planes to become a part of this victory celebration that awaited the entire Israeli military.

Before this, though, during the long hours of standing inside the command bunker with the other leaders of Israel, Ezekiel and Esther had reached the end of their endurance and almost collapsed from exhaustion. By that time, Ezekiel had already been awake for almost forty-eight hours straight, and Esther had been awake for almost as long.

General Green eventually noticed that they both were teetering on the very edge of passing out while standing on their feet. He turned and told them to both go to his quarters and get some sleep. He said that if they were needed, he would call for them.

Ezekiel and Esther were delighted. They were dead on their feet, but they were also married now. And they knew what that meant. That meant they would now be able to consummate their marriage as husband and wife, just as God had decreed.

After Ezekiel and his men took off, they quickly pointed their planes south toward Egypt. Once they got there, they began to drop the actual fires of *hell*—the same nuclear fusion that burns eternally inside of the actual boundaries of hell and which fuels our sun which is nothing more than an enormous molten lake of fire—down onto the remnants of the gathered armies that were intent on destroying Israel.

They bombed and strafed the combined armies until there was not much left at all of the defeated armies. Then, running low on fuel, they all turned to go back home. That is, all but one of their planes. One of their F-22s was missing. It was Ezekiel's.

After arriving back at Sharon Air Force Base, all nine of Ezekiel's men hurried back over to the command bunker. They wanted to be the first to offer their condolences to Esther. But Esther had already received the news that Ezekiel was missing. Since that time, she had been absolutely frantic, inconsolable, distraught, on the very edge of complete hysteria.

She was lying face down on the carpet of the bunker. General Green was kneeling down next to her, trying his best to console her. He had his hand on her back while stroking her long, brunette hair in slow, smooth strokes. He wasn't saying anything. His heart was breaking too. He loved Esther as if she were his own child.

*How brave she has been to have gone through what she has and still remained sane,* he thought. *It would have broken most people.*

Tears welled up in his eyes as he kneeled next to her, listening to her crying, "No, God. Not again. *No.* You can't have allowed this to happen to me again. Could you? What kind of a God are you to allow the love of my life to be taken away from me twice?"

She remained in this position for a long time, unmoving, wishing with everything inside that God would allow her to die too and wondering what she could use to end her own life. She did not want to go on living without Ezekiel. Her mind was tormented. All she could think about was how she had not accepted Ezekiel's overtures until now. She had rejected him for almost a full year. They could have been together for all of that time if she hadn't been so stubborn. She could have felt his wonderful arms around her all of this time if she had just given in and accepted his proposals.

"Oh why, God? *Why?*" she cried.

General Green leaned over and whispered in her ear, "Esther, my darling child, let me tell you something. I am going to issue an order to go find Ezekiel. I swear to you that we're going to do everything we can to find him. I'm going to divert a full company of soldiers from our defense forces, along with a complete squadron of planes and helicopters until we find him. And I promise you this, my darling child, we will not stop until we do find him. I promise you this."

But two months later, Ezekiel had still not been found, either dead or alive. They had eventually found his plane, but it was completely destroyed almost beyond recognition. There had been no sign of Ezekiel in the remnants of the aircraft. Nor was there any sign that he had ejected from his plane. They had located what was left of the ejection seat still inside of the burned-out exploded remains. By looking at his plane, they knew it would have been impossible to have survived such a disaster.

But still, there was a small modicum of hope. None of Ezekiel had been found. Even in the hottest fire, and even with the exploded ordnance that had blown the plane apart, there was no sign of Ezekiel at all, not even a finger or a scrap of bone.

*Surely we would have found* something *of Ezekiel if he was still in the wreckage,* they figured.

During this time, Esther had gone to bed and had not gotten out of it except to go to the restroom. She would barely eat anything; just enough to keep her alive. She couldn't sleep. If she did happen to close her eyes and dose off for a few minutes, Ezekiel's face would immediately come before her, plus, she would feel his arms wrapped around and pulling her close to him. At those times, she could swear she could smell his wonderful scent. But then, she would immediately wake up drenched in a cold sweat. After that, she would lay there, unable to go back to sleep, afraid to even try. To try to ease the pain, she would constantly think about how gentle and loving and sweet and kind he had been to her the one and only time they had become one in the eyes of God, the one and only time they had an opportunity to consummate their marriage.

Not long after that, she got sick. Very sick. It was only in the morning though, at least, most of the time. It seemed like every morning, she would get so nauseated and sick that what little food she had eaten would come back up.

General Green was beside himself with worry about her. Finally, he brought the best doctor in Israel to Esther's bedside. The doctor gave her a thorough examination. As he finished his examination he leaned back and looked directly into Esther's eyes. His own eyes had a sparkle and glint in them. With a big smile on his face, he declared, "Esther and General Green, I have some wonderful news. Yes, you, Esther, are going to have a baby. There is nothing wrong with you that a little more food and a little more time will heal."

At first, she was stunned, totally speechless. But as these words sank deeply into every cell and molecule of her entire being, she thought, *God didn't forsake me. He might have taken Ezekiel away from me, but in His mercy and love, He gave me a piece of Ezekiel that I'll have with me forever.*

utside of Esther's bedroom, the world as it had been known was now changed. What does the future hold? What kind of a new world would emerge out of the chaos, anarchy, and destruction that had just taken place? Would it be a better place? Would the new one-world government, which had been approved by almost all of the countries on earth, work better than the old governments and individual nations before this chaos began?

What about the new leader of this new one-world dictatorship, His Supreme Highness, Excellency Angel Abaddon, Supreme Leader of the United Confederation of Nations? Would he be a benevolent leader? Would he be able to bring stability back to the world? Would he be a kind and caring leader? Or would the power of such a lofty title and position turn him into another satanically-indwelt personality like Hitler and Stalin?

What about Israel? God had destroyed all of the Arab and Muslim nations that had joined forces with the king of the north, Russia, and the kings of the south. Not long after this, Israel began moving many of her troops and civilian populations into much of the areas that used to belong to the Arabs and Muslims. They were claiming as their rightful possession all of the land north of them up to the Euphrates River. This land used to belong to Lebanon, Syria, and Turkey.

To the east, they were claiming all of the land of Jordan, much of Saudi Arabia, and all of Iraq west of the Euphrates River. From there, they claimed all of the land south of the river until it emptied into the Persian Gulf.

To the south, they were claiming all of the land down to the great river of Egypt, the Nile River. This included all of the land west until the river emptied into the Mediterranean Sea and east as far as what used to be Ethiopia.

They were claiming this is the land their God had originally given to Abraham. These are the borders of what God had declared to Abraham in Genesis, chapter fifteen, verse eighteen, in which God said to Abraham, "In the same day the Lord made a covenant with Abram, saying, 'Unto thy seed have I given this land from the river of Egypt unto the great river, the river Euphrates.'"

The Israelis were saying that even if this wasn't written in their holy book, all of this new territory was theirs anyway due to the "spoils of war." They were also claiming all of the wealth inside of these borders as their own.

Because of all of this Israel has become a superpower equal to any other country. She has full control of the majority of the oil in the world within her new borders. For the rest of the countries of the world to continue to survive, the leader of the world, His Supreme Highness, Excellency Angel Abaddon, will be forced to sign a peace treaty with Israel.

With the Dome of the Rock mosque completely destroyed by the two missiles Hussein Immad launched, Israel is now free to build a new temple in the exact same spot where their old one once stood. Construction on the temple was ordered to begin immediately. The Torah was studied to make sure the temple would be built exactly according to Moses's original instructions, along with Moses becoming the general contractor overseeing the construction.

Moses and Ezekiel told Esther, and the rest of the people, to not give up hope about finding Ezekiel alive. The search for him would continue indefinitely until they did locate him. As far as was known, Ezekiel was the only Israeli casualty during Ezekiel's War. Because of this, hope sprung eternal that he would be found alive.

Moses and Elijah were also telling everyone who would listen that the world had entered into what is called, The Great Tribulation, which was described in perfect detail by the Apostle John in his book called Revelation. They were saying that the next seven years would be the worst years to ever take place on the earth, and they needed to prepare for it. They also opened a religious training center to prepare missionaries to spread the Gospel of Jesus Christ to the Jews. Before long, one hundred and forty-four thousand men and women had joined.

Moses and Elijah emphasized that the Gospel of Jesus needed to be preached to all corners of the world for Jesus to be able to return and set up His kingdom on the earth as king of the world. His kingdom will last a thousand years. It is called, the Millennium. Ezekiel and Esther's child will be called a "millennium's child" because she will enter the millennium as a small child.

Her birth and story, along with any unanswered questions, are told in the sequel to this book called, "Millennium's Child." Please go to www.twmanes.com to read an excerpt from it.